Shelter
Mountain Man's Love

STAND-ALONE NOVEL

A Western Historical Romance Book

by

Nora J. Callaway

Disclaimer & Copyright

This is a work of fiction. Names, characters, places and incidents either are products of the author's imagination or are used fictitiously. Any resemblance to actual events or locales or persons, living or dead, is entirely coincidental.

Table of Contents

Letter from Nora J. Callaway

"*How vain it is to sit down to write when you have not stood up to live.*" -Henry David Thoreau

I'm a lover of nature in the mornings and a writing soul at nights. My name is Nora J. Callaway and I come from Nevada, the beautiful Silver State.

I hold a BA in English Literature and an MA in Creative Writing. For years, I've wanted to get my stories out there, my own 'babies' as I like to call them, as inspired by my own experience leaving out West and my research of 19th-century American history.

All my life I have been breeding horses, cows and sheep and I've been tending to the land. It's time to tend now to my inner need to grow my stories, my heart-warming Western romance stories, and share them with the rest of you!

I'm here to learn and connect with others who enjoy a cup of black coffee, a humble sunset and a ride with a horse! Bless your hearts, as my nana used to say! Come on, hope in!

Until next time,

Nora J Callaway

Prologue

Deadwood, South Dakota

1881

Josie staggered out of the cattle barn, breathing hard. She braced her hand on the side of the barn and leaned her head forward to catch her wind. Managing the cattle on her own had not gotten any easier since...

She stopped herself from thinking about that and straightened. She smoothed her hands over her black dress, plucking off bits of straw. It was time to go check on her daughter, Ella.

She crossed from the cattle barn to the house, the sun beating down on the back of her neck, drying her sweat. She passed the chicken coop and the last two hens watched her go without making a single cluck. Before all of *this* happened, the hens would set up a fuss if they even heard her, hoping they were going to be fed. That she had been culling their numbers, roasting their family members in her oven, had them shy and suspicious. She felt bad for them even though they were just animals. She knew what it was like to have to be quiet to avoid trouble— and for it all to be in vain.

The pig would be next. Some of the cattle too, or she might just sell those and use the money to buy some nice, fresh vegetables.

She pushed open the door to the house. “Ella!” she called.

She heard someone move in a nearby room, heard a scuffling like feet shifting. The sound was too large to belong to a two-year-old waif.

Her heart hammered and the breath she had just managed to get back left her lungs again. There was an intruder, and she wouldn't be able to get to Owen's gun from the hallway closet in time. Her eyes darted around the foyer, searching for anything that could be used as a weapon, landing upon a candlestick on a small table. She snatched it up, holding it in front of her.

"Who's there?" she called out, voice shaking.

The heavy footsteps advanced, a shadow leaning out of the side room. The tall, slender form of a man emerged and Josie gasped when she recognized him. "Clive?"

Her dead husband's cousin looked at her with amber cat's eyes, then at the candlestick. "You fixin' to whack me one?"

Josie lowered the candlestick slowly. There was still something not right about this. She didn't know Clive very well and there was no reason for him to be in her house.

"Ella?" she called again.

"Mama?" Her little girl's voice came from deeper in the house, likely the bedroom where Josie had left her.

"You stay there," Josie said, speaking both to Ella and Clive. "Right where you are."

Clive crossed his arms over his narrow chest. "I didn't come to start no trouble, Josie. I came 'cause I know trouble's comin' and I want to help you."

Her stomach clenched and she tightened her grip on the candlestick. Outside, the chickens were making their lonely clucks, calling for sisters they no longer had.

"What are you talkin' about, Clive? What kind of trouble?"

“Let’s go in the parlor so your little girl don’t hear us.” Clive motioned to the room he had come out of.

Josie shook her head hard. “No, right here’s fine. What kind of trouble?”

She might not have known him well, but she knew what men were like. Her father, Owen, the ranch hands that used to work on the property: once they sat down and settled in, they meant to stay for a while. She wasn’t equipped to deal with a guest right then. There was so much she still had to do, chores that needed done, and then she had to figure out where dinner would be coming from, since the pantry was bare again.

Clive lowered his head, his eyes still on her. “I was at Owen’s funeral. Didn’t have the time to say nothin’ to you, but I’m real sorry for your loss. They ever find out who did it?”

Owen had been murdered right on the property a few months back and nothing had been the same since then. Worse, the sheriff never caught the culprit. Word around town was he had stopped investigating because there just weren’t any clues pointing to the criminal.

“No,” Josie said, short and clipped.

“It’s a real shame.” Clive rubbed his hand over his lank brown hair and heaved a heavy sigh. “He was always my favorite cousin. That’s why I’m here right now, and ‘cause I like you, Josie. You deserve fair warnin’.”

“What are you talking about? What kind of warnin’?” She frowned and shifted her fingers on the slim metal of the candlestick. She really couldn’t deal with anything else at the moment.

Clive reached into his back pocket and pulled out a letter, holding it out to her. "The Deadwood Bank owner came into my saloon the other night and went off on a bender, loosened his tongue. He told me that Owen owed money. A lot, Josie. He was gettin' roostered and makin' bets, takin' out loans and not paying them back. The bank is goin' to try to take the ranch away from you. I convinced him to hold off while I talked to you about it. All the details is in this letter here. You should read it."

Josie recoiled from the letter like Clive had just offered her a snake. Bile rose up her throat and she put her hand over her mouth to hold back a moan. Black spots appeared in her vision, floating at the edges.

When she was sure she could speak, she pulled her hand from her mouth. "That's not right. I knew our finances were bad, but.... Are you sure?"

"It's all in the letter." Clive repeated. He stepped closer to her and put his cool, faintly clammy hand on her wrist. His fingers curled around her like the jaws of a handcuff cinching shut and she lost her hold on the candlestick, dropping it to the ground with a heavy clatter.

Her marriage to Owen had given her plenty of experience with such firm, possessive touches. She yanked her arm to pull away, but he was strong and kept holding on.

"You don't got the money to pay any loans back, do you?" Clive asked, voice low, and didn't wait for an answer. "You're goin' to lose the ranch. What're you goin' to do then? You got your little girl to think of."

"I'll think of something. I won't lose the ranch." The ranch used to be her father's before it was hers and Owen's. She refused to just give up. "I'll go to the bank. I'll talk with them and maybe we can figure something out."

Clive tilted his head to the side slightly. "And if that don't work out? I came here 'cause I had an idea. You could come stay with me for a time. I'll give you work at the saloon so you can get back on your feet. What do you say?"

Josie put her hand to her face and closed her eyes. This was all far too much to take in right then. "I-- I need to think. Clive, thank you for coming. I'll read the letter and I'll talk to the bank. I'll see what I can do, but I'm not ready to give up. I won't leave the ranch."

He pursed his lips and released her arm. "Alright. Good luck to you, Josie, but I don't hold out much hope. Just know that the offer's there. A place to stay, steady work. You'll come around, I think."

Josie stepped to the side and held the front door open for him. "I do appreciate it. You've given me a head start and I thank you for that."

She stopped short of saying she owed him. If what he said was really true, getting into more debt, even of a personal kind, didn't seem wise.

Clive placed the letter on the table where the candlestick had been. She could smell him as he strode past, a mixture of old, dried whiskey and vegetable stew. He looked back over his shoulder at her, feline eyes narrowed to slits. She thought he was about to say something, but he continued on without a word.

She shut the door and leaned back against it, rubbing her wrist where Clive had gripped her. If he was anything like Owen had been, she was very glad not to have gone with him. But what was she going to do? If the bank wouldn't work with her because Owen had put them in such debt before his death, she would have to find a job off the ranch, maybe two jobs. She could sell some of the cattle, pawn off some of their tools and belongings.

Would it be enough?

What could she do if it wasn't?

"Mama?" Ella's voice broke through her dark thoughts like a ray of sunshine. With a series of tiny, pattering steps, Ella appeared in the hall, looking all around with her bright red curls bobbing. She spotted Josie by the door and raced over to her with arms outstretched to grab onto her.

Josie bent and lifted her precious daughter into her arms. Ella nestled in, holding onto her around the neck. Pure warmth filled Josie's chest and she pressed Ella to her chest. She breathed in the scent of Ella's hair and some of the panic that had been forming in her stomach was quelled.

Ella was the only gift Owen had ever given Josie, the most perfect present delivered almost a year after their nuptials.

Ella was a miniature version of her. Truly miniature, as she was small even for a two-year-old, clearly having inherited Josie's petite frame. Her skin was the color of milk, a reflection of Josie's Irish blood; Josie's own skin had gone to tan from working long hours out in the sun. Their bright red hair was the same but for Josie's being longer.

Ella leaned back in Josie's arms and beamed up at her, big green eyes sparkling like sunlight on forest leaves. Whenever Josie looked at herself in a mirror these days, that vividness seemed to have gone from her own eyes. And she had circles underneath hers that Ella did not.

"Mama sad?" Ella's smile fell and she pressed her small, soft hand to Josie's cheek.

Josie took that hand and kissed it all over, making Ella giggle and squirm in her arms. Her whole body filled up with that warmth from before, like fire flowing in her veins. She pressed Ella against her chest again and Ella lay her head on her shoulder, innocent, trusting. Josie stroked her back and swayed on her feet, from side to side.

Sad? She didn't have the time to be sad. She didn't have the time to be doubtful or scared.

She had to keep the ranch, for Ella's sake, just like Clive had said. Everything else had to be put aside to make sure her daughter had a good, safe life.

"Mama? Apple?" Ella was tugging on her.

"We don't have any apples right now." Josie kissed the top of her head. "You want some bread with butter?"

"Apple," Ella insisted.

"Bread and butter," Josie repeated, and took Ella with her into the kitchen to fix her a snack. She passed the letter on the table as she went and tightened her jaw.

Ella always napped after she ate and that meant uninterrupted time to read the darned thing. Then, tomorrow, Josie would head to the bank with her daughter in tow to ask for another loan, a loan extension, forgiveness on the debt, anything. She would take anything. She would work as hard as she had to, any job that she had to, and as long as she got to keep the ranch and had food for Ella, it would all be worth it.

Chapter One

One year later...

"Story, Mama, story."

Josie draped another blanket over Ella, the last blanket they had in the tiny cabin. Ella's cheeks and lips were pink, so she was warm enough, at least. Josie couldn't say the same about herself.

"What kind of story do you want, sweetie?" Josie tucked the blankets in around her daughter as best as she could with fingers stiff from the cold.

"Bear," Ella said. She snuggled into the blankets, blinking slowly. "Bear story."

Josie stroked her daughter's fiery hair, smiling a little, just for her, as if she wasn't being haunted by thoughts of what she was going to have to do later that night.

"Once," Josie said softly, "there was a little bear cub, a little girl bear, named Ella. Ella the bear cub lived with her mama bear in a cave. One day, when mama bear was away hunting, Ella discovered a secret tunnel at the back of the cave and crawled inside to see where it went."

Ella's attention was rapt in spite of her tiredness. She clung to wakefulness to know where the tunnel would take the little bear who shared her name. Josie continued to stroke the soft, red flames of her daughter's hair as she told the tale of how the bear cub followed the tunnel all the way to another cave where there was a big garden. Ella the bear brought back berries and other fruits to her own cave so that when mama bear showed up without any meat from her hunt, they still had something to eat.

"With their bellies full, the two bears curled up in their soft nest and fell fast asleep."

Ella was asleep, her head tilted to the side. At what point she had fallen asleep, Josie wasn't quite sure. She had been too busy making up the story to have noticed.

Josie bent and kissed her little girl on the forehead. Ella didn't stir. She always slept heavily, never waking until morning.

Josie was counting on that, as terrible of a risk as it was to take. She had no choice.

She stood and crossed the whole of the cabin in a few steps, reaching the door to the inhospitable outside. There, she took a last look back at her sleeping daughter to remind herself of why she was doing this. In her story, the bear family had *needed* food, just like her own family did. This was what had to be done for them to survive.

"Here we go," she whispered to herself.

Josie took a deep breath and pushed the door open, and the fierce wind pushed right back at her, almost slamming the door shut again. She twisted and put her shoulder against the door, heaving it open just enough to slip out.

The wind tore right through her coat, chasing away any warmth she might have had left until all that remained was the glow of love in her chest. Worn threadbare, the coat was never going to offer much protection from the elements. What she really desired was the dark brown color of the fabric, which would allow her to blend in with her surroundings.

Huge pine trees surrounded the cabin, thick black trunks shooting straight up from the earth before exploding into layers of wide branches. The branches blocked out most of the moonlight on clear nights, and on this night a thick blanket of cloud covered the heavens. She would have an even harder time seeing than usual. One wrong step and it would be all over for her, and no one would come to save Ella.

No one knew where they were.

Josie walked into the forest, the trees engulfing her. The ground was riddled with ferns and other low, creeping vegetation, all of which snagged at the hem of her dress like tiny claws. The ground was also covered in rocks, which were hidden beneath the ferns and coated in a layer of slippery pine needles. She clutched at the tree trunks as she made her way down the steep slope in front of the cabin, using them to keep herself upright as her shoes slid on the unseen stones.

It's quiet tonight, Josie thought. The mountain forests were typically noisy as heck with crickets chirping and other insects humming and whirring. She should have been hearing raccoons and foxes move about in the undergrowth, seen waving ferns in the distance as deer glided silently by. And always there would be owls hooting, and night birds shrieking.

It must have been the thick, black layer of clouds overhead, she reasoned. All the animals were tucked away in their homes, anticipating the rain just like she was. She had watched that storm coming for most of the day and had expected rainfall by then, but there hadn't been a single droplet. Very strange.

Reaching a large, flat boulder covered in moss that she used as a landmark, Josie turned to follow an old game trail, skirting around the edge of a meadow and plunging again into the trees before meeting up with a creek. She bent and scooped up a mouthful of the frigid trickle of water to wet her throat, then followed its chuckling course further down the mountain. Always down, always onward, no matter how her legs ached, no matter the chilled mountain air slowly turning her bones to icicles.

That was how to reach her version of the little bear's secret garden cave.

After another long while of walking, she reached the abrupt edge of a hill, over which the creek fell, splashing with increased vigor to become a waterfall at the bottom. A thin river flowed from the waterfall pool, running right through the middle of a valley. There was a ranch down there in the valley. The clouds overhead threw the features of the ranch into impenetrable shadows, but she had seen it in the daytime too and knew there was a cattle barn, a stable filled with horses, and two houses, one larger than the other.

There was no way to safely descend the hill from where she stood. She lingered anyway, watching the ranch for signs of activity. A warm light burned in the window of the main house but as she watched, she saw no movement.

Does that light mean there's someone still awake down there?

If only she could come back another time when there wasn't any light at all. But she had no choice. She couldn't wait any longer.

She turned and walked along the edge of the hill until she reached a spot where she could go down into the hills that made up the valley's longest wall. She stopped long before she reached the bottom, at a place where vines and moss-covered shattered stones, some of which were bigger than the cabin.

Josie sat on one of the boulders to catch her breath, as she always did. She put her head in her hands and thoughts came out from the shadows in the back of her mind, taunting her. Her shoulders drew up tight around her neck as she cringed.

Maybe if I had worked a little harder...

She had marched into that bank with her head held high, and walked out of there with it hanging low. The debts Owen had accrued were too great and the bank would give her no further loans. She had to start making payment, and fast.

She had worked two jobs, three sometimes. Butchered the last of the chickens and the pig. Sold off the cattle, all of the tools, most of her clothes, and anything else they didn't absolutely require for survival.

It still wasn't enough.

The ranch was taken.

There was only one place where they could go: her father's old hunting cabin up in the mountains above Deadwood. He had taken her there a few times before he died, before her marriage to Owen, and she had still remembered the way. It had started snowing on the day she and Ella made the journey with just what they could carry. Only Ella had given her the strength to plow onward through the drifts until, at last, they finally reached the cabin.

That was weeks ago and her own stupidity still amazed her. The cabin might have collapsed in the years since she had last been there. They really could have died, buried in the snow to never be seen again, and it would have been her fault.

We can still die.

"Get up, Josie," she muttered, and slapped her cheeks with both hands. She barely felt it.

Her joints groaned in protest as she moved to a portion of the ivy-covered stone on the side of a slope. She used her arm to push the ivy aside, revealing the gaping black mouth of a hidden tunnel.

She had stumbled upon the tunnel not long after first arriving at the cabin. After giving all of her food to Ella for the past couple days, there was finally nothing left, not so much as a crumb. Her stomach aching with hollowness, she had gone off to try and forage from the land, although she had no experience with that. Foraging proved to be harder than expected and she had walked for a very long time without even *seeing* a single berry.

On the verge of collapse, she had smelled it. Cooking meat. Mouth flooding with saliva, she had tracked the scent to this very spot in the hills and discovered it was wafting from the hidden tunnel. Drafts of air blowing through the tunnel had carried the scent all the way from the house down there in the valley.

Josie ducked into the tunnel, leaves tickling the back of her neck. The tunnel walls were earth and stone and she could easily touch both at one time. She trailed her hands along both walls and walked forward into the endless dark. Slithering shapes and specks of light danced before her. Her mind was playing tricks on her. She knew there was nothing in the tunnel but stone and soil and sometimes rats; she heard them squeaking sometimes, their tiny sharp claws skittering over rocks.

Her grasping hands encountered occasional gaps in the tunnel, other earthen halls branching off. Where they led and why they were there, she wasn't sure. She wasn't even sure why there were hidden tunnels at all, especially ones that went from the hills and down into the valley, into the cellar of the ranch house.

The first time she had snuck into the cellar, she thought she must have finally started hallucinating from hunger and imagining the bounty before her: barrels of apples and pears, potatoes, sacks of flour, beans, rice. Aged cheese on the shelves, cured meats hanging from a rack.

She had eaten an apple crouched in the mouth of the tunnel, devouring everything, even the stem and seeds, and then she had filled the pockets of her coat with as much food as would fit to take back to Ella.

The exhilaration of the find hadn't lasted long, quickly replaced with a burning shame. Her father had raised her with morals. When she was a child and all the other children were stealing candy from the general store, she never had, no matter how they laughed and called her a yellow belly.

But Ella changed things.

She tried so hard to feed her in other ways and she had endured her own hunger for days until she was forced to return to the tunnel, the cellar, to steal from whatever family lived in the house.

She could only comfort herself with the thought that one day she would pay them back. Even if they never figured out she was stealing from them, she would pay them back. She'd get another job soon, move into a better place, and save up the money she owed this family. For one final time, she'd sneak into the cellar and leave the money where they would find it.

For now, surviving came first.

She knew she was getting close to the cellar when the ground leveled out beneath her feet. She slowed now, feeling out with one hand in front of her. Her fingertips brushed against wood, a panel that covered the tunnel entrance. She slid it to the side and there was the cellar, ripe with the scents of salted meat and dried fruit.

She listened past the hammering of her heart and heard nothing. She swallowed hard and left the tunnel. She moved toward the barrel of apples, as it was always full and she felt like she could take from it easily.

Something moved behind her, something far larger than a rat.

Her heart jumped up into her throat. She froze. In the next instant, a huge arm wrapped around her waist from behind. A lightning bolt of the worst terror she had ever experienced shot through her and she opened her mouth to scream.

A bear paw of a hand clamped over her face, muffling her cries.

Into her ear, a man's husky voice whispered. "*Got you now, thief.*"

Chapter Two

Kerry Thompson was churning butter when Hunter walked over to her with the intent of complaining. The forty-eight year-old maid lifted and shoved the plunger down into the barrel in a steady and tireless pumping action. Strands of sandy blonde hair dropped loose from beneath her sunhat and hung in her eyes, making her seem strangely girlish.

Kerry spoke without looking at him, her attention on the horses frolicking in their corral. "Finally going to fire me, are you?"

"No," Hunter grunted. His complaint wasn't about her. "You'd just come back, anyhow."

Kerry laughed and nodded. She finally turned and looked up at him from her stool on the porch. "When you stomp around like that, I know there's trouble."

Hunter grunted again and shoved his hands into his pockets. Kerry had worked for his family for as long as he could remember and he trusted her completely, partly because he knew how stubborn she was. The woman would never do anything that she didn't want to. If she did want to do something, she would do it perfectly.

Kerry stopped churning the butter and rubbed her hands together, scattering tiny flecks of wood. "Go on, then, Hunter," she said. "What's on your mind?"

"It's the cellar," he said.

"Of course, it's the cellar." She sighed and rested her hands on her flabby stomach. Her arms were also flabby, her face like a lumpy piece of dough. Having five children softened a woman, Hunter supposed. Hardened her, too. "I'm not fully convinced that someone's breaking in."

"I am," he said. He lowered himself onto the porch, sitting next to Kerry's stool. He was still almost as tall as her despite her having the advantage. "I started keepin' track of when I think the food is going missin'. It's every four days or so. Well, five days ago, I marked up an apple with my knife and put it on top of the others in the barrel. When I checked next, it was gone."

"It could have been Harry getting himself something to eat," Kerry pointed out, naming Hunter's best ranch hand and friend. "Or maybe I had an apple. I don't remember every time I eat something."

"It disappeared overnight," Hunter said, stressing the point. "Neither you nor Harry are here overnight. Anyway, tonight I'm settin' up a trap for the thief."

"A trap?" Kerry removed her sunhat and produced a few pins from her pocket. She secured the strands of hair that had come loose and placed her hat back on her head. "What sort of a trap? You aren't planning on doing something foolish, are you?"

"No," he said, "it's not foolish. It's simple. If I'm right, the thief is going to come again tonight. I'm going to hide in the cellar and wait to see if they show up."

"What if they don't show up?" she asked.

"They will," Hunter insisted.

Kerry shook her head and pointed out across the ranch. Hunter followed her finger and at first he didn't know what she wanted him to look at.

"The sky, Hunter," Kerry said, sounding both patient and impatient at the same time.

Hunter saw it then, what Kerry was trying to get him to see. Just barely visible at the far edge of the soft blue morning sky was a strip of charcoal, a stain marring the pale blue. "So there's a storm comin'," he said. "If someone wants to steal, some rain ain't stoppin' them."

"It's not going to be just rain." Kerry gripped the butter churn plunger and got back to work, the thick cream sloshing inside the wooden churn. "When I was a girl, before I came to work on your pa's ranch, I broke my wrist playing with my brother, God watch over his soul. Now every time a big storm is coming, my wrist hurts something fierce."

Hunter watched her churning butter with vigor and raised his thick eyebrows. "Doesn't seem like it's botherin' you that much."

"Oh, I work through it." Kerry smiled and lifted one shoulder. "I don't let it stop me from doing my job. But it's been aching since yesterday and now there's those clouds. I've been watching them. They're slow, but they'll show up tonight and no one will want to be outside when they finally do. I imagine there'll be damages in the morning."

Hunter looked at the clouds on the horizon and narrowed his eyes. Kerry was incorrect on frustratingly few matters. If she said there would be a storm, there was going to be a storm. "Not everyone has a broken wrist to tell them when there's bad weather comin' in. I think the thief will come anyway, and when they do, I'll be in the cellar waitin' on them."

Kerry sighed. "Say the thief doesn't come. You'll be down there for hours when you're supposed to be sleeping. Then we'll all have to deal with you."

"No, I'll admit I was wrong and deal with my consequences." He huffed. She was looking at this in the wrong way. "Imagine if the thief does come and I catch them. We'll finally have the answer to this mystery."

"What if they have a weapon?"

"They won't have a chance to use it." Hunter pushed himself to his feet and stretched his arms. "They'll come through the tunnel. That's how they've been gettin' inside. I'll grab them right as they come out and that'll be the end of it. I'm tellin' you, Kerry, this is going to work."

"I do hope that it will work," Kerry said, with another little sigh. "Then you can stop talking about it. You pay me to clean your house, not listen to your ramblings."

Hunter waved his hand and walked away, her laughter following him as he went to the cattle barn to check on his herd. His presence in the barn set the cattle to stirring, shifting in their pens and stomping their hooves in the straw. Tails flicked and heads tossed, horns flashing in the light spilling through the high windows.

He walked along the pens, scanning the herd, searching for injuries and anything else that needed special attention. Satisfied, he went to the supply closet to get out the tools and cattle driving gear. He brought an armful of tools to a patch of sunlight and set them down to examine, checking for signs of wear and breakage that would otherwise make themselves known at the worst possible time.

When he was a boy, he had learned to take proper care of his equipment so it would take proper care of him. His father had stressed the importance of that and many other things, and under him, Hunter had learned how to run the ranch in a meticulous and orderly manner. He kept all his ranch hands and animals on a strict schedule. All tools and equipment had their own places and they were to be kept clean. He knew where everything was and when it should be there, and that was what had helped him to realize he had a thief.

The first time, it was only a suspicion, a sense of misgiving when he went down into the cellar to grab a wedge of cheese for the meal Kerry was cooking. He felt almost like he had walked into a dream on descending those steep cellar steps, where certain things were wrong that he just couldn't pinpoint. That had put him on edge, and when it happened again, he no longer held any doubts that someone had found the secret tunnels underneath the ranch.

Long before his father ever built the ranch, a crazy old man had come to the mountains to dig for gold, claiming he'd had a dream about it that was too real not to be true. He had created the tunnels that went into the hills and valley, digging like a mole. No plan, no crew, nothing but his own crazy ideas and a shovel. No one knew what had happened to that old man.

Hunter didn't even know if the story was true or something his father made up. No one outside the family knew of the tunnels, that he was aware of at least, which meant there were no records to check, no evidence that anything of the kind had ever occurred. The tunnels were just there.

He had explored them when he was a boy with the goal of mapping them out and had quickly given up after he was lost for a full day and had his hide tanned for making the whole ranch look for him. There seemed to be no pattern to how the tunnels were laid out or where they connected, and about half of them led to dead ends.

Whoever the thief was, he must have discovered the tunnels by accident and taken advantage of them.

Hunter clenched his jaw as he thought of an intruder sneaking onto *his* property and taking *his* hard-earned food.

That thief could be off telling any number of his criminal cohorts about the house that was so easy to break into. That would stop tonight. Just as Kerry had her broken wrist warning her of the coming storm, he had a nagging sensation inside him that told him of the oncoming robber.

But he had to wait.

He busied himself with work as the day wore on. Now that he was aware of it, he kept an eye on the incoming storm and could see its slow, threatening progress across the sky. The leading edge was gray, with swirls of boiling black ink just behind. The temperature plummeted to nearly freezing and a wind began to blow, stinging his eyes when he turned his face into it. The cattle grew increasingly restless in their barn and the horses became shy, almost wild, fighting against their handlers with bared teeth and flattened ears.

"Boss," Harry called out, approaching Hunter around sunset. He had his hat in his hand, his sweaty black hair standing on end. He wasn't quite as tall as Hunter and had to look up at him. "I think I should get a move on. The storm's picking up speed now. I want to beat it home if I can."

Hunter put his hands on his hips, thinking. It was a strange, bloody sunset, tendrils of fire licking into the smoke of the coming storm. The air was humid, thick, electric on the tongue. "It's going to get dark faster than normal because of those clouds. You should stay the night here or you'll be ridin' blind before long."

"Appreciate it," Harry said, nodding. "But I can't."

"Don't be a yack. You can," Hunter insisted. He couldn't have his best ranch hand getting into trouble. The others rallied around Harry and would be almost useless without him.

Hunter pointed at his little guest house, a short distance from the big main house. "Kerry's stayin' overnight because she's smart. You can stay too, in the main house with me. You can help me catch the thief."

"Much as I wish I could help so you'd stop talkin' about it, I really can't," Harry insisted. He shifted on his feet. "Grace is pregnant. I want to be home as much as I can."

Surprise fluttered through Hunter like a startled bird. He hadn't known Harry and his wife were trying for a child. "Well, congratulations. I suppose I really can't make you stay here. You best get a move on. Borrow one of the fresh horses. That'll give you a better chance of beatin' the storm."

"Thank you. And thanks." Harry put his hat on his head and tipped it with a flash of a smile. "I'll be back tomorrow in the morn' to see what the damage is. I'll pray it isn't much."

"It'll be what it'll be," Hunter said. "Go on. Ride fast. Ride safe."

Harry hurried for the stable and emerged a few minutes later on the back of one of Hunter's horses, a strong, wiry mare with swift hooves. He glanced up at the sky, then bent low over the mare's neck and urged her up to speed. They were soon gone, disappearing around a bend in the valley wall.

With darkness rapidly falling over the mountains, Hunter performed one last check of his land, ensuring doors were secured properly. He also stopped by the guest house to check on Kerry, though she waved him off and told him to go catch his thief.

He knew the thief wouldn't show until after dark. He went and stood out on the porch, watching as the storm finally covered the whole sky from end to end, blocking out the moon and the stars. The storm sat up there on top of the valley, pregnant with rain, yet so incredibly still.

A low peal of thunder rolled across the sky, a physical rumble more than a sound, and everything was still again.

The thief will take their chances, I think. The way this storm looks, it could pass right over us without doing anything at all.

Hunter went inside and went through the motions of retiring to bed, then went down to the cellar. He took up a spot against the wall next to the piece of wood covering the tunnel entrance and began his wait, listening for any sound that didn't belong. As the time passed, his frustrations reignited, filling his chest with fire. Who could the thief possibly be?

He clenched his jaw and his hands curled into fists. He didn't really care about their identity so long as this came to an end.

Maybe he should fill in the tunnels, at least the part that came right to his cellar. He wondered why he hadn't done so already. He would get right to work on that tomorrow.

As his thoughts wandered, he abruptly remembered that he had left a light burning upstairs and silently swore at himself. He needed to go and put that out, or the thief might not come.

Though, perhaps it would be fine. He often left a light on somewhere just in case he had to get up in the middle of the night for whatever reason. If someone was watching his house, they would know the light was normal. It would be fine.

Somewhere deep in the tunnel, earth crunched beneath a foot.

In an instant, all of his muscles tensed and his pulse increased. He held his breath, listening to the slow, methodical footsteps as the thief approached. He heard their breathing, rapid and unsteady. They were nervous, so it wasn't a seasoned thief. That was bad. Nervous people acted unpredictably.

Hunter readied himself, his legs braced for a lunge.

The thief stopped just at the piece of wood, their fingers scrabbling over the splintered surface like spiders. The wood was shifted aside slowly, bit by bit, and the intruder emerged, a small man in a dark coat. He paused and scanned the cellar, somehow not noticing Hunter standing right next to him.

Seemingly satisfied with their inspection, the thief walked out of the tunnel and headed deeper into the cellar.

Hunter didn't wait long enough to see his destination.

He rushed forward and grabbed the thief around the body, yanking him back and clamping his hand over his mouth to muffle the inevitable scream.

His smothering hand encountered a face more delicate than a man's. The lips were soft as he crushed them under his palm, the nose a tiny button, the chin weak. That was when he finally felt the body he had pressed up against his, the shape of the thief beneath their oversized coat.

It's a woman!

Hunter hesitated, doubt intervening, preventing him from continuing. The doubt didn't last and satisfaction took hold in its place. "Got you now, thief," he growled.

Never mind that she was a woman and he felt like he could break her in half without trying. He had her, and now he could put an end to this nonsense she had started.

Chapter Three

Josie knew better than to struggle as the huge man propelled her in front of him, shoving her across the cellar and up the stairs. His hand clamped on her shoulder pushed her almost faster than she could make her tired, aching feet go. Terror at this worst outcome wanted to freeze her in place like a spooked rabbit.

The light she had seen in the window illuminated the house with a dull orange glow as she emerged from the cellar, just off the kitchen. The dining room and parlor were a shadowed blur, glimpsed as the man spun her around and pushed her shoulders back against the wall. His hulking frame towered over her. He was a bear of a man, a monster of a person, broad-shouldered, thick-necked. His hair hung shaggy and mane-like around his face and his eyes were lumps of coal as he leaned over her and stared down.

"Your stealin' days are over," the man rumbled. His voice shook her, shook the whole house, making the wall vibrate at her back.

"Wait." Her voice emerged as a squeak. She cleared her throat and tried again. "Please, wait. It's not what you think."

He shook his enormous head. "Too lazy to work for your own food, that it? You're not going to like jail. They'll put you to work, straighten you out right quick."

Jail? She started shaking. An icy knife was stabbing her heart over and over.

The man let go of her. He seemed to have realized she wasn't going anywhere, too trembly to run away. "Come morning, I'm going to get the sheriff out here and have him deal with you."

"The sheriff? Morning?" Her eyes burned with useless, useless tears. They wouldn't have any effect on this brute of a man. She needed to have her wits about her now.

She bit her tongue until the urge to shed her pointless tears abated. She lifted her hands, the man watching her closely, and pushed her long, straight red hair back from her face. There were bits of twigs and leaves caught in the strands.

Her history with her deceased husband, her isolation for the past weeks, all of it made eye contact difficult, but she tried, focusing on his wide nose in the middle of his furious face. "Please, sir, listen to me. This really isn't what you think it is."

She heard him breathing, huge, rough huffs of air. He spoke slowly, as if she was an idiot child. "You got somethin' to say, then say it. Better be worth my while."

"I have a daughter," she blurted out. Her hands clutched tightly together, nails digging into her skin. "I had to take your food to feed her. I'm so sorry. I was planning on paying you back when I got the money to do so."

The man stared at her. It was hard to see his expression in the dull lighting, if he had one at all. He might as well have been wearing a mask for all that she was able to read him.

Now that she had started speaking, she found it hard to stop. "My daughter is in a cabin further up the mountain. She's all alone right now. I have to get back to her."

She thought she saw the man's black eyes widen ever so slightly, although it could have just been a trick of the flickering orange light. "You left your daughter by herself on a night like this?"

The house shook again, the wall vibrating at Josie's back. She started as she realized that it and the earlier rumble could only be one thing: thunder. And the chattering wasn't her teeth clicking rapidly together because she was trembling, but the strengthening patter of rain on the roof.

Josie put her hand over her mouth, nausea gripping her stomach. Black spots danced before her as she thought about what she had done. She was always aware of the huge risks of leaving a three-year-old alone, but she hadn't imagined a scenario like this. The thunder and wind would wake up Ella and when she cried out for Josie to comfort her, *Josie wouldn't come.*

How awful of a mother could she be, to not be there when her daughter cried for her? It was the worst betrayal she could imagine and it was all her fault.

Maybe Ella would forget and forgive her in time, but Josie would never, ever forgive herself. She had to do something to get out of this house and quickly.

A blaze of blue-white flashed outside the kitchen window in the same instant as thunder snarled, loud enough that Josie clapped her hands over her ears to muffle the brain-shaking pulsations of the angry sky. The tapping of rain on the roof turned into a downpour and a blast of wind whistled past the house.

Another flash of lightning split the sky, again accompanied by that horrific thunder, like the voice of God booming over the valley.

"Now I really can't get the sheriff until morning," he said.

She started to shake her head. Everything inside of her cried out for her to return to her daughter, a thousand voices urging her to go as fast as she could possibly go, race through the rain, brave the wind and thunder, until she reached the cabin and could hold Ella in her arms once more.

How to explain any of that to him? How to explain what it was like to be a mother? To have only this one person in the entire world who meant so much to her?

She looked at him and this time forced herself to meet his eyes. “Let me go to my daughter. I’ll come back in the morning. I swear I will. Just let me go to her now and I’ll accept my punishment in the morning, when she’s safe.”

“Heck, no. Your word is nothin’ to me. I’m not convinced you’ve even got a daughter,” he said.

“Her name is Ella,” she whispered. “Please.”

Silence from the man, though outside the winds were howling and the thunder was a constant roll of skyward drums.

“Leave.”

Josie snapped her head up. “What?”

He stepped away, giving her a reprieve from his oppressive presence. “Leave,” he said again. “Go, and don’t come back.”

Josie staggered to her feet. She almost fell and grabbed at the shaking wall to support herself. “You’re really letting me go?”

He turned away, putting his immense shoulder to her. “Got too much to worry about with the ranch in the mornin’ to deal with takin’ you to the sheriff. So get out of here. And I best not see you again or I’ll make sure you go to jail for a long time.”

"Th-thank you! Thank you!" She didn't stop to consider her luck, just in case he changed his mind. She turned around, searching for the front door.

"Take the tunnel." He grabbed her shoulder and pushed her to the cellar steps. "It's the last time you'll ever use it. *Go.*"

His command was the final push she needed. She fled down the steps, almost tripping at the bottom. She caught herself on the barrel of apples she had wanted to steal from and recoiled, both hands up in the air to show the man at the top of the steps that she hadn't taken one. She ran for the tunnel, calling out over her shoulder, "I swear I'll pay you back!" before she was inside and blind.

She had never moved so quickly through the tunnel, grabbing at the rocky walls and propelling herself forward. She tripped with every step, her feet catching on stones and uneven earth. She could no longer hear the rain, only her own rapid breaths.

Then she was pushing through the vines, rain soaking straight through her coat and dress, drenching her to her skin. The icy droplets stung where they pounded down upon her. Rivulets ran down the hills, collecting in puddles on the grass. She started the long, perilous climb back up the steep slopes, the wind shoving her from all sides, the rain trying to beat her into the mud. She could hardly see and held her arms out in front of her, navigating by feel and tiny glimpses through the freezing waterfall dropping from the sky.

There were tears on her face, mixing with the rain.

Her thoughts raced, mind spinning.

The cabin was so terribly old now, creaking, the wood rotting, the nails rusted. Would it outlast the winds? What if it was struck by lightning?

She toiled up the mountain for an eternity until, at last, she saw the cabin, a miserable shape illuminated by yet another flare of lightning. Her cry of dismay was lost in the storm, the air flying from her lungs, leaving her retching.

The door to the cabin was gone, whipped away by a gust of wind, and rain was pouring in. The whole structure swayed, the wooden slats bowing, clearly on the verge of crumpling.

A surge of pure energy awoke inside Josie. She dashed through the last of the trees and in through the doorway. A part of the roof fell, smashing into her arm, leaving a burning cut. The rain came in and another part of the roof dropped.

"Ella!" Josie screamed. She ran to the bed as the whole cabin groaned. She made out the lump of her daughter curled beneath the blankets, soaked with the rain blowing in through a hole in the wall where a section had blown off. With a series of creaks and pops, the roof folded in on itself, collapsing.

Josie threw herself on top of Ella.

The roof crashed down all around her, landing hard on her back. Something about the impact seemed odd, but there was no time to think about it as the shattered remnants of the roof continued to crumple and fold. After a few rapid heartbeats, everything settled.

Ella was sobbing, incoherent.

Josie lifted her arm to feel for the piece of roof on top of her. They couldn't stay in the wreckage for long. She had to take Ella away somewhere.

The tunnels.

They could hide in the tunnels until the storm passed.

Her groping hand encountered something very solid on top of her. And warm.

She twisted around, looking over her shoulder, and gasped.

The man hulked over her, supporting an enormous section of the roof on his wide shoulders. With a roar, he heaved it off, sending it knocking into the other debris, causing another cascade of collapsing. He reached past Josie and grasped Ella's arm.

"What are you doing?" Josie shouted to be heard over the storm. "Let go of her!"

He stared at her and pulled Ella to himself, lifting her up against his chest. Josie's heart raced. Her little girl was so small, so vulnerable.

"Let's go," the man growled, and looked around. Almost the whole structure of the cabin had been downed, only a few walls and bits of structure remaining. He used his legs to kick a path clear and Josie trailed behind him. They picked their way out of the wreck of the cabin and then the man started off back down the mountain, still with Ella clasped to his chest.

Josie had no idea where they were going, but wherever Ella was, she needed to be. The overwhelming surge of energy she had experienced previously was fading fast. She struggled onward regardless as lightning slashed the black heavens and rain poured in waterfalls off the pine branches, until they came to the hills. The man meant to take them back to his house.

Why? Why was he doing this? She had stolen from him multiple times and not only had he let her go, he had followed her, risking his own life to save her and her daughter. There was no reason for him to have done that.

She wanted to be thankful, but it seemed too good to be true. There had to be some catch, because no stranger was that kind unless they wanted something.

"You comin'?" Hunter stared back at her from inside the tunnel, holding the vines up out of the way with his spare arm.

"Yes," Josie said quickly, and rushed in after him. Her questions would have to wait. Getting to safety was what mattered most.

Chapter Four

They climbed the cellar stairs. The man turned and thrust Ella into Josie's arms. Ella had ceased crying and lay limp and silent against her, wracked with shivers. Josie grabbed her and pulled her in close, holding the back of her head.

"Stay here," the man commanded. He brushed around them and Josie heard a door slamming.

She looked around, uncertain of what she was meant to do. They were creating a puddle on the wood flooring from all the rainwater pouring off them. Anywhere they went, they would create a terrible mess.

Josie pressed her cheek to Ella's head and closed her eyes. *You're safe. I'm safe. We've made it through. For now.*

The door slammed again, making her jump, and the man walked back into the kitchen, now with a small, rotund woman hurrying along behind him on her short legs. Her blonde hair was plastered to her skull from the rain. Blue eyes shimmering out from behind sodden, straggling hairs held concern and a great deal of confusion.

"Hunter, what is going on?" she asked, looking around. "What's happened? Your arm is bleeding. And who are they?"

Josie jerked her head up. Hunter. Not only was it an appropriate name for such a fearsome person, she realized she knew it. Having grown up on a ranch in the area, she'd heard of most of the other ranchers. Word was that Hunter tended to keep to himself on his secluded ranch and didn't often go to town... just like her. In the past few years especially, when she was married to Owen, she'd barely gotten off her property.

She hadn't even known this was where his ranch was and she certainly wouldn't have recognized him. The descriptions of him as broad and tall hadn't painted a picture even close to reality.

It doesn't matter, anyway, she thought. *Knowing who he is doesn't make this any better.*

Hunter glanced down at his arm. A gash near his elbow leaked blood, which diluted into pink swirls on his soaked skin. "Don't mind that. Check them over, Kerry."

Kerry's lips pressed together and she straightened, though she didn't become any taller by doing so. "Fetch towels. Rags. Old bedsheets. Anything. Everyone needs to get dry or you'll all get terribly sick."

Hunter moved off.

"And bring more lights," Kerry called. She turned to Josie and looked up at her; Josie wasn't used to anyone having to look up at her. "Your name, dear?"

"Josie," she whispered.

Kerry stared at her and made a brief lifting motion with her hand. Josie understood and spoke her name louder.

"And the little girl?"

"Ella." This was all so terribly confusing and she was afraid, fear gripping her heart in its claws. She had to try to be strong and focus on what mattered, which was getting help for Ella.

"Can you help us?" Josie asked. "Please, Kerry."

"Dear, you don't even need to ask. That's why Hunter brought me." Kerry put her hand on Josie's wrist, her touch warm and gentle. "Let's go into the parlor. Don't mind the mess for now."

For now.

Josie trailed after Kerry, leaving streaks of water on the floor. It was almost worse to be out of the rain. Her clothes stuck to her skin, chafing as she moved.

The parlor was the room in the house where the light was burning, a lantern left to blaze. Kerry clucked her tongue like a disapproving mother hen. "I always tell him not to leave fires unattended, even candles, but does he listen?"

Kerry turned to Josie and motioned to Ella, still limp and shivering. "Will you allow me to undress the poor thing? She needs to get warm and the first step is getting dry."

Josie nodded and together they undressed Ella. Hunter strode into the parlor with an armful of rags and blankets. Kerry took a blanket and draped it over Ella and started to dry her hair, rubbing vigorously. Ella began to cry at the brisk treatment and her wails were music to Josie's ears.

Kerry seemed to agree with Josie. "If she's got the strength to cry, she's goin' to be fine. She's just cold and frightened. I only see a little scratch on the back of her hand there."

Josie closed her eyes as a wave of relief struck her. She swayed on her feet and put her hand to her face. "I was so worried," she gasped.

"Sit down," Hunter growled.

Josie flinched at his tone. "The furniture."

"Sit down," he repeated, and she had little choice but to obey. She sat on a chair and felt her dress and coat begin to soak through the cushion right away.

Kerry bundled Ella in a dry blanket and placed her down on another chair. “She’ll be just fine. Now you, Josie.”

Her face flamed and she shook her head. She couldn’t undress in front of this man, and not in front of Kerry, either. Not in front of her daughter. No.

“Take off the coat,” Kerry said, narrowing her eyes. “Or I’ll do it myself.”

That was something she could do, at least. Josie shrugged out of the coat and she realized how heavy it had been, soaked with rain. She could breathe easier without it.

Kerry stood in front of her and picked up her arm, turning it this way and that. “You’re covered in scratches. And on your face, too. Hunter, get a bottle of whiskey. And we need more light in here. Start a fire in the fireplace.”

Hunter gave a grunt and walked off. Josie watched him go, until a stinging on her arms drew her attention back to Kerry. Kerry dabbed at her bleeding cuts with an old rag, frowning. Josie hadn’t been aware of how hurt she was until then, dozens of cuts on her skin, including a nasty scrape on the back of her right hand.

It must have been all those trees I ran through.

Thunder snapped and she flinched, and Kerry flinched in response to her.

After a moment, Kerry said, “What were you doin’ outside, Josie? In this weather?”

Hunter returned with a bottle of whiskey, setting it down on a table with a heavy thud. He went to the fireplace that Josie hadn’t even noticed before and crouched down. A fire was soon sparking to life, growing as he fed it.

Kerry picked up the bottle of whiskey and poured a good amount on a rag. The dab of the alcohol-soaked rag on Josie's arms made her cuts sting worse and she hissed in a sharp breath between her teeth.

"Sorry," Kerry apologized. "It's got to be done."

"I know," Josie murmured. An infection would be very bad.

To distract herself from her burning cuts, she started talking, telling Kerry the same things that she had told Hunter before he decided to let her go. She considered stressing that she had eaten as little of the stolen food as she could manage, giving most of it to Ella, but it didn't matter. It was all thievery in the end.

Kerry touched the rag to a scratch on Josie's cheek, her eyes big and moist. "Poor things."

Josie swallowed hard and turned her head away.

"Poor things?" Hunter must have been listening while he worked on the fire. He barked a sudden laugh that made Josie's heart jump into her throat. There was no kindness in that laugh.

Kerry shot him a glare and he turned back to the fire, stirring the burning logs. Kerry picked up a blanket and draped it around Josie's shoulders. "Go stand in front of the fire. Get as warm as you can. Hunter, come here."

Josie stayed where she was because Hunter was still at the fireplace. Even shaking from the cold, she wasn't going to get near him.

Hunter at last left the fire, walking over to Kerry. "I'm fine."

"Well, I heard that a whole cabin fell on top of you. Best to make sure, don't you think?" Kerry waved the rag, stained with whiskey, smeared with Josie's blood.

With Hunter out of the way, Josie hurried to the fire. The snapping flames sent out a wave of heat and she moved even closer, until it was almost unbearable. She turned around and saw Ella in the chair and shifted it closer to the fire to warm her up as well. Ella stirred, turning her sweet face toward the warmth.

Outside, the storm raged on.

"Well, you're also fine." Kerry's voice broke into Josie's moment of peace before the fire and she half-turned.

Josie put her hand to her mouth as she saw Hunter had removed his shirt. The skin stretched tight over his broad chest and every muscle in his abdomen was visible. The lines of his body were sharpened by the shifting lights and shadows thrown from the fireplace, particularly the protruding tendons in his neck and at his wrists. It was no wonder he had been able to protect her and Ella from the collapsing cabin; he was every bit as muscular as a bull.

Hunter picked up a rag and rubbed it over his glistening shaggy hair. "Thanks. You can go back to the guest house now."

Kerry pressed her lips together and Josie experienced a swirl of anxiety. If Kerry left, she and Ella would be all alone with Hunter and she still didn't trust him. He had saved them, yes, but she was supposed to have left and never come back. He might really get the sheriff now and she would be sent off to jail.

"Maybe they should come to the guest house with me," Kerry said.

Hunter held up his hand. "No point gettin' them all soaked again. They'll stay here."

"Josie is still soaking wet," Kerry pointed out.

"She can... borrow some of Ma's old things." Hunter ran his hand through his damp hair. "Go, Kerry."

Kerry sighed and leaned around him, looking at Josie. "You look after that little girl of yours. Children are precious."

Josie put her hand on the chair where Ella drowsed fitfully. Precious was a good word. Ella was what Josie valued most in the world. She ached to think of what might have happened if any part of this night had gone differently. "I will. Thank you"

"What was I going to do, stand by and watch you two suffer?" Kerry flashed a soft smile. She turned and gave Hunter a look that Josie couldn't see, but it made him snort. Kerry continued to look at him for a long, long moment until he lifted his hands, and then she turned and left the parlor. Josie watched her go until she was cut off from sight, and she heard the door open and shut.

Hunter turned to her. "Follow me. Bring your daughter."

"Where are we going?"

Rather than answer her, he started to walk away.

Resigned to obeying him, just like she had obeyed every other man in her life, Josie bent and lifted Ella into her arms. Ella curled against her and Josie held the back of her head, stroking her damp curls.

Hunter was waiting outside of the parlor for her. When she moved to follow him, he took her down a hall, into a room where a lantern already burned on the windowsill. Though sparsely decorated, it was a nice room, neat and tidy. The big blue-and-white quilt over the lower half of the bed looked very comfortable and Josie would have liked nothing more than to crawl beneath it and go to sleep.

Hunter moved to the corner of the room, hands in his pockets. “This is your room. You can stay here with your daughter.”

Josie hurried to the bed and placed Ella down. The mattress was soft and Ella sank down into it. Josie put a hand on her back, needing to be in contact with her, to reassure herself Ella was actually there, and watched her slip off into sleep. Finally safe, for now.

Her throat tight, Josie looked up at Hunter. “We'll leave in the morning. You'll never see us again.”

“No.”

No? What did he mean no? Did that mean he'd be getting the law involved? Or was he about to suggest something else? She opened her mouth to ask, black dread in her stomach.

“After you've done caused me so much trouble, you're not gettin' to walk out of here. No, ma'am.” He clenched his jaw. You're goin' to be doin' things for me from now on.”

Her heart was pounding. “I don't understand.”

Why didn't he just say what he meant?

Hunter folded his muscular arms over his chest. Some of his injuries were much worse than the ones Josie had sustained during her run through the forest, since he had taken the brunt of the cabin collapse. The biggest cuts were still bleeding and she saw dark red marks that would surely turn into bruises. By stealing from him, she was ultimately responsible for the harm that had come to him.

Hunter said, “No home, no cabin. You've got no food, nothin'. Since you got no choice, you're goin' to stay here as my maid. You can pay me back for your thievery with hard, honest work.”

Josie lowered her head. "I see. I understand now. I accept."

How could she do anything other than accept? She would have to work for him, and she didn't know or understand him, but there would be a roof over their heads and food for them to eat. This was ultimately the best possible outcome. Though, some things could never be paid back. She could never make up for the harm she had caused to him, to everyone, on this night.

Tears threatened to fall, but didn't. She was too tired to cry.

"I'll bring you some of Ma's old clothes," Hunter said. A muscle in his cheek twitched. "You can get out of your wet things, hang 'em up to dry by the fireplace. Ma was taller than you, but it'll work out. Suppose you can hem a dress or two if you need to."

"I don't know how to thank you." She kept her head down. He was letting them stay in his big house when he could have sent them both to the guest house with Kerry, or put them in the stable with the horses.

He's making sure I can't get away without him knowing about it.

Hunter left and Josie got up from the bed, not wanting her wet, soiled clothes to stain the blankets more than they already had. She was a maid now and she would have to take care of that tomorrow, along with whatever else Hunter desired from her. A trickle of fear went down her spine— or it could have just been rainwater.

Heavy footsteps announced Hunter's return. He dropped an armful of dresses on top of the small chest of drawers and stepped back. "Need anythin' else?"

She wordlessly shook her head.

He nodded and left the room again, this time pulling the door shut behind himself.

Josie looked over at her daughter. “Ella?” she whispered.

Ella didn’t stir.

Satisfied that she was fully asleep and unlikely to wake up, Josie quickly stripped off her wet clothes and put on one of the new ones. The dress was only new to her though, as the style and design were decidedly out of date by ten or more years. The bodice was too big, the skirt much too long.

It would do for sleeping in, she supposed.

Josie draped her wet clothes across the windowsill. She probably wouldn’t be wearing them again, she supposed. The mud and bloodstains would never come out, and all the little rips and tears would take too much effort to mend. The best thing to do was wear these new clothes and adjust them with some hemming. There ought to be sewing supplies somewhere.

A problem for the morning.

Josie looked at the bed where Ella slept and ached to join her. However, tired as she was, she wasn’t actually ready to go to bed.

There was a small mirror on top of the dresser, neatly polished, reflecting the lantern light on its silvery surface. Josie walked over and bent down to look at her face. Her scratches weren’t too bad. They would heal quickly, faster than the last injury she’d had on her face.

She touched the corner of her eye where a small white scar split her tanned skin, a faint hook like a bird’s talon. She had gotten that scratch on the same day as Owen was murdered, when she had messed up his breakfast by overcooking his eggs. As flawed of a man as he was, he had never been able to let it go when she made mistakes. She had always paid the price.

If Owen had ever caught me stealing...

Josie pulled away from the mirror, biting her lower lip. It didn't make any sense to her why Hunter was being so kind, going so far out of his way for her and Ella. Her instinct was to think he had something nefarious in mind, but she couldn't actually think of anything that he might do to her. If he was going to harm her, wouldn't he have already done so?

Yet, the past had her wary. A man could hide his true nature, like Owen had done at first.

She was going to have to be very, very careful. At the first sign of trouble, she was getting out of there whether her debts were paid or not.

Chapter Five

Hunter sat in a chair in the parlor next to the fire and lifted his arm, grimacing. When Kerry was checking over him he had rushed her, not wanting to be fussed over. There had been too much going on to spend extra time on himself. He had been careful not to show any reaction when Kerry touched his wrist, but it had taken a lot of effort. His wrist throbbed with every beat of his heart. He had been too distracted to know when it happened, though of course it must have been when he caught the collapsing portion of the roof.

He rubbed his arm, praying it wouldn't swell and prevent him from working.

He leaned back in his chair, resting his head on the back. He needed to leave the house soon, so Kerry wouldn't get the wrong idea about him staying overnight with an unfamiliar woman. But he couldn't stay in the guesthouse with Kerry, either.

The stable it is, he thought, rubbing his arm again. *In a minute, I'll go.*

Soft hay to lay his head on, apples to chow on if he got hungry. It wouldn't be the first time he'd slept out there in the stable, though the last time was when he was much younger.

His mind turned to the woman. *Josie.* That was what Kerry had called her. She must have learned Josie's name during one of the times he was fetching supplies elsewhere in the house.

Did he know of a Josie? Wasn't there a small-time rancher with a daughter named something like that? He couldn't be sure. He kept to himself too much to know what everyone else was up to.

Whether he knew her or not wasn't the puzzle he needed to solve. His own actions were. Why had he followed her out into the storm? It wasn't a conscious decision. The urge had come over him only a minute after she had left through the tunnel in the cellar, too powerful to resist. His father had raised him on logic and most of the time that was how Hunter operated. There were still those times when instinct took over, when he felt more like an animal than a man of reason. Tonight had been one of those nights.

Considering it now, he figured it had to do with the child. Once he knew the girl was in a vulnerable situation, he simply had to help. Josie, too, had been in great danger, going back out into such weather. It wouldn't have been right not to assist and he was glad he had done so. Josie and the girl were both so much smaller than him. Their injuries would have been far greater than his aching wrist. The cold would have finished them off.

He was glad to have helped them and brought them to safety. He wouldn't be going easy on Josie, though. She was still a thief and she still owed him. Even more now.

Somehow, perhaps because it was unnaturally quiet when compared to the storm, Hunter heard a door opening inside his house. He strained his hearing and caught approaching footsteps. He sat upright as Josie appeared around the corner, looking child-sized in his mother's old dress. She wrapped her arms around herself and peered at him from inside the tangled curtain of her hair.

"I'm not sneaking out," she said, her voice quiet and a touch hoarse. "I just wanted some water."

Life was full of such ironies. Rain pouring down all around and yet there wasn't a drink for her.

"In the kitchen." Hunter inclined his head.

She scurried past him, the hem of her dress fluttering over the floor. He continued to listen as she moved through the house, heard her shuffling about in the kitchen. He wasn't worried about her making a break for it. She wasn't stupid enough to go back outside and she didn't have her daughter with her.

She walked back into the parlor, holding a wooden ladle. "I brought you some water, too. If you're thirsty."

Hunter took the ladle and drank the cool, sweet water in a few swallows. She stood there, watching him, shifting slightly on her bare feet. He handed the ladle back to her and as he did, he angled his arm the wrong way. The flash of pain was fierce and he winced before he could get ahold of himself and prevent his feelings from showing on his face.

Josie dropped the ladle, her hands flying to her cheeks. "You're hurtin'?"

"It's nothin'," he said, and waved her away with his working arm. "Go back to your room. Busy day for you tomorrow. Best rest up."

She shook her head. "Is it your cuts? That one there looks really painful."

She was awful stubborn for someone who had nearly died in a house collapse. He waved her away again. "Go to your room."

She tilted her head, staring so intensely that he was the one who started to get uncomfortable. "Did you hurt your arm when the roof came down?"

"Does it matter?" Where was this pushiness coming from? What right did she think she had to ask him anything?

"It does matter!" Her voice rose ever so slightly, almost nearing normal volume. She looked all around and went over to the pile of rags and scrap cloths he had yet to put away. She picked out a rag and used her teeth to nip through the threads along one edge. She continued the tear, ripping a long, ragged strip off, and repeated the process. "It's going to start swelling in the night and you won't be able to use it at all in the morning. We need to wrap it up."

"I can do it myself. Go back to sleep." He reached for the pile of fabric strips she was creating. He should have thought of wrapping his wrist himself instead of just hoping he would be fine. There was too much on his mind and that had fallen to the side with so much else going on.

"I don't really trust that you will do it." Josie picked up her scraps and approached the side of his chair, taking tiny, exhausted steps. "I won't be able to sleep if the job isn't done right."

"Hope you feel that way about your maid duties," he said. "I don't count half-done work as proper work."

"I always work hard." Her eyelids lowered and her mouth formed a hard line.

The sudden darkness of her expression unsettled him in a way he didn't understand. And hadn't she said she had lost their house and ranch? That didn't sound like the story of a hard worker to him.

She pressed the end of a fabric strip to his wrist, her fingertips gentle, and started to wrap it around his forearm, firmly, but not too tightly. When she was done, she tucked in the ends so they wouldn't come undone.

Hunter moved his arm around to test her work for himself and nodded his satisfaction. “Decent enough.”

“I know about wounds.” Her head was lowered, her hands clasped together.

Hunter snorted. Sure, she did. “You got such skills, you should be a pill’s assistant, not stealing.”

“I wish that I could,” she said, bitterly. “But you can’t bring your child to your job as a nurse.”

“And why would you have had to bring her with you?”

“Because then Ella would be alone.” Josie sank into a seat and hugged her arms around her middle.

“I don’t understand what you’re sayin’.” Maybe it was time to stop this useless jawing and get some real information.

“What I mean is...” Josie raked her hands through her hair. “My husband, Owen.” she said. “He was murdered a year ago.”

Hunter let out a low whistle, his heart twinging. “Now you mention that, I think I heard about it. And they never caught who did it. That’s a darned shame.”

“After he died, I found out we were in a lot of debt.”

Now, how had they gotten into such debt in the first place?

“I tried to find work, but I had to bring Ella with me to my jobs. But bosses don’t like that.” She rubbed her face. “It’s a long story. It doesn’t matter anymore. The bank took the ranch. Ella and I left.”

Her voice died, leaving only the crackling of the fire in the fireplace. Hunter realized he was leaning forward to listen to her. He sat back and crossed one leg over the other knee.

"Seems odd to be goin' up the mountain after somethin' like that. How did you find the cabin? You didn't build it."

"It was my father's," she replied. "His old hunting cabin, before he got sick and died. He took me to it a few times."

Josie stood up abruptly. "I think I'll go back to the room now. Try to keep your arm over your head while you sleep and don't move it too much. You might need to keep it wrapped up for a few days."

Hunter nodded and she slipped away. He heard the door shut and though he listened for a while after that, there were no other sounds from inside the house.

He took his leave then, sprinting across the dark, muddy ground until he got to the stable. The horses were surprised to see him, whinnying in alarm and stamping their hooves, but quieted down after a bit.

He made himself a bed in the hay and lay down for a few hours until the storm broke apart just before sunrise. Dawn's yellow and pink tones were muted, as if the sun was uncertain if it should come out of hiding yet.

Pieces of debris were ripped from the stable and barn covered the muddy ground. Deep puddles had formed in even the slightest of divots. A section of fence was damaged, too. But, overall, the state of the ranch could have been far worse than it was. He had good craftsmanship and constant maintenance to thank for that.

Hunter went to the guest house first. The porch had disappeared inside a puddle so large it was practically a lake. He slogged up to the door and knocked. "Kerry?" he called. "You awake?"

The door opened and Kerry stood there, her hair half-done. She held a few pins in her mouth and spoke around them. "Survived the storm, I did. Disappointed?"

"Relieved," he said. "Goin' to be too busy to have given you a proper burial."

Kerry finished putting her hair up with that mystifying, practiced ease that women had. When Hunter groomed himself, he always had to look in the mirror.

"How's Josie?" Kerry asked. "And Ella? And why is your wrist wrapped up?"

He ignored the last question. "I got them settled in one of my spare rooms. Figure they're still asleep. Probably going to wake up hungry soon."

"I get the hint." Kerry laughed softly and touched his arm. "I'll make my way over and work on breakfast. A big breakfast. Looks like I might need a boat to get over there, though."

Hunter pretended to notice her diminutive stature for the first time and scratched his head. "I guess I could carry you pick-back."

Her light touch turned into a swat. "I'll strangle you if you try to pick me up."

Hunter grabbed her arm and examined it. "You couldn't get these all the way around my neck."

"I would certainly try!"

With the help of a stick that she made Hunter fetch, Kerry waded through the puddle by sticking to the shallowest parts. She complained all the while, which he tuned out.

When they got to the house, Kerry went straight into the kitchen and busied herself with preparing breakfast. As she mixed up a cornmeal batter, she said, "What do you think they'll do after breakfast? Where are they going to go? You said their cabin collapsed. Can it be repaired?"

"Not at all," Hunter said. "It was already old and on the verge of fallin' apart. It's not even good firewood now. As for what they're goin' to do, I wanted to talk to you about that."

"I'm listening." Kerry set down the bowl of batter and set to cracking chicken eggs in another, smaller bowl.

"I told Josie she's going to work as my maid. I'd appreciate it if you would show her around the ranch and fill her in on all the chores she's expected to do. She's goin' to be livin' here with me so I can make sure she don't run off without working off what she owes me."

Kerry's mouth opened and she stared at him, still holding a cracked eggshell. "Well, that's... But you've already got me for a maid. Do you really need another?"

"There's no other work I would want to give her." She had lived on a ranch, but how much did she actually know about caring for the animals? Her husband and hired help would have taken care of those tasks while she kept the house and watched over their child.

"The two of you can figure out a schedule between you," Hunter said. "I'll expect you to work together until she gets the hang of things, and then you can decide how you want it done. Continue workin' together, trade off, it doesn't matter to me."

"I understand." Kerry gave him a sideways look. "Now, why're you doing all of this for her, Hunter? It seems like all of this is more trouble than it's worth for you."

He clenched his jaw and said nothing, though she almost certainly didn't actually need his answer to figure out his reasons. She had spent too much time with him, knew him too well.

Having a new member of staff and a child under his roof was absolutely going to be a pain, but given his own childhood and what he had gone through, he couldn't allow the little girl to suffer.

A soft voice came from behind him. "Making breakfast, Kerry? I'll help."

Josie walked into the kitchen, eyes flicking back and forth between Kerry and Hunter. His heart skipped a beat, although he wasn't sure why. Perhaps because of his misgivings. Perhaps out of sympathy for how ragged and exhausted she looked with her red hair tangled and her dress rumpled from sleeping. The scratches covering her arms and face were particularly vivid in the morning, dark scarlet slashes and dashes on her sun-browned skin.

Kerry quickly rearranged her expression into a soft smile. "Is Ella still asleep?"

"Yes."

"Good. Yes, you can help." Kerry swept her arm around the kitchen. "I hear you're going to be the new maid. I'll show you where everything is."

Josie nodded and walked to Kerry's side, making an effort to stay as far away from Hunter as possible.

There were hoofbeats outside, approaching, splashing through mud and water.

Josie shrank in on herself, clutching her thin body with her injured arms. She quivered all over and her mouth opened, emitting rapid gasps. "Who is that? Is it the sheriff?"

She looked like a frightened rabbit cornered by a hunting dog. Hunter held up his hands and motioned for her to calm down, alarm stirring in his chest. It didn't seem right for her to have such an extreme reaction, even if she was afraid. He began to wonder about all the things he didn't know about her, the life she had lived between her husband's murder and now. What had she done? What had she seen?

Kerry put her arm around Josie, patting her. "That will be Harry, won't it?" To Josie, she said, "Harry is a ranch hand. A good man."

Josie clutched herself tighter and seemed to make an effort to stop shaking.

Hunter couldn't bear the sight of her like that any longer and she probably didn't want him staring at her while she calmed down, anyway. He turned away. "Goin' to go talk with him. Call when breakfast is ready."

He left, heading out as Harry rode up on the horse he had borrowed. They met by the stable and Harry dismounted, landing in the mud. He frowned down at his boots, then lifted his head and flashed a smile for his boss.

Hunter nodded at him. "You got home on time?"

"The storm held off plenty long enough," Harry said. "How's the ranch this morning?"

"I don't know."

"You don't know?" Harry frowned and leaned in, suddenly concerned, and Hunter understood why. It wasn't his way to not know how things were going on his own ranch.

Hunter motioned for Harry to follow him into the stable and as they started to get the gear off the horse and return her to her stall, Hunter explained the events of the previous night after Harry had left.

"That is something else, boss," Harry remarked. He wiped mud and water from the mare's legs and rubbed her muscles to help with any soreness. "I had no idea you had a heart."

Hunter frowned at him. "You keep up with that and I'll tell Kerry not to give you any breakfast."

"She'll do it anyway just to rub you the wrong way." Harry smirked and guided the mare into her stall. He patted her neck as she dropped her head to drink deeply from her water. "You're really going to let that woman stay in your house?"

"Don't see any other way for this to work out." Hunter reminded himself to get the mare more water before he got too busy with other tasks. "I'm not sendin' a little girl like that off to an orphanage. And now I know the reason behind the stealin', it doesn't seem right to send Josie to jail."

"That all sounds about right," Harry said, still smirking. "How purty is this lady, anyway?"

Hunter scowled, prickling with irritation. "Not too purty. Bit like a rat that's been dragged through the mud."

Harry elbowed him, starting to laugh. His eyes sparked with humor that Hunter wasn't sharing. "She'll be a lot purtier when she's cleaned up, right?"

"You want to look like a rat dragged through the mud, too?" Hunter stepped toward him, growling. This was enough fooling around for one morning.

Harry moved back, still laughing, not seeming threatened at all. "Bet you if she was an old crone, you'd have handed her off to the sheriff by now."

Hunter threw his hands into the air, the prickling irritation becoming disgust, then pain as his wrist reminded him he had injured it. "I'm goin' off to check the cattle. Breakfast is soon. Suppose you'll see her then and know she's nothin' special."

Harry's chuckles followed him out of the stable. Hunter strode toward the cattle barn, skirting around deep pools of muddy water. The herd heard him approaching; he heard them shifting around, stomping and snorting in anticipation of his arrival.

He reached out to push the barn door open and saw his wrist wrapped up nice and neat in those fabric strips. The ends hadn't come undone at all while he slept and his pain was much less when he didn't gesture too sharply. Josie had done a good job.

Maybe she really does know about wounds, he thought, and didn't at all like what that might mean.

Chapter Six

Josie trailed after Kerry as the older woman guided her from the henhouse back to the ranch, both of them holding eggs in their aprons. Josie's head spun with everything she had been learning over the past several hours.

Hunter's ranch was almost twice as large as the one she had lived on with Owen and there were many more animals, more buildings, and more chores to fit into each day. How Kerry kept up with it on her own mystified Josie. How Josie was supposed to hold her own at all gave her pangs of worry in her stomach. She tried to remember what she had already learned, but her memories were like scrambled eggs, all blurry and mushy.

"Josie? Are you listening?"

Josie jerked her head up as Kerry spoke to her. She realized that she had stopped walking and hurried to join the other maid on the porch in front of the main house. "I- I was listening," Josie stammered. "You were saying...."

Oh, no! I can't remember! I wasn't paying attention at all.

Kerry clucked her tongue and shook her head. "Let's get these inside," she said, entering the house.

Josie followed after her, and they carefully put their eggs into a basket in the kitchen. Kerry dusted her hands off, scattering bits of straw and little feathers, and turned to face Josie.

Josie tensed, ducking her head down and lifting up her shoulders. She was already failing. She deserved to be reprimanded.

Warmth on her shoulder.

"Now, would you relax?" Kerry's voice was gentle, as soothing as her painless touch. "Goodness, you're acting like I'm about to hit you."

Josie flinched and turned her head away, tears stinging, her nostrils burning. "I'm sorry."

There was a long pause, and then Kerry sighed and pulled her hand back. "I see. That's how it is, is it?"

Her heart pounding, Josie prayed they wouldn't discuss this. She didn't want to talk about it. She didn't know what she could say, if there was even any point in saying anything at all. She needed to do better, that was the only thing that mattered.

Kerry cleared her throat and Josie risked a look at her, finding the other woman's face soft, her lips pursed in thought. She looked away again.

"It's fine to be overwhelmed," Kerry said in her gentle way. "There's a lot that's happened to you just in the past day, never mind everything that's come before."

"Kerry, please," Josie muttered.

"Now, you hold on and let me finish saying what I've got to say." A businesslike tone overrode the gentleness and that was somehow more comforting to Josie, to be treated like a normal woman.

"It's my job to teach you how to do *your* job," Kerry said. "And because I am good at my job, I know that you aren't goin' to learn everything in one day. Or even one week. There will be messes made. You're probably goin' to burn some of the meals you cook. You're goin' to forget things. And it's all okay, because nothing in this world is ever perfect, you hear? You just stick with me and do your best. You'll make it through."

Josie looked down at the once-pristine floor now scattered with bits of detritus from the chicken coop. “It’s nice of you to say. I worry Hunter won’t think the same.”

“You don’t worry about him. He won’t mess with us too much. He does his work and we’ll do ours. That’s how his pa ran this place and that’s how he runs it, too.” Kerry went to a nearby closet, one Josie had learned was there and had since forgotten about, and returned with a broom and dustpan.

Josie leaned back on the counter and watched her work, listened to the scratch of the broom over the wooden floorboard.

When Kerry had finished, she said, “I believe it’s time that we started making a bread dough so it’ll be ready for dinner tonight. Where’d that baby of yours get off to? She might like to help out.”

Josie looked around, realizing that she hadn’t seen or heard Ella in far too long. Minutes, at least. Her heart began to thump. “Well, I- I don’t know where she is. What if she’s gotten lost?”

“I guess we’d best go and find her.” Kerry led the way out of the house. Josie kept right behind her, stepping on her heels. “I believe she was still with us when we were at the henhouse. We’ll go there first.”

Josie sloshed through the muddy puddles, splashing her borrowed dress. She craned her head around for some sign of her daughter. The ranch was so large and if Ella had gone wondering, there would be no telling where she had gone. And what if she had gone to the river and fallen in?

“Now, don’t you go losin’ your head. Look over there.” Kerry pointed.

Josie whirled around and saw Ella wrapped up in the little blanket she was wearing for a dress until other clothes could be found for her. The girl crouched at the edge of a big, shallow puddle in which a number of birds were wading and bathing. Relieved, Josie started over to fetch her.

A shadow fell over Ella as Hunter stepped out from the nearby shed. He approached and stood over her, and the birds scattered.

Hunter dropped his big hand onto Ella's shoulder. Her chubby little legs almost crumpled under the sudden weight falling upon her and she squealed out in surprise and looked up.

"Hi!" Ella chirped. She smiled and pointed up at the wide, clear sky. "Birds up there!"

"Birds," Hunter rumbled. "That's right. Where's your mother?"

Josie at last reached Ella and lifted her up off the ground and into her arms. "I'm here. She wandered off."

"Saw birds, Mama," Ella said, and wriggled around in her arms. Josie held her tighter so she couldn't get away again.

Hunter stared at her daughter. "She likes birds?"

"She likes all animals," Josie said. Her cheeks were beginning to feel warm. She turned to go back to Kerry.

"Like birds best," Ella said, and rested her head on Josie's shoulder.

Josie was a few steps away when Hunter spoke again. "I like birds, too."

“What?” Josie looked back, but he was already moving off, paying no more attention to them. Had she even heard him correctly?

“Bye-bye,” Ella called out to Hunter, waving. Kerry chuckled, while Josie was confused. Why did Ella seem to like him already? She had been shy around Owen, rightfully so, and had shown little interest in the few other men she had seen in her short life. What made Hunter so different that she would smile at and talk to him?

Back in the house, Josie took Ella to a chair in the parlor, set her down, and crouched in front of her. “Ella, you must always stay where I can see you. Understand?”

Ella tipped her head. “Why?”

“Because.” Josie held her by the shoulders. “It’s not safe. Stay with Mama.”

“I like big house.” Ella kicked her legs and wiggled in Josie’s grasp. “Nice house.”

“We can only stay here if you behave.”

Kerry walked over. “She’ll remember. Until she forgets. Don’t stress so much over it, dear.”

“You keep telling me things like that, but I have to.” Josie stood and lifted Ella into her arms. Caring for Ella was the only steady work she had, and was coincidentally her most important work, and she needed to be good at it for both their sakes. “Ella, we’re going to make some bread now. You can help us mix everything up.”

Ella said, “Want see birds,” and put her arms around Josie’s neck.

“Maybe later we can look for more birds.”

They all went into the kitchen to work on the bread and kept themselves busy with other chores until it was time for dinner. They set the table and Josie took on the responsibility of serving, wanting to give Kerry a break. She brought the bread and then the sausages and fried potatoes. She was bringing the corn when her foot came down on the hem of her dress and she stumbled.

Hunter was on his feet in an instant, grabbing the bowl of corn out of her hands just as she started to drop it. Their fingers brushed together with a jolt of sensation that shot straight up Josie's arm.

Josie righted herself and clutched her still-tingling hand with the other. Everyone was looking at her, even Ella, and she realized how close she had come to tossing a bowl of hot corn kernels all over the table. Heat rose to her face and she huddled her shoulders up. She wished she could leave so they wouldn't look at her anymore, though of course that wouldn't have helped.

Hunter moved first, lifting a spoon and serving himself a generous helping of corn, nearly half the bowl. He began to eat, completely silent. She had no idea what that meant. Was he angry with her for almost creating a huge mess?

Owen would have been.

Kerry pulled out the chair next to her and motioned for Josie to sit. "No harm done," Kerry said. "Tomorrow, before we do anything else, we will work on getting your clothes to fit you properly. And I will bring some clothes that my grandchildren don't use anymore, for Ella."

"You really don't have to do that." Josie lifted her fork and poked at a piece of sausage. Savory, steaming juices ran from the holes left behind by the fork tines.

"But I will." Kerry nudged her and smiled.

They ate their meal. Ella devoured everything that was put on her plate, plus another helping of potatoes. Her voracious appetite filled Josie with relief. At long last, her daughter had enough to eat.

Hunter finished his food and left the table. Josie and Kerry began to work on cleaning up while Ella sat in her chair and munched another slice of bread.

Heavy footsteps announced Hunter's return.

"Here," he said.

Ella squealed out. "A bird!"

Josie turned and her heart leaped in her throat as Hunter was once more looming over her daughter. Then, she saw that Ella was holding something in both hands, beaming at whatever it was.

"What is that?" Josie walked over and took it from Ella, who whined and waved her arms, trying to get it back.

It was a doll shaped like a bird, rustic and clearly old, though well-crafted out of fabric and stuffed to a pleasing plumpness.

Hunter put his hands in his pockets. "For her, since she was so interested in the birds outside. Used to be mine when I was a boy. Figure Ella will get more use out of it now than I do these days." He shifted on his feet. Josie would have thought he was embarrassed if she hadn't known better. A man like him surely wasn't capable of embarrassment.

Josie held out the bird for Hunter to take it back. Though her heart hurt to do it, she knew what had to be done. "We can't accept this."

He glared at her with his black, baleful eyes. "Why?

"Mama!" Ella whined, trying to reach the toy.

Josie kept it out of her reach. She wouldn't have the resolve to take it back another time. "We aren't in a position to accept gifts. Take it back."

"No." Hunter set his jaw. "I ain't goin' to. You won't owe me anythin' for it. Anyway, it's not for you. You don't get to decide to give it back."

Ella continued to whine and her small hands curled into fists. Josie could feel a tantrum coming and she really didn't have the energy to deal with that. Why was Hunter making this so difficult? Even if the toy was a gift, they would be indebted to him just a little more. It was a different sort of owing, more personal, and she didn't want anything personal to be between them.

Hunter turned away. "You want her to have toys and be happy, don't you?"

"Of course I want her to be happy," Josie protested, and knew she had lost the argument by saying so. Hunter flashed a smirk and walked away.

Sighing, Josie crouched down and offered the bird to Ella. "Now, Ella..."

Ella didn't wait for her to finish. She snatched the toy in both hands and leaped out of her chair to go show Kerry. "Look, look, a bird!" she crowed.

Kerry bent down with her hands on her knees, laughing. "I see, yes. Very pretty. Take good care of it."

Josie looked at the floor and put her hand to her head., rubbing to soothe away the developing headache. What a stubborn, irritating man.

Chapter Seven

Hunter set down his steaming mug of coffee on a side table and sat in the huge chair that used to be his father's. When there were calm moments between chores, and late at night before bed, his father used to sit in the office and drink either coffee or whiskey. He would read one of the many books on the shelves, or pore over financial documents. Hunter was rarely ever allowed into the room while his father was in there, even when he had become a grown man. The office had come to seem like a mystical place, his father a mysterious and manly figure partaking in mysterious and manly activities.

Now that the office was Hunter's, he knew how normal it was, how ordinary his father had been. Still, there remained a bit of that magic. He sat in silence in perhaps the most important room in the house and unwound from the day's activities, sheltered from the hustle and bustle of the ranch. He could be still. He could do anything he wanted, but most often he chose to be still to better enjoy the quiet.

He picked a book that he had been reading off the side table and opened it with that ever-satisfying spine crackle, and the luxurious fluttering of thick pages. He ran his finger over the page, observing the neat, printed words without reading them, just admiring their shape and form upon the paper.

His father was not the kind of man to spend excessively. The opposite, in fact. However, the man was unable to resist the allure of a well-bound book and would purchase them whenever a traveling salesman came into town with them amongst his wares. The books in the office ranged from beautiful Bibles with embroidered covers to adventure tales, short story collections, and informational tomes on business and livestock.

The one Hunter had been reading was one he had read before, a refreshing and often humorous look at the true, honest challenges of running a ranch. Whenever life was especially stressful, he liked to get down this book and read a few chapters to remind himself that life was difficult for *everyone* and he was doing just fine, all things considered.

Hunter drank some of his coffee and settled in to read. He was just turning the page when the office door shifted in its frame. He glanced up and watched the door move inward another few inches.

Seeing as Kerry had gone off home already, there was only one person who could be out there. Or it was a rat.

Hunter put his book down, open, on his knee. "Come in."

The door bobbed open a little further and a small shadow fell into the room. A little face poked through the gap.

Hunter sat upright. "Ella?"

Saying her name was evidently the invitation she needed. She slid through the gap she had made and walked over to him. The stuffed bird he had gifted to her in spite of Josie's protests was tucked beneath her arm.

His mother had made him that toy, though his father had said he was too old for such things. Hunter had kept it, but not played with it. His chest warmed now to see the toy at last serving its purpose.

Ella walked over to him and grabbed the arm of his chair. She craned her head to look at his book and Hunter picked it up to show her. She reached for the book and wrapped her small hand around part of it. "Story?"

Her forwardness and confidence made him lift his eyebrows. She didn't seem to care that he was a stranger to her. Maybe that went to show how good of a mother Josie had been, in spite of her circumstances.

Or maybe he just didn't know anything about little girls. They could all be like this.

"It has stories in it." Hunter glanced over at the doorway, expecting to see Josie. She wasn't there, which surprised him. "Where's your mother?"

Ella ignored his question and started trying to climb up onto the chair, hiking her leg up. Hunter watched this process for a few moments, puzzled, before supposing he had better help. He put his hands beneath Ella's arms and lifted her so she could sit on the arm of the chair. She reached for his book again. "Story."

"Uh, yes, there are stories. Where's Josie?" He leaned his head down to make eye contact with her. Such pretty green eyes. Her red hair bobbed when she moved, which was often. She was going to be a heartbreaker when she grew up.

Ella stretched out her arm and poked his cheek. "Story for Ella?"

Hunter finally figured out what she wanted from him. "You want me to read you a story?"

Ella nodded and slid off the chair arm, tucking herself in against his side. He stared down at her, this tiny waif he could crush if he happened to move the wrong way. He tightened his muscles to keep very still and lifted the book. He leafed through the pages until he found one of the stories that he thought Ella would enjoy, since she liked birds so much. It also happened to be one of the shorter tales, so he could finish quickly and then take her back to her mother. Josie didn't trust him and she wouldn't like this one bit. But what else could he do? Say no and upset Ella, maybe make her cry?

Hunter cleared his throat and began to read aloud from the book. The author had had a particularly rough day— Hunter carefully skipped over the reason, that being the unexpected deaths of two calves due to a lone wolf attack. One of his favorite chickens, his best laying hen, was missing, which the author feared might also be a result of the wolf attack. Despite searching for the hen, he was unable to find her. At the end of the day, the author went to his favorite chair to smoke his corncob pipe. When he sat, something crunched underneath him and made his rear all wet.

"Standin' up," Hunter read, "I saw the broken remnants of an egg that had been laid not so very long ago, now smeared into the chair cushion."

Ella giggled with both hands of her mouth, her toes wiggling.

Hunter felt his own smile coming on. "I realized the egg had still been warm and I looked around just in time for Spotty, that favored hen of mine, to come flying down off the cabinet right into my face, peckin' me as revenge for sitting on her egg. She would not listen what I tried to tell her that I was only doin' as I had seen the other chickens do on many an occasion."

Ella squealed with laughter and let her head fall against his shoulder. The sight of her in such stitches made him laugh, too. He chucked under her chin with his finger and she squirmed around, her eyes squinted shut. He had no idea if that meant she liked it and pulled his hand away.

The moral of the story was a bit more serious than its content. The author went on to relate how he had just had to laugh at his own misadventure despite the terrible day he'd had. It still wasn't a good day, far from it, but humor could be found even in the midst of such darkness.

Not that Ella would understand that, even if he had included the part about the wolf attack. All she knew was that a funny man had sat on an egg and gotten all messy.

And that's all that she should know, he thought, looking down at her as she went limp and breathless against his side. *No more hardship. No turmoil or hunger or fear, not while you're under this roof. Your mother's still afraid, but you don't have anything to worry about while I'm around.*

He felt a sudden presence, the prickling of eyes watching him. He looked up and Josie was there in the doorway, her arms crossed over her chest. He had no idea how long she had actually been there.

She stepped into the office, coming into the light of the lamp he had lit to read by. In this quiet and thoughtful space that was his office, he found himself noticing some new things about her.

She had a scar next to her eye, a little hook like a bird's talon. She had probably gotten it when she was a child and played too roughly. He had a number of similar small scars, himself.

There were freckles on the bridge of her nose.

Josie walked over and the light of his lamp caught in her straight red hair, highlighting flashes of amber and marigold. "I'm sorry." Her voice was tired. "She keeps on ducking away when I'm not looking."

"You'll have to put a lead on her if this keeps up."

She lowered her head, the flaming curtain of her soft, clean hair hiding her face from him. "I really am sorry that she's bothering you so much."

"I was makin' a joke." Hunter put his book aside and stood, lifting Ella with him. He held her in the crook of his arm, where she was small enough to fit just right.

"Oh. Sorry."

Hunter huffed. "You can't keep apologizin' for everythin', Josie."

"Well, what am I supposed to do?" She raked her fingers clawlike through her hair. "When everything is still so wrong. Nothing is how it should be."

Hunter looked down at her daughter and Ella blinked up at him, green eyes wide and curious. "Apologizin' doesn't fix any of it. What's done is done. Only thing to do now is look forward."

Josie said nothing, still looking down with her back bent and her shoulders slumped. He felt a twinge of sympathy for her, a soft ache in his heart. Maybe he should have read the story to *her,* not Ella. She was the one who needed to learn to find the spots of brightness amidst all the dark.

Ella was tugging on his arm, trying to get his attention. He looked down at her. "What is it?"

Her smile stretched from ear to ear. "Bedtime," she announced.

"Yes," Josie said quickly. "It's late for you. Come here." She held out her arms.

Hunter started to hand her off, but Ella wrapped both arms around his and clung tightly. "Hunter do it," she said.

"Hunter does what?" Hunter asked, mystified.

"She wants you to take her to bed." Josie massaged her temples, her face scrunched. "It's fine, just hand her over and I'll do it."

"No, I'll do it. Can't be that hard." Hunter stepped around Josie despite her quick, muttered protests, and took Ella to her room. The bed was made up very neatly and he had to tug hard with his free hand to pull the blankets down.

Ella let go of him and he placed her down on the mattress. Memories surged up from the back of his mind and he was just a boy again, five or six, lying in bed and looking up at his mother as she tucked him in. She had pulled up the blankets and used her hands to fold them beneath his body, encasing him in a cocoon of warmth. He had felt so safe, so secure.

When his mother had leaned over him to kiss his forehead, he had been certain nothing bad would ever happen to him.

Hunter bent and lifted the blankets over her, being sure to tuck them in around her. "There," he said. "How's that?"

Ella's eyes were already closing, a sweet, satisfied smile on her lips. Hunter was certain she knew she had gotten her way and was proud of herself.

Josie motioned for him to follow her out of the room. Hunter shut the door behind them and faced her. "Learn anythin'?" he asked.

She blinked and seemed startled. "Was I supposed to be learning? I know how to put my daughter to bed."

Hunter gestured to himself. "I'm not a monster. Just a man. You don't have to be worried about Ella bein' around me. I'm not goin' to eat her."

He watched as color rose to her cheeks, making her freckles stand out starkly. "I didn't think that."

"That was also a joke. You'll learn how to make them someday, maybe."

"I know how to make jokes!" The red spots on her cheeks flared even more hotly.

Hunter waved his hand and turned to leave. He wanted to read a little more, finish his coffee.

"Wait." Josie's voice beseeched him, suddenly softer than before. He looked over his shoulder at her. Her eyes flicked up to meet his before darting away again.

Something inside of him flipped over as their eyes glanced across each other, utterly baffling him as to what it could be.

"Thank you," Josie said. "For being kind to her."

"It's nothin'. It's just the right thing."

He walked away and went back into his office. He leaned his head on his hand and stared at the far wall, considering these feelings inside him, making little sense out of them. In the end, it was all too confusing and he set the mystery aside for the time being. Best just to go on as he had been rather than bother figuring all of this out. Josie was just going to leave eventually, anyway.

Chapter Eight

Wrapping her hands around the thick stalk, Josie pulled hard and watched as the weed slid out of the garden soil. The tangled web of roots just kept coming until at last they let loose of the soil with a jolt that nearly had her on her rump. She held it up, admiring its size. "That's a big one," she said to herself, and then laughed a little as she realized how she was talking like a fisherman with a prize catch.

Josie tossed the weed aside and sat back on her haunches. The day was warm, with little trace of last week's storm aside from some lingering humidity. Kerry had let her borrow a sunhat, which kept her shoulders cool.

Josie adjusted the hat on her head and looked out across the ranch. One by one, she had met all the ranch hands who worked on Hunter's property. Not just Harry, but Ezra, the nineteen year-old with a limp; Charles, who was such a cowboy that it was almost farce; Butch, fatherly and gentle, and several others who came and went. She had come to learn that they were all hard workers, as Hunter would tolerate nothing else. They had quickly made all the necessary repairs on the ranch and now everything was better than new.

She had learned other things as well, like the layout of the house and the actual ranch, and the laundry schedule. She was starting to figure out how to make large-enough meals for the men, who were likely to be present for breakfast or dinner depending on their schedules and inclinations. And she was learning how to plan those meals in advance too, thanks to Kerry's instruction.

Crouched there in the garden, Josie was struck by the idea that, for the first time in *years,* life was easy. She didn't have to worry about work, food, a place to sleep.

She still felt as though she should be scared. All of this could end in moments whenever Hunter decided she had paid him back.

Perhaps Hunter would decide he liked having a second maid around. He also seemed fond of Ella, and Ella was definitely fond of him, for whatever reason. Maybe they would be invited to stay.

"How are you getting along?" Kerry walked over, holding out a canteen. "Looks like you're nearly finished with the weeding to me."

"Yes, nearly done. Just a little patch over there left to do. I can see the weeds from here." Josie took a drink from the canteen. The cool water that flowed into her mouth had been subtly sweetened. She wiped her mouth and looked for Ella to call her over to get a drink, too.

Ella crouched on the ground not far from the garden, one of the ranch hands, Charles, standing nearby and watching over her. That was another benefit of being on the ranch that Josie hadn't considered at first, which she now was very happy about. More people around meant more eyes on her daughter.

Charles noticed Josie looking and tipped his hat to her. "Howdy," he called in a voice turned rough by drink and tobacco. "Need somethin'?"

"How is she?" Josie pointed at Ella.

"Happy as can be, ma'am. Dirty as can be, too." Charles flashed a grin and slapped his knee.

Kerry chuckled. "She'll need a bath later. So will you after working out in the sun like this, even with my hat."

"I don't feel like having a warm bath," Josie said. She walked over to the other section of the garden that needed tending to and bent down to get to work. She dug her fingers into the warm, loamy soil. "Maybe before dinner, we'll go freshen up at the river. It's so nice to have a source of running water right on the ranch."

"Oh, yes. I think that was one of the features of the valley that originally drew Hunter's grandparents here in the first place." Kerry had walked with her and stood idly by. "It's not quite a normal spot for a ranch. Not as much room to graze the cattle and you can't really *make* more room, either. But the walls offer protection and the river provides fresh water. And fish. You done any fishing ever?"

Josie shook her head. She scraped around the base of a stubborn weed to free the roots a little. "I always thought hunting and fishing were what men did."

"Men's duties, women's duties. The lines blur sometimes." Kerry dismissed the notion with a wave of the hand. "No women out on the frontier with the cowboys. The men learn pretty quick how to sew and mend clothes and to cook."

"Spoken from experience?" Josie looked up at her.

Kerry patted her on the shoulder. "My husband. Love him now. Hated him when he was young. He went off to be a cowboy. Came back to Deadwood five years later with a different attitude, different thoughts. That's when I finally gave in and let him court me, once he saw how hard it was to do some of these 'womanly duties'."

Josie finished with the weeds and stood. She dusted the dirt from her hands, the brown plume briefly hanging in the air before dissipating. "So, what about fishing?"

"Oh, right. Well, sometimes when all the men go off on a cattle drive, I do some fishing in the river. Hunter doesn't like fish much, but it's a nice change of pace. Maybe you'll join me next time." Kerry smiled at her.

"Maybe I will." If she was still in the area when that opportunity came about.

Kerry looked up at the sky and clicked her tongue. "Well, I don't like to make you go back inside when you're enjoying the sun, but there's dinner preparations waiting to be done."

"I'm ready to go inside. I hope Ella is, too." Josie looked for her again.

Ella was in the same spot as before, though standing now. She had something in her hand that Josie couldn't quite make out, and she was looking at something.

Josie looked, too. Hunter was walking past, his back to her daughter.

Josie's chest went tight. She didn't know why, and she wasn't in control of herself as she strode toward Ella. She just felt like something was about to happen, like an event was lining up, all the pieces falling into place. She had often felt like that around Owen, like she was watching a train speeding toward broken tracks and there wasn't anything she could do to stop the coming derailment.

Ella lifted her arm and threw what she had been holding. A rock, just the perfect size to fit in a toddler's fist, flew from her hand and struck Hunter on the side of the head.

Hunter whirled around, his brows low over dark, glowering eyes. He advanced on Ella with his shoulders squared, pointing at her. "Hey!" he shouted. "Now what was that for?"

Ella's mouth fell open and she stared up at Hunter in shock as he towered over her.

Josie reached her then, snatching Ella up into her arms. She pressed her hand to the back of Ella's head as Hunter's angry shout echoed in her head, throbbing. Her eye, the one with the scar, was twitching wildly.

Hunter had only ever been kind in his own way, but the shouting. She couldn't stand that. Because if he shouted over a rock being thrown, what else might he shout over?

The echo of his yell in her head twisted, became Owen.

It wouldn't stop at shouting. It never did.

Clutching Ella tightly against her, aware that all eyes were on her and simply not caring, she hurried back to the house.

Chapter Nine

The look that came over Ella's face after Hunter's shout was familiar to him in a terrible way. He hunted, as all men did, and on the occasions when he walked up to finish off an injured, dying rabbit or deer, that was the look they wore, terror mixed with a breed of acceptance, a fear of their inevitable fate.

To see that look on the face of a little girl as a result of something he had done sickened him. His stomach turned over and he tasted bile at the back of his throat.

Was it wrong, what he had done? It both looked and felt wrong, yet how could it be, when that was what he had grown up with? His father had always shouted at him when he had made a mistake because shouting was easy to understand. The louder a yell, the more trouble Hunter was in.

So why, now, was his stomach so bitter with guilt? He wasn't the one who had made the mistake. He wasn't the one who had thrown a rock that hit someone. The side of his head was still stinging, proof that he was the one who had every right to be angry.

Josie marched up to Ella's side, her back stiff like an angry cat's, and forcefully yanked her daughter up into her arms. She clamped Ella's face to her shoulder and whirled away, rushing in the direction of the house. But in the instant before she turned, Hunter caught the look on her face and it was identical to the one her daughter wore.

He hadn't even shouted at *her*. She had no reason to look like that.

What is going on?

He looked around and everyone was staring at him, Kerry and Charles, and now Harry too, walking up and shaking his head at him.

"You got something to say?" Hunter demanded, pointing at Harry. His breath was hot in his lungs. "If you do, say it. Otherwise, you hobble your lip and get back to your work. This doesn't concern you."

Harry heaved a sigh and held up his hands. "Don't want you yellin' at me, now," he said.

"Now, what do you mean by that?"

Harry shrugged. He had hobbled his lip, as instructed.

Hunter waved his hand, dismissing Harry, and continued walking to the shed where he had been headed originally, though he could no longer remember what exactly he was going there for. He threw the door open and stepped inside, hands on his hips, staring at the racks, waiting for his purpose there to jump out at him.

The questions in his mind were too thick, a flock of black starlings preventing him from seeing past. He thought about Josie again, the injured-animal glaze of fear in her eyes, the taut stretch of her lips into something that almost resembled a grin.

She was an odd woman; he had thought that about her from the very start. She was uptight and stubborn, with these strange moments of vulnerability. He never knew what side of her he was going to get, and not knowing where to stand with her was a constant frustration for him. He wanted everything to make sense and she just didn't.

His own mother had been yelled at by his father on many an occasion and she had never snatched him up and run off, so why was that Josie's inclination?

And he couldn't forget her strange comment on the first night she was in his house, when she told him that she knew about wounds. He still didn't know what she had meant by that.

If only he knew more about her past, he might be able to understand her better and to figure out why she had such extreme reactions to the strangest things.

But he didn't need to understand her, that was the thing. Their arrangement was that she would work for him and he wouldn't go to the law. That was it.

Restraining a growl, Hunter stepped out of the shed and shoved the doors closed again. He left the building without anything that he had meant to get, an act that would have earned him a hide-tanning from his father when he was a boy.

Harry walked up to him, thumbs hooked into his belt. "You might want to go see what's happenin' at the house."

Hunter frowned at him. "Who said you could unhobble your lip?"

"Didn't you hear what I said?" Harry pointed at the house. "Josie's in there. I saw her walkin' around through the windows. I think she was carrying somethin' but I don't know what. I don't get a good feelin' from it, though."

Hunter kicked at the dust and muttered a profanity under his breath. "I don't got the time to deal with these womanly problems."

"You brought her on. Those are your problems now, too." Harry scoffed and hooked his thumbs into his belt once more, turning away. "Quit beatin' the devil around the stump and go in there to talk to her."

Harry strode off, which left Hunter alone outside. The other ranch hands had gone, and Kerry was out of sight, too.

Hunter looked at his house and heaved a sigh, then started across to it. It was what a man did when no one was watching him that mattered the most. He would see what was going on with Josie and hopefully put an end to it before she got the whole ranch out of sorts.

Approaching the house, he heard shrieking coming from within and his heart lurched up into his throat. He picked up his pace and burst in through the door, following the sound down the hall to the room he had given Josie to sleep in. Looking through the open doorway, he saw Ella sprawled out in the middle of the floor, waving her arms and kicking her legs. Josie was walking past her with a dress draped over one arm, seemingly unaware of her screaming child.

Josie placed the dress on the bed and started to fold it. She stiffened and looked up at Hunter. An echo of that earlier terrified expression flickered over her face, before settling into a weary and accepting mask. She looked away and resumed folding the dress.

"Josie?" Hunter raised his voice to be heard over Ella's fit.

Josie flinched, jerking her head to the side.

Ella's next shriek ended in a gulping sob. She rolled over onto her side and lifted her red, tearstained face. She saw Hunter and her eyes flew open again. She scrabbled up onto her feet and Hunter winced, expecting her to run away from him, and then she was running toward him, putting her arms around his leg and squeezing tight.

She had already forgiven him for scaring her?

Yet another mystery these two posed. Why was it that Ella had become attached to him so quickly? He could understand her opening up to him after he had shown her some attention, but she was the one who had initiated all the interactions between them thus far— good and bad.

Hunter stretched his hand down, meaning to stroke Ella's hair or touch her shoulder, he wasn't sure. Josie rushed over, grabbing Ella up in her arms again and taking her to the bed. "Stay there," Josie said, her voice tight. "For once, Ella, stay where I tell you."

Ella's face scrunched up and her hands turned into fists. The tears started rolling again, dripping off her chubby chin. "Hunter!" she cried, plaintive as a lost fawn. "No go! No go!"

"I ain't goin' anywhere," Hunter said, more confused than ever.

"No, we are," Josie shot back. She finished folding the dress and strode across to the dresser, grabbing miniature clothes from one of the drawers— Ella's clothes, borrowed from Kerry's grandchildren. Shapeless dresses mostly, white and beige, with little ruffles and ribbons sewn on to pretty them up.

"Where are you goin'?"

Josie slapped a tan dress down onto the pile she was making and whirled to face him. Her eyes were rimmed with red, her mouth turned down. "I don't know. We'll figure it out. We aren't staying here any longer."

Hunter frowned and scratched the side of his head. The spot where the rock had hit him no longer hurt. He didn't even feel any swelling. "Why not?"

"You can't be serious." Josie put her hand to her face and shook her head. She resumed piling up the clothes.

"I am serious. You're madder than a hornet right now and I don't know why." He leaned his hip on the doorframe, going back and forth between watching Ella and Josie. The girl had given up on her fit and was crying softly, occasionally muttering something in her child's tongue that he would never be able to decipher.

"If you can't even think of why, then there's no hope for this." Josie braced herself on the bed and spoke to the clothing stack, her hair hiding her face from him. "I know I still owe you a lot. When I find work elsewhere, I'll send money. I won't just disappear without paying it all off."

"You are the one who can't be serious right now, Josie. You're goin' to put yourself and Ella in an even worse situation than before. You don't even have a cabin to go to now."

"What I'm doing is taking Ella out of another bad situation we've found ourselves in." She straightened and pushed her hair back. Her jaw was set, a faint flame ignited in her tired green eyes. She really believed in what she was saying, in what she was about to do.

"I've learned from last time. We'll go into town, to the church. The priest can help us. And we're going as soon as I find something to put our clothes in." She hesitated. "I'll send more money for the clothes and everything."

"You can take one of the old sacks from down in the cellar." If she really thought she was going to do this, he saw no reason not to help her. He could only make the situation better for her. "Don't got to pay me back for that."

She nodded. "Okay. Then, I'll get one in a minute. Leave us be now, please."

He stood there looking at her and he thought that there should be something he should say. Did he apologize for something he hadn't done? Did he wish her good luck in this fool's errand of hers? Nothing seemed right or appropriate, so he turned and left the room, and left the house.

Kerry was coming up the porch as he left, huffing for breath. She must have been doing something strenuous, though just by looking at her, he couldn't see what that was. She looked up and skidded to a halt in front of him. "Is she still in there?"

"Yes," he said, "she is. You goin' to try to stop her?"

"Not exactly." She swatted at his side. "Move. I need to go talk to her."

Hunter held his ground for the moment. "Do you know what's going on with her?"

Kerry stared up at him as if he was the dumbest man in the entire state. "Yes, I do."

"How?"

"Because, Hunter. A woman always knows." Kerry apparently lost her patience with waiting for him to move and slipped past him, bumping into him on the way.

So it is womanly problems, of a sort.

There really wasn't anything that he could do about it, then. He'd be sorry to see the two of them go, but this was something he knew nothing about. It was best to stay out of it.

Chapter Ten

Josie headed for the door with Ella's hand in hers, the sack of their meager belongings tossed over one shoulder. Someone stood in the foyer, blocking their way.

"Kerry," Josie said. She appealed to the older woman with her eyes, silently begging her to see logic and let them pass.

"Josie." Kerry put her hands on her considerable hips. "I know you think you're doing the right thing, but this isn't it."

"I can decide that for myself." Josie shifted the sack on her shoulder. The weight of it was very light, but the rough fabric scraped the skin on her neck. She supposed she would be rubbed raw by the time they got to town, to the church, where she would rest until the priest saw her and she could ask him for help.

Kerry sighed. "You won't at least consider waiting until tomorrow morning for a fresh start?"

"I can't." Her voice cracked. She cleared her throat. "The way he yelled at Ella. She didn't hit him with that rock on purpose. And how much could it have hurt him? She's a little girl. But he yelled at her and he looked so angry with her."

"I'm sure it was only the surprise," Kerry said. "You would have been surprised, too."

"You're making excuses for him." Josie gritted her teeth.

"No. I'm just tryin' to explain." Kerry bent and cupped the side of Ella's face in her hand and smiled at her, then straightened again. "No one could be mad at that sweet little face for long. What you think is an oncoming storm has already passed by."

"Maybe." She wasn't convinced. Even if this incident of yelling was just a sudden lightning strike, she didn't trust it. There was always more that could come.

"If you're really thinkin' of doing this and I can't stop you, then I had best make sure you can be safe." Kerry removed a folded handkerchief from her pocket and held it out. "You take this."

Eyebrows furrowing, Josie took the handkerchief. Something crinkled within the folds. She peeled back a lacy layer and caught a flash of distinctive sage-green printing on paper. "No! I can't take your money!"

"It's your money," Kerry said, backing away as Josie tried to push it into her hands to return it. "I know Hunter wasn't paying you because you were still working to pay him back. I thought ahead, as I knew you might leave when you were done, or maybe sometime after. I started putting aside some of my pay here and there to give you when you left, to give you a head start. If you're really committed to leaving now, you can have the money now, though it's not as much as I'd like. I didn't have the time I thought I would."

Josie folded the handkerchief over the money again and put it in one of her pockets for safekeeping. She knew she couldn't turn it down. "I'll pay you back."

"The Lord Himself will pay me back in his own way." Kerry smiled and waved her hand. "There should be just enough there to get you a room at the hotel in town for a night or two, and some hot meals. The rest is up to you."

Josie blinked away hot tears and held out her arm. Kerry embraced her, squeezing her tight and patting her back. Her body was warm and soft. If Josie had had a mother, she imagined this was what a hug from her would have felt like.

I won't let you down, Kerry. I'll do my best.

Josie pulled away and took in a deep breath, then let it slowly out. “We have a long way to go until we get to town. We better get started.”

“I’d reckon so. Want me to keep you company? I can go with you until the edge of the valley,” Kerry offered.

Josie shook her head. “I appreciate it, but it’s best for Ella, for everyone, if we just go our separate ways now.”

Kerry looked her up and down, lips pursed. Josie shifted on her feet and looked past her, through the open front door, trying to gauge the light and how many hours they had until sundown.

Kerry stepped aside. “I’ve got faith in you. You’re strong. Good luck.”

“Thank you,” Josie said. She gave a gentle tug on Ella’s arm. “We’re going now. Say goodbye.”

Ella stared blankly ahead, her cheeks still damp with tears. She had stopped crying around the time Josie put their clothes into the old sack, as if she realized that it was useless to keep throwing a fuss. Or, more likely, she was just tired.

Josie walked with her outside. The hairs on the back of her neck prickled. She resisted the urge to look around and see who was watching. She didn’t want to see Hunter.

Slowly, to account for Ella’s smaller steps, they skirted along the high hills that formed the edge of the valley wall, around the edge of the ranch. As they went further, Josie noticed the grasses growing taller and wilder, snagging at her legs, in some areas reaching up over Ella’s head. There wouldn’t be as much ranch activity going on in this area normally, which meant the grass wasn’t trodden flat or grazed down. Though, she did see some faint paths marked here and there where someone had gone through. Crossing one of those paths, she saw hoofprints marked in the soil.

The hills dropped around them, gentling. Deadwood was a cluster of buildings in the near distance, surrounded by trees that were very much alive in spite of the town's name. Josie knew there was some story behind the name's, though she couldn't remember what it was. Right now, what the town meant to her was safety.

Josie turned them to cut across a field where they could join with the winding road in and out of town, to make their journey easier. The sky above was still that high, pure blue, free of clouds, but she didn't trust it to last. Sunset fell with surprising speed and suddenness over the mountains and the weather could do strange things.

There was a resistance on her arm. Josie stopped and looked around at Ella. Ella had stopped in her tracks, her head down, her hair a mass of flames around her head.

"Ella?"

Ella sat down with a huff in the middle of the grass.

Josie dropped the sack of clothes and crouched in front of her daughter. She touched two fingers beneath her chin and lifted until their eyes met. "Ella, what are you doing?"

"Feet hurt," Ella grumbled. "No more walk."

"We're going to town. We're almost there now." Josie smoothed Ella's hair down, and the wind tugged it out of place again. "Come on, my Ella."

Ella pushed her fingers into the soil and pouted.

Is there anyone in the world who has found a way to make children listen?

Josie bent and lifted Ella into her arms, and Ella held onto her around her neck. As her daughter rested her head on Josie's shoulder, she could feel her smiling. Of course, this was exactly what Ella had wanted all along.

Josie rubbed her cheek on Ella's. "Well, it's a nice day for the walk, at least," she murmured. She snagged their sack and moved on in the direction of the road.

Something shot through the grass in front of her and she tried not to think about what it might have been. Once, early on in her marriage, Owen had found a snake in their chicken coop and brought it into the house to frighten her with it, ultimately throwing the hideous serpent at her. For weeks, she imagined hissing noises inside their house and would have to search every small corner to reassure herself nothing was there.

She still hated snakes.

Although, as she put some distance between herself and the potential snake, she figured the snake Owen had thrown at her had done nothing wrong. Owen was the one who had wronged her. He had always wronged her, even as he tried to make it seem like she was the one doing wrong to him.

Josie shuddered.

Ella stirred in her arms. "Mama?"

"Hush." Josie kissed the side of her head and she was still again.

Josie's legs ached as she crested the final hill and started down the last slope to town. People covered the streets, on foot and astride horses, women in dresses and men in their vests and breeches. A man with a fancy hat stood next to a wagon, making wild gestures with his hands as he spoke to a butcher still wearing a bloodstained apron. The fancy man motioned to the back of his wagon, and he went around behind with the butcher. A few moments later, the butcher walked away, shaking his head. Some sort of business deal gone wrong, perhaps.

A group of children ran into the general store and emerged soon after with fistfuls of candy, their laughter high and sweet. Dogs and cats roamed, the cats slinking in the shadows, the dogs loping about as they pleased, fur dusty, pink tongues dangling from their mouths.

"Now, who is that?"

Josie looked around and saw two women staring at her. Their cheeks went red upon realizing they were caught and they hurried away with their shopping baskets.

Josie dropped her head, staring at the dusty street. Eyes burned into her from all directions and her face flamed. If she looked around again, she would see them all staring at her, especially the women, wondering who she was and where she had come from, and where was the father of her child.

She lived in this town, but she wasn't a part of it, not since she married Owen. She was more of a stranger than the man in the expensive hat. He at least thought he belonged. Josie knew she didn't.

Maybe one day, if she tried hard enough, if she worked hard enough, she would belong.

She crossed to the other side of the street as she passed the noisy saloon, avoiding the leering men sitting out front. Clive was probably in there, working at the bar, serving his loyal customers. That was where she thought he would be anyway, as he seemed too nosy to sit in the back in an office working with numbers all day. The way he had gotten the owner of the Deadwood Bank to tell him all that information about the ranch and then brought it to Josie was clear evidence of that.

The hotel at the corner was a shabby building with a façade faded by wind and weather. A few men stood outside, smoking, grumbling to each other. Josie hurried past them, waving her hand to clear the smoke. It wasn't enough and Ella started to cough.

"That little lady ain't illy, is she? Ain't got the consumption?" A gruff voice inside the stuffy building drew Josie's attention to a shadowy desk, behind which sat the widest man she had ever seen. His small, beady eyes blazed like burning coals from beneath the heavy ridge of his brows.

"She's not sick," Josie said quickly. "It's just the smoke."

The man heaved his bulk to his feet, his chair groaning as it was relieved of his weight. He lumbered forward like a bull. He smelled strongly of aftershave, tickling Josie's nose and bringing water to her eyes. "Ain't I know you? The Smithson girl?"

She started at the sound of her maiden name.

The man laughed, then coughed, hacking raggedly. He bent forward over his gut, his face turning the color of a tomato. Josie bit the inside of her cheek, her heart skipping beats. She had been in town for less than an hour and this man was going to die in front of her.

She rushed over to a chair and set Ella down on it, placing the sack of their belongings in her lap. "Stay here and hold this," she commanded.

"Why?" Ella asked.

Josie didn't bother answering the question and hurried to the desk the man had been sitting at. A mug sat atop a mess of wrinkled papers, droplets beaded up on the smooth surface. She grabbed the mug and swatted away one of the papers that stuck to it and went back to the man. She only smelled the alcohol when she was already by his side. She would have preferred for it to be water, but she didn't think she had the time to go and find some. It would have to be whiskey.

"Here, drink some." She pushed the mug into the man's meaty hands.

He grasped the mug and pulled the rim to his mouth, swallowing a gulp of the whiskey as if it was water. He gasped and coughed again, then took another drink. Some of the alarming red color began to fade from his round face.

Josie put her hand on his back, tentative. She sensed no harmful intentions from this poor man. "Will you be okay?"

He drank again, long and deep, his throat bobbing, and wiped his mouth on the back of his hand. "Don't worry. I ain't got the consumption neither."

"I didn't think so."

"Just took me by surprise, the look on your face." He coughed and frowned into the mug. He turned it upside-down and not a single drop came out. "I knew your father. Good man. Shame that he done went and left the ranch to that Owen feller."

"Owen was murdered," Josie said quietly.

This man she didn't even know thought little of Owen. Had other people known that he was trouble?

She didn't look forward to having this same conversation over and over again with everyone she spoke to. She didn't want to think that people had known and done nothing to warn her. But what could they have done? Would she have even listened? It was her father who wanted her to marry Owen and she would never have disobeyed him like that, not when he was dying and depending on her to make his passing easier.

The man's voice drew her out of his thoughts. "Ayuh, I recall that now. That's a shame, too. Done left you and the nipper there all alone."

He extended his hand. "Name's Arthur. What can I do for you?"

"Josie." She took Arthur's very warm and clammy hand and shook with him. "I need a room for a day or two."

"Got a room right down that hall there you can have." He waved his hand across the room. "Second door. It's two dollars a night. Pay each morn' for the next night or you ain't gettin' back in."

Josie nodded and reached into her pocket to get out her handkerchief with the money inside. She unfolded two bills and handed them over.

Arthur removed one of the dollars and gave it back to her. "A discount on account of you bein' so kind, ma'am."

She lowered her head. She hadn't been kind to get something back in return.

Arthur cleared his throat, looking away. "Breakfast and dinner's included in the price. First come, first served. Dinner's in about an hour tonight. Goin' to be served in that room back here. You best go to your room and get settled in."

Arthur moved away, navigating with surprising grace behind his desk to remove a key from the wall. He returned and handed it over to her, the metal heavy and cool laying in her palm. "You let me know if there's anythin' you need."

"Thank you, Arthur." Josie turned and went to Ella, lifting her and the sack again. Her arms protested at being put to work again. She gritted her teeth against the soreness, so close to the end of their journey. She couldn't give up yet.

She went down the dingy hallway, feeling Arthur watching her. She fumbled with the key and managed to slot it into the lock and pushed the door open.

Dust hung thick in the air, big drifting motes the size of day-old chicks. A gray film covered the top of the ancient, scarred trunk at the foot of the equally ancient bed. Josie approached the bed and studied the thin, holey sheets, the mattress with straw poking out through ripped seams.

At least there's no bugs.

Josie placed Ella down on the bed, which creaked loudly in the small and silent room. She rubbed at her lower back, stretching to try and ease some of the accumulated strain.

"Bad." Ella's small voice rose up. "Bad room."

Josie sat down on the bed next to her; the mattress was so thin she felt as if she was sitting on the bare wooden bedframe. She wrapped an arm around Ella and drew her to her side, stroking her hair. "It's only for a little while, my dear."

Ella grumbled and wriggled to free herself. Josie let go of her and Ella hopped off the bed, heading straight for the door. Josie hopped up to intercept her, making a note to lock the door and hide the key so Ella couldn't sneak away in the night.

Ella whined her frustration and dug her head into Josie's shoulder. "Hunter, where Hunter?"

Josie rubbed her back, a lump in her throat. So much she couldn't explain, so much Ella wouldn't understand...and hopefully would never have to.

Ella heaved a huge sigh and cuddled into Josie. With their bodies pressed together, Josie felt it when Ella's stomach rumbled. Her own stomach twisted with hunger and she laughed softly under her breath. Of course, that was why Ella was being so ornery.

"We'll have dinner soon." Josie stroked her hair, the silky flames sliding between her fingers. "And then we'll get some rest. Would you like that? Are you tired?"

Ella said nothing. Josie hugged her tighter. To her, getting some rest sounded even more appealing than dinner.

Rest tonight, then try to find work tomorrow morning. She didn't know where she would find it, but she had to go looking. Kerry's money wouldn't last forever.

Chapter Eleven

Hunter stared down at the food on the plate in front of him, absently rubbing at his forehead where an ache was lingering. Butter was slowly melting into one of Kerry's famous fluffy biscuits, seeping into the layers. Normally, he didn't wait long enough for the butter to even soften. He had no appetite that morning at all. The fried eggs and bacon also held no appeal for him.

Kerry sat across from him at the table, also not eating. They were the only ones. Harry had eaten at home before coming out to the ranch, and Ezra had turned down the offer to join them. A sour stomach, he had said, probably as a result of drinking too much the night before, although he wouldn't say so. His bloodshot eyes and the pasty cast to his skin had spoken the truth for him.

Hunter grabbed his coffee and swallowed the powerful black brew in a few gulps, burning his throat in the process. He wiped his mouth and pushed back from the table.

Kerry lifted her head. There were more wrinkles at the corners of her mouth than normal, creases formed by the strength of her frown. "Tell me what I did all this cookin' for if no one is goin' to eat a bite."

"Save it for lunch. Ezra'll be over his 'sour stomach' by then, I'd guess." Hunter shrugged. "Sometimes a man just isn't hungry."

"The only time a man isn't hungry is when he's got a bellyful of guilt." Kerry pushed back from her chair and stood. She snatched hers and Hunter's plates off the table and took them back into the kitchen.

Hunter's ears burned like she was his mother scolding him. He followed her into the kitchen and stood over her. "I don't got any guilt. I didn't do anythin' wrong."

"You aren't the only one who gets to decide that." Kerry started to wrap up the uneaten food, staring hard at her work. "Josie felt like you wronged her. You pretended like her feelin's didn't matter, but they did and they do. No matter what you think, she thinks differently."

His head throbbed with every beat of his heart, his pulse in his ears like a dull stabbing. He pinched the bridge of his nose and squeezed his eyes shut. "She didn't want to stay."

"She was fine with stayin' until you yelled."

"Ella needed to learn."

Kerry rounded on him, holding a butter knife in hand. "Well, you ain't her mother!" she exclaimed.

Silence.

Hunter took the flat of the butter knife blade between two fingers and lifted it from Kerry's grasp. She sighed and leaned on the counter, rubbing at her face. "Now you got me yelling, too."

He looked at her, this woman who had always been so strong and capable, a solid presence in his life for years and years, now seemingly losing control of her composure. And why? Well, there was only one thing that had changed, making it easy to narrow down the cause.

"You really cared for Josie," Hunter said. "You're worried about her. You weren't eatin' and you love your own cookin' as much as the rest of us."

"Yes, I'm worried for her. She was much better off here. I was hopin' she would stay for a time, until she had a good place to go to. Or she could have stayed here for as long as she wanted."

"Well, it's not your ranch. You wouldn't have been the one to decide that."

Kerry took the butter knife back from him and placed it in the sink for washing, along with the dirtied dishes and other utensils. "You liked having her around, too. You can't deny that, Hunter."

"I don't know where you got that idea from." This discussion had gone on for long enough. Josie had left them yesterday. She could have gotten on a train and been across the country by this point. There was no use in talking about her.

Kerry picked up a gingham-patterned towel and swatted at him with it. "Get out of here. Go take care of what actually matters to you," she said, her words terse.

Shaking his head, Hunter let her be, heading to the foyer to put on his boots before stepping outside. Ezra was wheeling a 'barrow of dirtied straw out of the stable and off to the compost pile, the ripe, yet not entirely unpleasant odor of manure trailing after him.

The cattle were lowing in their barn, sounding moody, frustrated. Hunter went in that direction and found Hunter working there, feeding them, though not quickly enough for their liking. He pitched in and soon the fuss was quieted, replaced by the sounds of chewing and contented grunting.

Harry thumped the side of his boot on the barn wall to dislodge a half-dried cow patty from the bottom. "How in tarnation did they get that out here? I swear they're throwing it, sometimes."

Hunter smirked. “After all this time, you still haven’t figured out how to watch where you step.”

Harry kicked the smashed pieces of the patty at him. Hunter stepped away and grabbed a shovel, scooping up the manure and dumping it into a nearby wheelbarrow. “You want to mess around with this stuff so much, you can clean up in here after we take them out to graze.”

“Bit stuffy in here, but it beats staying outside in the sun.” Harry grabbed the shovel out of his hand and leaned it up against the wall. “Hey, how are you holdin’ up?”

Hunter frowned. “With what?”

“Well, you were getting to be pretty fond of that little girl, I thought,” Harry said, and Hunter groaned. “What? You trying to tell me that you weren’t? She was fond of you, at least. Always wanting to follow you around, like a duckling.”

“Once or twice, she did, I guess.”

“That’s all you noticed, sure. But Josie was always runnin’ after her and bringin’ her back into the house. Guess the little girl had a strong will. She just wasn’t goin’ to give up.” Harry chuckled. “I hope my kid is easier to manage than that.”

“Maybe it’s a good thing they left, then. A ranch is no place for a small child.”

“You and me were small children once.” Harry adjusted his hat.

Hunter put his hand on his head, suddenly realizing he had forgotten his own hat. “Shoot. I’ll be back.”

Harry laughed. “Yeah, I think you’re losing some hair in your old age. Best get your hat so the top of your head doesn’t burn.”

Hunter left the barn and walked back to the house. He ran his fingers through his hair as he walked, trying to feel if he really was getting thinner hair or if Harry was making a fool out of him. He felt nothing out of the ordinary, thankfully. He was only thirty-one and his father had still had a full head of hair when he died at fifty-nine.

Kerry was in the kitchen, washing the dishes. Hunter walked on the balls of his feet to avoid her hearing him and went to his room to grab his hat. Settling it atop his head, he started on his way back.

Both times, he passed the door to the guest room where Josie and Ella had stayed, but it was only on the way back that he saw the door was slightly ajar. He reached to pull it shut all the way, and then some other urge took over him and he pushed it open all the way.

Everything was exactly as it had been before the pair had come to stay, the bed neatly made, the top of the dresser polished.

He started to turn away, then noticed something was out of place after all. There was something underneath the bed.

He stepped into the room and got on his knees to reach underneath. His groping fingers snagged a soft object and he pulled it out.

He held the stuffed bird he had given to Ella. Josie must have made her leave it behind.

He stroked a finger over the neat rows of stitching his mother had made one at a time. He had never noticed before the painstaking care that had gone into making each stitch identical to the others. The body of the fabric was soft blue, with the wings made from different scraps, though with matching white undersides. The eyes were mismatched buttons.

I wanted Ella to have this.

Josie would use any money she got to buy essentials, not toys.

A hand fell onto his shoulder. He looked up at Kerry. Her soft blue gaze locked with his. She held out her hand for the toy and he gave it to her, rising to his feet.

"I really wanted Ella to have that," he said. His voice came out stiffly. "I don't know why. It's like you said. I'm not her parent."

Kerry fiddled with one of the button eyes. Even years and years after being first sewn on, the eye was still firmly attached. "You could go give it to her."

"I don't know where they've gone off to."

"I gave Josie some of my money and told her to go to the hotel in town. She should be there. If you want to find her." Kerry returned the stuffed bird to him. How small it looked in the palm of his hand, and how large in Ella's arms. "You're stubborn, but you're a good man, Hunter. You know you were havin' feelings for her."

"Feelings?" He laughed, incredulous. "No. You couldn't be more wrong. I don't have time for that nonsense, and even if I did, I wouldn't be spending my time on a thief and a widow."

"What would it matter that she's a widow?" Kerry asked. "She had no control over that. She didn't murder her husband."

"What I mean is..." He stopped and scratched the back of his head, beneath the brim of his hat. What did he even mean? "I don't think about settlin' down like that. It especially never crossed my mind to court a woman who's already been married, already had another man's child.

That's like gettin' involved in someone else's business when I should be mindin' my own."

"Things happen out of our control all the time."

"I know that, and you know I know that. What's your point, Kerry? I need to get back to work."

Kerry lifted her shoulders and stepped out into the hallway. "Whether you have feelings for Josie or not, we both know you should take that toy to Ella. Maybe you'll wind up talkin' to Josie and you'll tell her you're sorry for yelling. Maybe you'll tell her that we all already miss having her around and want her to come on back home."

Kerry walked away, leaving Hunter alone in the empty room. He looked down at the toy bird, turning her last word over and over in his head, examining it.

Home.

He hadn't thought about his ranch being Josie's and Ella's home. He had thought of it as a temporary arrangement. Something that would inevitably end. And maybe it would have ended on its own, but that should have been something decided in the future. Instead, he had chased Josie away.

He tucked the toy into his pocket and went back to the barn. There must have been an odd look on his face, causing Harry to squint at him.

"You okay, boss?" Harry asked.

"I am." Hunter nodded slowly. "I just remembered I got some business in Deadwood. Let's get these cattle out to graze so I can get on my way. I'd like to be back by sundown."

"Sundown, huh?" Harry hooked his thumbs into his belt. "It's just after breakfast. That must be some business. Mind telling me about it?"

“I’d rather just get to work and get this handled.” Hunter set his jaw and Harry got the message.

They set off to the stable to saddle up a couple of horses for driving the cattle. Hunter tightened straps and did up buckles without needing to think about it, his mind occupied with figuring out what exactly he would say to Josie when he found her.

If he found her. She might not actually be in Deadwood. Then what would he do? He couldn’t let it end this way now that he had realized his errors. He would fix what he had done, somehow.

Chapter Twelve

Whistling, Clive wiped down the bar counter with a clean cloth. The saloon had just quieted down after the last of the lunch crowd left, leaving just him and a single customer, a roostered, jobless old pod slumped across a table in the back corner next to the dead fireplace. While he did prefer the chaos and activity of the crowds that came around mealtimes, he had always found there to be something special about these between-times.

Something to do with potential, maybe.

Not a lot of things in Deadwood had much potential these days, but when he was in his saloon thinking about all the customers to come later that night, the future had a shine to it.

Rapid footsteps approaching the saloon doors drew his attention from his idle work. He looked up and waited, expecting to see the sheriff or one of his men. The law came in on a somewhat regular basis, sneaking sips of whiskey while on the job. Or they came in because of their job, seeking information on the participants of a brawl, chasing down some other criminal activity. There used to be a fair few murders in the town years back, in the middle of the gold rush.

And there were still murders every now and again.

Like his cousin Owen's murder.

The saloon door burst open and a small, scrawny man with the nervous manner of a squirrel came scampering up to the bar.

"Buck!" Clive exclaimed. He was the brother of the man who ran the hotel in town, Arthur. The two were as unalike as brothers could ever be. The rumor around town was always that they didn't have the same father.

"How's the store, Buck?"

Buck hopped onto one of the stools at the bar. "Same as always," he said. His voice was a high chittering. "Ladies comin' in all the time with them little troublemakers. Makes me fit to be tied, I tell you."

Clive made a sympathetic sound. Buck worked at the general store. They saw very different people at their jobs. The women who came into the saloon were not the sort to have children and be doing daily shopping.

"I learned somethin' that's of interest to you today." Buck leaned over the counter, hands flat on the polished surface, no doubt smudging it with his greasy fingers. "Heared it from Arthur, I did. I'll tell you if you give me a shot of tonsil varnish."

Clive had heard this bargain a time or two. He sometimes took pity on the rodenty man, sometimes not, depending on how generous he was feeling. Everyone knew Buck only ate enough to stay alive, and imbibed enough to put a normal man under the ground. He would do anything to get a drink.

Clive decided he was feeling generous that day. He turned to the shelves behind him and selected a small glass and a bottle of medium-quality whiskey— not the worst, not his best. He poured a bit of the dark amber liquor into the glass and slid it across to Buck.

Buck tossed it back like it was water and slapped the glass down with a thump on the counter. "Someone came to stay at the hotel yesterday," he announced. "And she's stayin' another night, 'cause she paid for the room again this morn'."

"Who was it?" Clive added another dribble into the glass. That was all that he felt like giving out for free and he moved to put the bottle back on the shelf.

"Josie Murphy."

Clive's entire body went stiff as he pulled in a sudden, sharp breath. The whiskey bottle fell from his stiff and cold fingers, smashing on the floor at his feet. Glass shards sprayed in all directions, sparkling with whiskey droplets. He felt his pulse began to tick rapidly at his throat as a film of gray and red filtered into his vision, blinding him. His ears rang.

Owen's widow. The beautiful woman Owen hadn't deserved. The woman who hardly gave Clive a glance, even when he went out of his way to forewarn her about the bank taking her ranch from her.

He had tried so hard to forget about her, he really did. So many times. And now she was back?

"Clive? Clive?"

The frantic voice pierced through the ringing in Clive's head. He blinked hard and looked around. Buck stared at him, though the man at the table in the back hadn't stirred at the crash of shattering glass.

"Clive?" Buck spoke timidly. He leaned over the counter and stared at the smashed bottle.

Clive held his face, digging his fingers in hard. He couldn't seem to feel his feet. It was as if they were just gone and he was floating there. "Uh?"

"I'm goin' to get the doctor." Buck jumped up off his stool.

No.

Somehow, he was able to get enough control over himself to hold out his arm, reaching for Buck. "Don't. Don't get the doctor. I'm fine."

"You don't sound fine."

"Of course, I'm fine." Clive forced cheer into his voice. Buck stared at him, but he was no longer running for the doctor and that was good.

"Are you sure? You, uh, you went pale right as I was tellin' you about Josie." Buck shifted on his feet, looking over at the door. "Maybe I should still get the doctor."

"No. My hand just slipped, is all. And I was thinkin' about how it was a waste of liquor." Not true, not true at all, but now Buck was nodding along, agreeing about the waste. Clive knew he had him. Such a simple man, with such simple needs.

Clive grabbed a bottle of whiskey that was little more than water and thumped it down on the counter. "You know what, I should go pay a visit to Owen's widow. It's been too long since I seen her last. You keep an eye on things for me, Buck. Help yourself to some of this."

Buck licked his lips, looking at the whiskey like it was water and he was the thirstiest man alive. He extended his small, bony hand and wrapped it around the neck of the bottle, pulling it closer to himself. "I should be gettin' back to work. I just comed to tell you about Josie, is all."

"And I do appreciate it." More than Buck could ever know. Clive pointed at the bottle. "Why work to pay for it when I'm givin' it to you for free so long as you stay here and keep an eye on things, make sure John back there doesn't stop breathin'?"

"I never knew you was a man of logic, Clive." Buck unscrewed the top off the bottle and lifted the mouth to his lips.

Clive smirked to himself and left the saloon. He barely felt the hot sun beating down on his shoulders and the top of his head, where he was developing an early bald spot. He set his eyes on the hotel and marched straight for it. A boy ran out onto the street in front of him, and he kept right on going, knocking the boy to the dust as he passed. He ignored the child's pained cries, and ignored the glares the mother threw in his direction as she rushed by. There was only one sight he wanted to see and that was Josie's face. The only sound he wanted to hear was Josie's voice.

When his cousin Owen was just a working hand on Henry Smithson's ranch, he started talking about the rancher's pretty daughter. Once when Clive was visiting, he happened to see her and that was it for him. He had fallen right in love.

Her gorgeous hair. He wanted to embrace her and smell it.

Her pretty green eyes. He wanted to stare into them for hours.

But she hadn't paid much attention to him even as he made more trips back to the ranch, inventing reasons that he had to be there. Most women didn't pay him *any* attention at all. At twenty-nine, he had never successfully courted anyone. He was just too ordinary. He wasn't muscular or very tall, and his hair and eyes were both the drab brown of a muddy creek. But when Josie did look at him or talk to him, his heart would quiver in his chest, and not stop quivering for hours.

Then, Henry Smithson died, and left his ranch and daughter to Owen. Clive had done his best to move on. He had his saloon to take care of during the day and the company of soiled doves on the nights when he was too lonely.

Josie had just kept drawing him back in. Just like she was doing right now, even if she didn't know it.

Clive threw the hotel doors open. Arthur jolted in surprise, almost overturning his desk. "Clive! What've you got your wiggle on for?"

"Is Josie really here?"

"Oh, guess you might want to see her. Second door there."

Clive walked past while Arthur did an awful job of hiding that he was watching him, and he went right up to Josie's door and pounded his fist on it.

Someone spoke inside, a child. That was right. He kept forgetting that she'd had a child with Owen.

The door opened and thoughts of the kid left him once more as he saw Josie standing there, beautiful as a sunrise with her flaming red hair pulled back into a bun. Her eyes widened and he leaned in slightly, amazed by all the different shades of green caught in them, dark and light, amber-tinted and purest emerald.

"Clive." Josie sounded as surprised to see him as he had been to hear she was back. "What are you doing here?"

He put his hand on the door frame. His heart pounded and his face was hot. "I heard you were in town. What are *you* doin' here? In a hotel?"

Josie looked over her shoulder, probably checking on her child. Clive admired the slender line of her neck. He thought he might be able to encircle it entirely with one hand.

Josie looked back at him and let out a soft sigh. "Just stayin' for a few days. Lookin' for work. Arthur's letting me help clean the rooms for some dimes."

Flames ignited around his heart. It wasn't fair that that *pig* got to spend time with her. "You could have come to me, you know. I'd pay you better. Let you stay with me for free. I wanted to help you back when I first told you about the house and I still mean it."

"I know. Thank you for that." She dropped her head.

She's too embarrassed to accept my help because she knows me. That's it.

"Where've you been?" Clive asked. "People were talkin' about how they saw you around often, lookin' for work, and then you just vanished. And now you're back. Did you go somewhere?"

"I went away for a bit."

That's it? That's all I get?

He fought to keep his hands from becoming fists. He thought so much about her and spent so much of his time thinking about her, and she would still hardly talk to him. It wasn't fair.

His view of the hotel room past Josie doubled and then tripled as he lost focus. The film of gray and red returned, like looking at the world past a blazing fire.

"...Hunter."

He snapped out of it and blinked hard. "What? Who?"

Josie frowned, and it didn't suit her face at all. She needed to be smiling. "I said that recently, I've been staying on that ranch in the valley nearby. The one owned by Hunter."

He barely restrained a groan that bubbled up in his throat. Why, why did she seem so accepting of other men and not of him?

"Hunter Carson. Isn't he strange?" Clive asked pointedly. "Keeps to himself and everythin'. No one knows much about him. You're safer in town."

She said nothing. He had to think that she agreed and was too polite to say so. "You would be even safer with me, you know. There's no point to you workin' for cheap and stayin' in strange places."

"Clive..." Josie stopped speaking and looked past him.

He could feel someone moving down the hall toward them, hear their heavy footsteps. He moved closer to the doorway to let them pass. Whoever it was stopped right behind him, close enough to feel their hot breath steaming on the back of his neck. He spun around, sharp words already on his tongue, spilling over.

Hunter hulked over him, shaggy hair protruding from beneath his old threadbare Stetson. His black eyes were filled with the savagery of wild animals.

Clive shrank back, breathing hard and fast. The twist of Hunter's mouth into a predatory snarl had him shaking in his shoes.

Josie whispered something faintly behind Clive, and he remembered. He straightened his back and squared his shoulders. He had handled some frightening criminals and unhinged drunks in his time owning the saloon. He could handle Hunter, too. He had to. Josie must have left his valley ranch for a reason.

"What do you want?" Clive demanded.

Hunter inclined his head toward Josie and it was like watching a boulder shift downward on a mountainside. "I'm bringin' my maid home."

"It doesn't seem like she wants to go back to your place. If she wanted to be there, she wouldn't have left."

Hunter lifted one eyebrow. "Who are you?"

"Clive."

"Oh, I see. You're her husband's cousin." Hunter nodded as if he understood something. "This isn't any of your business. You should leave."

"I'm not leavin'," he snapped. "I was here and talkin' with her first. You can wait your turn."

"No one is taking turns with me." Josie spoke sharply, and Clive swiveled, staring at her. She shot him a glare and he had no idea why. He was trying to help her.

"Clive," Josie said, "I appreciate it, but I'm not takin' you up on your offer. Maybe we'll talk more later. I need to see what Hunter wants."

Just like that, he had gotten the mitten. His heart was a pincushion, stabbed with needles. He stepped back and Hunter moved in to take his spot, already replacing him.

"Alright. We will talk more later. You can believe that, Josie." Clive took another step away. "As for you, Hunter, you'd best watch your back."

"I always do," Hunter growled.

Clive scoffed and left them to whatever it was they had to talk about. Josie would have the good sense to send Hunter away. He hoped. And he hoped Buck's information was right, that Josie was going to be staying in the hotel again that night. If she found better work than what Arthur offered, she would stay in town and he could see her more often. Maybe he would get her to see the smartest thing for her to do was work for him, and stay with him.

Maybe he could finally make her his, after all this time.

Now *that* was a bright and shiny future he could look forward to.

Chapter Thirteen

"Hunter, Hunter, Hunter!"

Ella dashed between Josie's legs and threw herself at Hunter, latching on and climbing him like a chipmunk going up a tall, broad oak. He put his arm underneath her and lifted, and she sat there with her legs kicking, beaming up at him, as pleased with herself as any child had ever been.

Josie watched this, helpless to put a stop to it. Part of her didn't want to, anyway. All last night and earlier that day, Ella had been withdrawn, a turtle in her shell, hardly speaking, hardly eating. Having her bright and eager daughter back to normal was almost worth Hunter being around, except that he was the one who caused the problems originally.

"You left this behind." Hunter produced that darned stuffed bird from his pocket and handed it to Ella. She squealed in delight and snatched it up in both hands.

How many times do I have to give that back to him?

Almost as if he heard her thoughts, Hunter lifted his head and stared at her. "You got to ask yourself if this is really an argument you want to spend your energy on."

It wasn't, she conceded. There was definitely something more important to focus on. "What are you doing here, Hunter? You told Clive that you were going to bring me home? I'm sorry, that's just not happening."

"Mostly, I said that to get Clive to go away. Seemed like he was botherin' you."

Josie sighed. "He wasn't, not really. He's just always been a nosey parker. I don't think he knows when he isn't wanted around, but he doesn't mean any harm."

Hunter grunted. "Long as he wasn't botherin' you, I suppose. How you been doin'? I know that Kerry gave you some tin to spend."

"I've been fine."

"And Ella?" Hunter looked down at her daughter, and she beamed up at him.

Josie held up her hands. "You would think that she's been just fine this entire time. I don't know why she likes you so much. After you yelled at her, too."

Hunter shrugged. "I don't know what to say on that. She just does. I like her too, by the way."

"You *yelled* at her. How can that mean you like her?" She squared her shoulders. "It's all for show until things go wrong, is that it?"

Hunter kept looking at Ella as he shifted his feet on the floor. "It was a lapse in judgment. Everyone's prone to them."

Josie held out her arms. "Give her to me."

Hunter spoke to Ella. "Got to give you back to your mother now." As he moved to hand her off, Ella protested and clutched her arms tightly around his neck.

"Heck. Ella..." Josie rubbed her forehead where a vein was throbbing. "Why did you have to come here? I need to get some rest before it's time to help the cooks set up for dinner. But now Ella will be upset when you leave and I won't get any rest at all."

Hunter managed to lower Ella to the ground, where she stood clutching at his hand. He tipped his head back and stared up at the ceiling. His thin lips moved with a muted whisper. “I’m sorry.”

Josie’s heart stopped as she heard those words. She couldn’t fully believe that she had heard them. She must have imagined them. "What?"

"I’m sorry,” Hunter repeated, his rough voice low. He pushed his hair out of his face. The darkness in his gaze had softened in some way she couldn’t quite identify. “That’s the real reason I came out here. Not to force you to come back if you didn’t want to, but to tell you that I was sorry. I ain’t used to having children around on the ranch. I’m used to dealin’ with men and with Kerry. When I lose my temper, they don’t get hurt. But I hurt Ella. I know I did. I’m sorry to her, and I’m sorry to you, Josie. I am.”

The floor was unsteady beneath her feet and she grabbed onto the doorframe to support herself. No man had ever admitted a mistake in front of her before, much less actually apologized. Owen certainly never had, and her own father preferred to say nothing and move on. Yet here was Hunter, saying he was sorry, explaining himself in a way that wasn’t an excuse.

She had absolutely no idea what to make of it and that frightened her. She wanted to understand her position in life, even if that position was a bad one. Hunter was making her question things, instead.

“You don’t got to accept my apology.” He turned slightly away, clearing his throat. “But, listen. Kerry’s concerned about you, and she liked havin’ your help. She won’t say anything about it, but she’s older and slowing down. It was nice for her to have someone younger around. If you did want to come back, she’d be glad to have you.”

"And what about you? Would you want me to come back?"

Hunter reached to her. She resisted a flinch, holding her ground. He brushed his thick, warm fingers over the back of her wrist before pulling away. Her skin burned where he had touched, three individual scorched lines of contact.

"I understand if you don't," he said, each word slow. His eyebrows furrowed together, his forehead creasing into long, tanned mountain ridges. "But I don't like how things went. I can't say I'll be perfect from now on, but I would like you to come on home if you want to. We can all try again."

Home.

Was that really what Hunter's ranch was? Home?

Can I trust him?

Josie crouched and took Ella's hand in both of hers. "What do you say?" she asked quietly. "Do you want to go home with Hunter?"

Ella bounced on her feet, her nose scrunching with her smile. "Yes! Hunter home, good home."

What was it that Kerry had said? "*She'll remember, until she forgets.*"

Ella had already forgotten, forgiven Hunter, and she was the one who had been wronged the most by his actions. What she wanted should matter most.

Josie briefly closed her eyes, then opened them and got up. "Okay. We'll come back. Tomorrow."

"Tomorrow?" Hunter frowned. "Why not now?"

"I told Arthur that I would be helping with dinner." Josie indicated the front room of the hotel with a tip of her head. "It wouldn't be good for be to just abandon him and the cooks. And by the time I'm finished, it will be dark out. Maybe you can go around at night without worryin' about it, but some of us can't."

"I'd protect you. But I understand your decision to stay. And I respect your work ethic." Hunter smiled slightly. The sharp angles of his jawline eased. Faint wrinkles appeared at the corners of his eyes.

Josie looked at him, wondering at this transformation. He was much less of a bear when he smiled even this small amount.

He was handsome, even.

"I never did tell you that." Hunter's voice made her focus again. "When I first said you were goin' to be workin' for me, I didn't expect much. But you've been puttin' a lot of effort in and I like that about you."

"Thank you," she said softly.

"Well, I'll go back on to the ranch." Hunter touched Ella on the shoulder, so very gently. "You're comin' home tomorrow. I'll be back at dawn with an extra horse for you to ride. I can't imagine it was fun to walk out the way here with such short legs."

Josie laughed. "It was fine for her. I was carrying her before we got too far from the valley. We never would have made it here otherwise."

"You're one brave lady, Josie." Hunter flashed that small smile of his again and started to walk away, his steps heavy on the wooden floorboards. "Tomorrow at dawn. Don't forget, or I'll be here knockin'."

"I won't forget," Josie called after him. Ella tried to follow him and she picked her up, holding her close.

Hunter grumbled a quick farewell to Arthur and then he was out of sight, the banging of the hotel door marking his exit.

Josie stepped back into her room with Ella and let out a long breath, willing her heart to calm down.

Is going back the right thing to do?

Ella climbed up onto the bed with the stuffed bird, stroking the mismatched fabric wings. She was smiling.

It *was* the best thing, Josie thought. She still didn't fully trust Hunter, but there was just something about him, the way he interacted with Ella, his apology, his smile. He wasn't a bad man. Distant, rough, but not bad.

There was still a lot she didn't know about him. It could be there was something in his past that made him act how he did. And if that was true, maybe she could relate to him more than she first thought.

Chapter Fourteen

High above the valley, mingling with the clouds, an eagle soared with wings outstretched, sunset light glinting off the brown feathers. As it was so high up, identifying it could have been difficult, but its dark coloration all over led Hunter to believe it was a golden eagle. A bald eagle would have had a more obviously pale head.

The breeze blowing down from the mountains carried a hint of damp, signaling possible rain later that night or even early the next day. Some rain would be good. As much work as Kerry, and especially Josie, were putting into maintaining the garden, they couldn't defy the sun. Rain would refresh the ground more than they could, no matter how many buckets of water they poured on the crops.

Hunter crossed one knee over the other. He sat in an old weathered chair, a creaky, ancient thing still plenty more comfortable than that stool Kerry used when she churned butter. The stool acted as a small table currently, with his mug set on top.

He picked up the mug and sipped the cool liquid inside. Whiskey, not coffee, to relax him after the long day he'd had, getting up well before sunrise to saddle horses and head into town for Josie and her daughter.

The door to the house opened. He spoke without looking. "You think we can have fried apples with breakfast tomorrow, Kerry?"

"I think we can." Josie's soft voice reached his ears.

He set his drink down and glanced up at her. "Well, you ain't Kerry."

"No, but I do like fried apples. I'd be happy to make some." Josie lingered just outside the doorway, her hands clasped behind her back.

"You want to sit for a short while?" He moved his mug off the stool and waved her over.

She drifted past him, her skirt fluttering around her ankles, and perched primly on the stool with her hands folded now in her lap.

"Where's Ella?" he asked her.

"Inside. Kerry's teaching her how to wash dishes." She smiled slightly. "Mostly, it's an excuse for her to play with the soap bubbles."

He chuckled. "She's sure got a personality, doesn't she? Knows what she wants and how to get it."

Josie nodded, silent.

Hunter extended his mug toward. "You want some?"

She leaned over and sniffed disdainfully, then sat back. "No, thank you."

"Alright." He sipped and looked up at the sky. The eagle was gone, lost amidst the clouds.

This conversation would be similarly lost if he didn't do something about it. He didn't want her to go back inside just yet.

"Why was Clive at your door when I showed up yesterday?" he asked. "I know he's your husband's cousin, but what was he doing there?"

"He was just being friendly," Josie said. She smoothed her dress over her lap. "He's always been friendly to me. He's the one who let me know just how bad our debt was. Without him, I wouldn't have been able to hold onto the ranch as long as I did."

"Sounds kind." Although, he hadn't really liked the look of Clive at all. Maybe it was the way he had been pressing in on Josie, standing closer than was proper. Definitely it was the way he had been eyeing her up, like a piece of meat on a butcher's slab.

"Back then, he offered for us to come stay with him. He made the same offer yesterday."

Hunter tilted his head, frowning, mulling over this. "You turned him down the first time."

"I didn't want to be a burden."

"Were you going to turn him down yesterday too, before I arrived?"

"It doesn't matter now, does it? I'm back here."

His frown deepened. "Well, no, it don't matter, but I'm curious, is all."

"Well, I did turn him down again. Even though he was offering me work at the saloon and a place to stay. But maybe I should have, instead of coming back here."

Hunter turned in his chair to face her. "What?" he demanded. "Do you regret comin' back?"

Incredibly, she was smiling, and for the first time he noticed the slight gap between her front teeth. "Well, see, Clive is better than you in some ways that I find admirable."

"Better than me? That little man? In what ways?"

Josie pushed a long strand of red hair back from her face. “He’s much better with communicating. He told me everything real clearly. I knew exactly what he wanted.”

“I’m clear, too,” Hunter grumbled. “It’s just that no one’s listening properly.”

“Now, see, when you mumble like that...” She laughed softly, the sound like music. “Clive has a better attitude, too. He’s always nice and friendly.”

“Friendly doesn’t mean anythin’.”

“Yes, it does. That’s how he gets people to come back to the saloon.”

“His customers come back for the drink.”

“They could get drinks elsewhere if they didn’t like his place.”

“You sure are defendin’ him a lot.” Hunter finished his drink and leaned over to set his mug down. Straightening, he saw Josie was laughing again, trying to hide it behind her hand.

She was doing this on purpose, getting him riled up.

“Maybe he is kind and whatnot, but I can’t see him runnin’ after you in a storm to catch your cabin as it fell down.”

Her laughter slowly faded and when it was gone, the silence in its absence was especially loud. “I can’t see that, either.”

“So that’s something in my favor.”

“Is it a competition now?” The smile returned at least, just a flash.

"He couldn't handle all the work we do out here. What's more is that I am more handsome than he is." He chuckled at his own words. Good looks had never made any man a hard worker, never earned him a profit. It was a useless measurement of worth.

"I can't disagree with that," Josie whispered. Her face turned red and she put her hand over her mouth again.

"Well, now." He reached over and touched the back of her hand. "I didn't know you saw me that way."

"I don't!" She drew her hand away and rubbed both of them together. "I was just statin' a fact. It doesn't mean anything."

"You're right. But it's nice to know." He paused. He sensed that there was something between them now, a tension. She was embarrassed, hiding from him, and he didn't want her to be uncomfortable. If he could do something to make them even, she would feel better.

"I think you're beautiful," he said.

"Oh, no, you can't mean that. I'm not." She ducked her head, shaking it hard.

"I do mean it, because you are!" he insisted. "Much too purty to be with Clive. He doesn't deserve you like that."

"I never said anything about *being* with him."

"A man pays you that much attention and offers you things like he does, that's what is on his mind." Hunter gritted his teeth. He really didn't enjoy thinking of that. Josie was strong, but she was vulnerable. An insistent man like Clive could take advantage of her even if he didn't mean to.

Now he was very, very glad to have her back home. This was where she belonged. If she left again, to go off with Clive or to start a new life, it would be her decision.

"You said you like birds?" Josie spoke timidly. She was trying to change their conversation.

"I do. I was watchin' an eagle fly around earlier, but he got too high for me to see him any longer."

"Oh, that's what you were doing."

She was watching me. He pressed his lips together to hold back a grin. She really did think he was handsome.

"Well, what are those birds up there on top of the stable?"

Hunter squinted at the tiny birds Josie indicated with a sweeping gesture. "Hard to tell, but I know there's a nest under the roof over there on that side. Some finches have laid their eggs there. The finches are the ones with red on their heads and chests. So, I'd say that one is likely a finch. And those other three are probably just crows."

"And what is that?"

Josie stood, pointing at a patch of cloud. A bird soared in circles in and out of the clouds, gradually descending. Then, a second bird joined, wings outstretched to catch the drafts. A third came moments later, all of them marking out circles above the same patch of land, weaving in and out of the others' paths. They were like juggled balls, graceful and unsettling in their pattern.

Hunter rose from his chair. "Those are vultures. They're watching somethin'."

"Vultures?" Josie swallowed hard. "Is there something... dead over there?"

"Dead or dyin', they got their eyes on it." He took her by the shoulder and guided her the few steps to the door. She offered no resistance at all. "I'm goin' to check on it. You head back inside and play with your daughter. If Kerry wants to know where I went, you can tell her."

"Be careful." Josie flashed a little smile that didn't quite reach her eyes before she stepped into the house and shut the door behind herself.

Hunter went to the edge of the porch and watched those vultures spiraling over something either dead or about to die. They were only birds, just animals acting on instinct. Why, then, did the sight of them fill his stomach with black dread?

He hopped off the porch and went to the stable, the birds on the roof scattering with his approach. He ducked inside and grabbed his favorite horse, the only one who reliably carried his weight time after time, a huge gray gelding. He saddled up and a few minutes later was headed off for the area the vultures were watching. There were four of them up there by that point, all flying much lower.

The gelding shied beneath Hunter, sidestepping and tossing his head with a snort.

"Hey, now, Granite." Hunter patted his horse's neck. He dismounted and, holding the reins tight, inspected the grass before them. They were not far from one of his grazing areas. He'd had his cattle herd nearby just earlier that day.

Granite tossed his head again and stamped a hoof, agitated by something. Hunter took another step forward and he saw it, at last, what was upsetting his usually steady and reliable horse.

Blood on the grass blades, vivid dark rubies. A trail of blood led away, speckles and splotches of it. The grass had been trampled as whatever was bleeding stumbled on.

Hunter moved to a tree, leading Granite away from the blood. He looped the reins around a crooked branch and left the horse there, following the trail around a thicket to the other side, where the ground sloped to form a hollow. The divot filled with water whenever it rained. The only thing in there right now, huddled at the bottom, was a dead animal covered in flies. A vulture perched on top, beak red, already feasting.

Hunter picked up a stone that fit in the palm of his hand and tossed it at the vulture, hitting it broadside on the dark wing. The bird took off with a rusty screech, wings thudding against the air.

Hunter pulled a handkerchief from his pocket and covered his mouth as he descended into the hollow. The tree branches overhead cast stripes of shadow over the dead animal, which was already black in coloration, though with some white spots on the rump. He moved around to the side and finally saw the grievous wound that had killed the creature.

His creature. One of his bulls. Not the best in the herd, but a good one. It must have wandered away from the herd and been attacked, but by what? The wound didn't immediately strike him as having been inflicted by another animal, though he couldn't have said for certain.

Slowly, he leaned his head back. Through the branches, he saw the waiting vultures right overhead, eager to continue their eating. Revulsion rose up the back of his throat and he turned away from the scene, ascending the shallow sloping walls of the hollow.

Let the carrion eaters have their way. He wouldn't be dragging the carcass back and butchering it like he might have under other circumstances. This meat was spoiled, tainted by dread.

Hunter walked away without looking back, heading for where he had left his horse. He would return in the morning to bury the remains and hopefully put this in the past. Everything was supposed to be better now. He believed that it would be, but it was hard when there seemed to be a shadow at his back, looming over all.

Chapter Fifteen

Humming a little under her breath, Josie wiped down the kitchen counters with a damp cloth. Sunshine flowed in through the window over the sink basin, puddling on the floor. Ella sat in the middle of the puddle of sunshine with the skirt of her dress spread out all around her, playing with some of Kerry's yarn balls and, of course, the stuffed bird from Hunter.

Someone entered the house and Josie stiffened, listening closely to the thumping of the footsteps approaching the kitchen. She recognized the uneven gate and her shoulders relaxed. "Hi, Ezra," she called.

Ezra limped into the kitchen and stood in the doorway. He held his hat by his side in one hand. Sweat glistened on his forehead, dampening his fine blond hair flat to the top of his head. "Howdy, Miss Josie, Miss Ella. Awful hot out there today."

"It sure is," Josie agreed. The house was cooler and a breeze ran through, keeping the temperature on the side of pleasant. "You want to fill up your canteen?"

"That'd be good, please." Ezra unclipped the canteen from his belt and held it out. Josie took it from him and he crouched down to Ella's level, picking up one of the yarn balls. "I see you're bein' a big help to your ma."

"Any time that she isn't wandering off on her own is helpin' me." Josie brought the canteen to a bucket of what she had learned was called Kerry's special water, a mix of plain water, a sprinkling of sugar, and a pinch of salt. Kerry always made up a batch of it on especially hot and sweaty days, swearing that it was better for thirst than normal water. She had taught Josie how to make it, but this was the first batch she had made on her own and she hoped she had done it right.

Josie brought Ezra's canteen back and he took it with a nod. "I ain't seen Kerry today," he said.

"She sent word that one of her grandchildren took ill last night and she wouldn't be able to come."

"It's just been you workin' today, then." Ezra put his hat back on his head and smiled. "I wouldn't have ever knowed. You're doing a good job."

Josie put her hand to her heart as warmth bloomed in her chest. "Thank you for saying so. I'm doing my best."

"I best get back out there before Hunter comes a'lookin' for me." Ezra tipped his hat and walked out.

Josie went back to her cleaning with a widening smile that hurt her cheeks. When she first heard that Kerry wouldn't be there, panic had whipped up inside her like the first gusts of a tornado. She had calmed herself by thinking of all the routines and schedules she had learned over the weeks, realizing that she knew what to do even when she was on her own.

And she had done everything. Fixed bacon, eggs, and fried potatoes for breakfast, tidied up the chicken coop, washed the bedsheets and hung them up to dry, and fed the men lunch. Now she was almost done tidying up after them, and she would move on to cleaning the rest of the house.

Hunter hadn't said anything about how good she was doing, but she had thought she was doing very well, and Ezra's comments reassured her further.

Ella gave up on her toys and sprawled out in the middle of the floor. Josie walked around her to get a broom and dustpan. "Time to sweep up all this mess," she announced.

Ella lay there, giggling, her hair spread out across the floorboards.

Josie swept the floor ahead of her, then gently tapped at Ella's sides with the stiff strands of broomcorn. "Oh, my, that's a real big mess right here. Seems to be stuck to the floor. I'll have to..."

Josie crouched and pretended to use the dustpan to try and scoop Ella off the floor. Squealing, Ella sat up and put her arms around her neck. "Mama! I not dirt!"

Josie laughed and hugged her tight. "Don't lay on the floor, then, or I'll think you are!" She straightened with Ella in her arms and kissed her cheeks. "Are you all tuckered out, my dear? It might be time for you to take a nap."

Ella yawned and leaned her head against Josie's neck. "Nap," she murmured.

Josie stroked her soft hair and took her to their bedroom. She placed Ella down and covered her up, tucking her in just right. She recalled how difficult this simple task had been when they were staying in the freezing cabin. Their situation had surely changed for the better, even if that change had come about in an unconventional manner.

Leaning down, Josie pressed a soft kiss to Ella's forehead, breathing in her scents of soap and sunshine. "I love you."

"Love you, Mama." Ella closed her eyes.

Josie lingered by her side until her breathing slowed, her sweet face relaxing in sleep. She left as quietly as she could, leaving the door open just the slightest bit.

She picked up her broom again and swept the kitchen floor, this time without a toddler in her way impeding her progress. She moved on to the other rooms, sweeping the floors and tidying up anything that was out of place. By now, she knew Hunter liked his things to be just so. Truthfully, that made the job a bit easier, as she didn't have to guess where to put anything or hunt for something that wasn't where it should have been.

She worked her way toward Hunter's office and edged her way inside. She paused in her sweeping as she immediately noticed something out of place, a book on the floor next to the desk. It lay open, with the spine up, some of the pages curled underneath. Clearly, it must have been placed on the edge of the desk and had been knocked over, or fallen on its own.

Having heard Hunter talk about the books before and how his father had enjoyed buying them, she knew they were important. She leaned her broom up against the wall and strode over, lifting the heavy leatherbound tome off the floor. She smoothed the curled and bent pages with her thumb, hoping they hadn't been damaged.

The words on the page caught her attention, not their content but their composition. They weren't printed, rather written by hand in a tight, tidy, flowing script. The writing style was distinctly manly, lacking any fanciful loops and flourishes.

She fluttered the pages, making note of the headings at the top of every page or so. Dates, time moving backwards as she reached the front of the book. What she held was actually a journal.

Hunter's journal? He didn't seem like the type to dedicate the time to writing down his thoughts. Or was it a ledger of some kind?

Josie looked back at the doorway. No one was there to see her taking a peek inside. She could hear the men outside if she really strained her ears, their distant shouts and laughter as they worked.

She sat down at the chair at the desk and slid her finger between the dry, yellowed pages. She flipped to a random spot toward the beginning of the journal and bent forward to read.

"Jenny told me today that she is with child. The Lord truly has blessed us this year. The ranch is performing as well as it ever has and we were able to buy ourselves a new wagon. I do not have the words to express my joy. May my wife's pregnancy be easy, and may my child be the son I have always wished for."

Josie looked up from the book, her heart pounding hard enough to shake her whole body. She listened for the men again, heard their shouts once more.

Her thoughts were a jumble as she tried to make sense of what she had just read. If this was really Hunter's journal that she held, his words placed down so carefully upon the pages, then she truly knew nothing about him.

He'd had a wife? He had never spoken of her, nor of a son. Had something happened to them that was so terrible, it didn't bear speaking of?

But even if he didn't want to talk about what had happened, surely Kerry would have said something by now. Unless she, too, didn't want to speak of the past?

Josie flipped further into the book, the months flickering by.

"My son was born in the small hours of the morning today. Jenny labored since the night before last. She was not able to

speak or to hold our son by the end of it, and she bled much. But she is alive and my son is alive. He is heavy as a newborn calf and lively. I do believe if I placed him upon the ground, he would get up and walk away. A nurse remains with us in the house to assist while Jenny rests and recovers. Would that I could remain with her, but the animals will not care for themselves and I do not trust my workers not to laze around without me there."

Josie checked the date again. March 11, but there was no year given. None of the entries had years. The events described in the journal could have happened ten years ago, or just the prior spring.

There was still much of the journal remaining. If she read on, she might find clues as to when these writings had taken place.

She flipped forward several more entries and bent to read again.

"Well, now."

Before her eyes could focus upon the words, Hunter's rumbling voice rolled through the office, shaking her bones like a peal of thunder. Josie jerked her head up, suddenly unable to breathe. She knew exactly what it looked like, what she had been caught doing. Her stomach burned as Hunter stepped into the room, crossing to her in only a few steps. He snatched the book from her hands and slapped it shut.

"Is this what you do when no one is around and watchin' you? You go snooping through other people's personal belongings?" Hunter growled.

"It was laying on the floor. I picked it up and..." Her voice shook. "I shouldn't have looked. You're right."

"Yes ma'am, I am right." He thudded over to a shelf and shoved the book into the gap where it evidently belonged. "I don't know what you read, but it's none of your business. And from now on, you aren't allowed in here. I'll do my own cleanin'."

He had every right to be upset with her, but what she had read was filling her mind. She needed to know, no matter how angry it might make him.

Hunter started to leave the room. She stood and hurried after him, grabbing his arm. His muscle tensed under her touch and he wrenched away from her. The force of the movement almost pulled her off her feet. She grabbed onto the wall, steadying herself. Words jumped up into her throat and the feel of them was treacherous, as if by speaking them she would be putting herself in danger, but she couldn't stop herself.

"Did you have a family?"

His back stiffened. "Whatever you read, it's none of your business, I said. Forget all of it."

"But if you had a family, where are they now? What happened?"

"Josie." His breathing turned ragged. "You really don't know what you're askin' about. You've got the wrong idea of things."

"Then tell me what the right way is," she whispered. "I deserve to know, don't I?"

He shook his head and walked away. She stared at his receding back, her head still full of questions she desperately wanted answered.

But maybe he was right and it was better that she didn't know. It was none of her business what life he had led.

The door banged shut, freeing her from her frozen state. She crept back inside to grab her broom, and then left in a hurry, just in case he came back to try and catch her snooping around again. She resumed her cleaning, but her heart was no longer in it. She kept thinking on what she had read, struggling to make sense of it, of Hunter's reactions, of anything.

Chapter Sixteen

"Dinner was good."

Josie froze at the sink as Hunter spoke from behind her. She ducked her head and scrubbed furiously at a plate, silent.

He restrained a sigh and turned away. He had sure messed up again. She hadn't spoken to him or even looked at him since he caught her being a nosey parker in his office earlier. She wouldn't even get near him.

She was aware of him though, like a mother deer with a fawn was aware of wolves in the area. Ella seemed not to notice the tension between them and she kept going up to him like she always did, wanting to play, to speak with him in her tiny voice. As they interacted, he could feel Josie shooting him worried stares like she thought he was going to start yelling again.

Even now, washing the dishes, her entire body was tensed as if she expected to need to run away at any moment.

Clearly, he should leave her alone.

He went to his office and sat at the desk. The urge to move awoke inside him almost at once and he stood again with a growl. There wasn't much room for pacing in there, and he didn't think that it would do Josie any good to hear him stomping around.

He approached the bookshelves and ran his hand over the bound spines. His father's journal jumped out at him, one of many leather notebooks he had filled out throughout his life. Hunter did enjoy reading them on occasion, but only some of them.

This one in his hand, aged, still beautiful, was not one of the enjoyable journals.

He had picked it up the night before, evidently not paying enough attention to realize which one it was. When he did realize, he had set it down in a hurry. That was how it had fallen on the floor, where Josie had felt obligated to pick it up. He could understand that, though not the snooping.

And the conclusions she had evidently drawn were ridiculous.

How could she know any better? I didn't explain.

He closed his eyes. He was meant to be learning from his mistakes and instead, he had repeated the same one. What if Josie decided to leave again? He wouldn't be able to convince her to come back again.

Opening his eyes, he looked at the journal in his hand and knew what he had to do.

He had to wait.

He selected a few of his father's other notebooks and set them out on his desk, then sat and listened to Josie moving around in the house. Water ran repeatedly into the sink basin as she scrubbed and rinsed the dishes from dinner. She remained in the kitchen for a long while, her movements ebbing in and out of his hearing range.

Eventually, he heard her approaching, murmuring softly. Little chirping sounds let him know that she had Ella. They went into their bedroom, and it was a long while until he heard Josie coming out again.

Hunter rose, his heart skipping beats, his chest tight. He picked up the stack of journals and left the office.

Josie spun around at the end of the hall, her eyes widening. "Hunter!" she gasped. "I didn't know you were in the house. I thought you were working outside."

He rubbed his neck with his free hand. "Didn't mean to startle you. I got to talk to you about somethin."

She swallowed hard and looked around. Her hands fluttered down by her sides, fingers flexing. "Okay. What about?"

"Let's go into the parlor."

She hurried ahead of him. Several lanterns burned, the shadows catching and releasing her as she nearly ran to the parlor. Hunter grabbed one of the lanterns as he passed by and brought it into the parlor. He moved to the fireplace and used the lantern flame to get the logs burning. The dancing amber glow flooded the parlor, washing over Josie where she perched on the very edge of a chair, fingers skittering around together in her lap.

Where the light fell upon her hair, he could see all sorts of different colors held inside the red. Sunset colors, gold and vivid orange, copper and cherry.

The absurd urge to stroke her hair came through him. He turned away and picked up the books he had brought with him.

"The journal you read," he said. "I didn't write that. That was my father's."

The fire crackled, hungrily gnawing the logs. There was a pop and sparks scattered. Hunter watched those bright bits of glow shower the hearth and then die, turn to ash.

"How could I have known?" Josie's voice was barely audible over the fire. "There weren't any years written down."

"There were." He flipped open the journal that she had started to read and handed it to her. "You must not have seen it. He only marked the changing year on January 1. These were written so very long ago."

"Oh." She stroked her finger over the numbers marking the year. "I read the parts about a pregnant wife, and the birth of a son. I thought... but that son was you."

"Yes." He sat in the chair next to hers and heaved a huge sigh. "It wasn't your fault that you read the journal. The way I left it out, it was like a baited trap."

"I still shouldn't have read it, but yes, it was." She almost sounded amused, but when he looked at her, her expression was passive.

Hunter reached over and turned a few pages for her until he reached the journal entry he wanted her to read. She glanced at him, her eyebrows lowered, silently asking for permission. He nodded.

She bent over the book and read it aloud, her voice so very soft, barely a breath.

"Jenny has not been right since she brought our son into this world. She does not leave her bed. She does not feed Hunter. I have had to hire a wet nurse to ensure my son does not die. But he thrives. I pray that tomorrow my wife will leave her bed to see this for herself. She does not ask after him. She does not even seem to realize she has a child."

Hunter turned the pages again. Josie read once more, this time without asking his permission.

"Today, I came home to find Hunter alone in his cradle, soiled and hungry. I could not find Jenny anywhere in the house. My search for her lasted nearly two hours before I found her by the river. She did not speak when I asked her

what she was doing there, nor did she move when I told her to come home. I had to lead her by the hand. Our son will be one year old tomorrow. When will Jenny at last recover from this illness? The doctors have said it is an illness of the mind and time is what she needs, but how much longer will this last?"

Josie rubbed at her eyes. "The birth was hard on her. It... hurt her inside. It hurt her mind."

"She was never the same," Hunter said. He plucked at a loose thread on the cover of one of the other journals. "Pa wrote extensively on that, year after year. She was a good mother to me, but I was too young to see all the flaws. I couldn't see that she was broken. I didn't know it was abnormal for a woman to spend weeks in her bed, to weep at the sight of her child."

"How terrible," Josie whispered.

Hunter took the journal from her and handed her another, finding the right page once more. He knew where everything was, having read these many times before. He often skipped the painful parts, but he still knew where they were.

"Hunter is a bad egg, the laziest child I have ever had the misfortune to meet. That this is my own son pains me. How can it be that he does not work hard and neglects his chores? When I was his age, my own father was sending me into town on my own."

"I was six when this was written," Hunter said. He showed her several more entries written in a similar vein, letting her read the sources of his pain. Each word was a strike to his heart, far more agonizing to be heard aloud than read in silence and privacy.

Then, a final entry, a break in the pattern. Jagged writing, a haphazard scrawl, dateless.

"Jenny went away in the night. She left a note. I burned it without reading it. All of this is Hunter's fault. Had he not been born, I would still have my love here with me."

Josie dropped the journal, shaking her head. "She left? I can't believe that! I would never, ever abandon Ella no matter how hard things were. Everything I've done is for her. How could any woman not feel the same way about their own child?"

Hunter took the book and stacked it with the others. "I don't know," he grunted. "She was just never right. She clearly didn't want to be here anymore, so she left when I was ten."

"Oh, Hunter, I'm so sorry." Josie bit her lower lip and took his hand, squeezing his fingers.

Her hand on his sent warmth up through his veins. He carefully curled his hand around hers, not wanting to hurt her. "You read there that Pa blamed me. He never did stop blamin' me. He hated me."

"No, I'm sure he didn't hate you!" Her voice rose slightly. "No matter what, he couldn't have hated you. You were his flesh and blood."

"He sure didn't love me." Hunter lowered his head. "Nothin' I ever did was good enough. I think the only reason he left me the ranch is because there wasn't anyone else."

He could still hear his father's shouts echoing in his head all these years later, still feel the dark, watchful presence at his back waiting for the opportunities to point out his mistakes.

Yelling was all he had known from the moment his mother left him alone with his father. That was why he had yelled at

Ella when she hit him with the rock. It was what his father would have done, what he had been taught to do.

But the look on Ella's face and Josie's reactions had told him he was wrong for what he had done.

Now he didn't know what to do, what was right or wrong.

I don't know how to explain myself to you, Josie.

Hunter cleared his throat and sat up straighter. "I got mad at you when I saw you in my office lookin' at this stuff. I didn't want you to know. But then I thought that maybe you deserved to know. You can take these, if you want. And there's others, too. You can read everythin' my pa ever wrote about me."

"No. I don't think I will. It would just upset me." She took her hand away, and he hadn't the time to lament its absence before her arms were around him, her small, soft and warm shape leaning into him.

He went very still as she struggled to encompass his girth with her shorter arms. He felt her breathing, her heart beating. Her scent was sweet wildflowers and soap, a comforting, yet strange scent he was unable to compare to anything else when he spent all his days working with animals and men. He was used to fur and musk, sweat and leather.

Even his own mother hadn't smelled like this. She had always smelled of sleep and medicines, the tinctures doctors gave her in an attempt to restore her energy.

He breathed her in and lifted his arm to wrap around her shoulders. She leaned her head on him, her soft hair against his neck. "Thank you, for sharing with me."

"You're welcome." His throat was very tight.

She drew back, leaving him cold, abruptly alone. Her cheeks were flushed. "I- I think I had best finish preparing for tomorrow and then get some rest."

"Me, too." He stood and picked up the books. There was so much else he could have told her, if only he had known how to say it, if only there was time for it.

Maybe he'd get to it some other time.

He went back to his office, leaving her sitting there by the fire, her eyes watching him until he pulled the door shut behind himself.

One by one, he slotted the journals back onto the shelf where they belonged.

Chapter Seventeen

"Josie!"

She looked up from tending to the garden as Hunter's voice rang out. She immediately checked for Ella and saw her playing in the dirt, causing no trouble. Relief swept through her and she stood as Hunter strode toward her.

"Just got back from town?" she asked.

"I did. And I am just fine, so you don't got to look at me like that." He flashed that smile of his that she was seeing more and more often these days. The warmth in it made an echoing warmth develop in her middle and she smiled back at him.

He had gone into town to settle some dealing or other with another rancher. A peaceful dealing, he had reassured her, though she had been worried until seeing him unharmed and in good spirits.

"I stopped by the post office and you actually got a letter." Hunter took the envelope from his back pocket and handed it to her.

"Really, now?" Josie took the letter. There was no address to let her know where it had come from. She pointed that out and Hunter nodded.

"Bit odd, but could just mean someone in town went there personally to drop it off for you. Family, maybe?"

"Well, I don't know. I don't really have any family around anymore." She tucked the letter into her apron to look at later. "Thank you for bringin' it."

"Welcome." Hunter looked past her and she followed his gaze to Ella sitting in the patch of dirt, having a grand old time and perhaps sampling the soil quality if the smudges around her mouth were any hint. "I don't suppose you got any plans for the day ahead?"

"Well, of course, I have plans," Josie said, surprised by the insinuation. "There's laundry to be folded and I'll need to prepare dinner with Kerry. And we're goin' to make a few batches of cookies."

"I meant special plans."

"Special plans?" she repeated. "No. Why would I have special plans?"

Hunter still wasn't looking at her as he spoke, though he now wasn't looking at Ella, either. He stared into the distance in the valley, past the barn and stable. "There's somethin' that I want your opinion on. It's goin' to mess with the schedule a little, but that's just how it has to be."

"I don't understand, exactly," Josie said, frowning. He was being vague again, not making much sense. What could he want her opinion on, and why would that mess with the schedule?

"Yesterday, there was somethin' I noticed while I was with the cattle at the pasture. I didn't have time to go look at it properly. It's part of the fence. You've been on a ranch before. You know how those fences get. Always bein' blown down and needin' repairs."

"You want me to help you make repairs on the fence? Why don't you just get Charles to do that with you?"

"Because I don't want Charles to go with me. I want you to go." He looked at her then, his black eyes clear as the night sky. She was falling into them, mesmerized, having never seen them so bright and open before.

"I want a woman's touch on this," Hunter said. "The men'd just tell me what they think I want to hear from them. I know you'd tell me the truth."

"The truth about the fence?"

"If the fence needs to be replaced entirely," he said. "If it's worth doin' it now all at once to make sure it's strong and can last the next winter. Or if we just keep waiting to see what happens."

"Well, I never did have much to do with that part of keeping the ranch," she said, doubts nagging at her. "But I suppose I could... go with you and take a look. But what's this about messing up the schedule?"

He removed his hat and scratched at his head, then firmly settled the hat back on. "Just how it works out. Lots of work left to do today, so the only time we'd be able to go out to that fence is during dinnertime."

"Oh, I see." Josie hesitated.

Hunter slapped his palm on his thigh. "I know that you're thinking about leavin' Kerry with all that work, but you have to remember that she did it all without you around for years and years. She can handle herself. Of course, if you don't want to go, you don't have to, but I thought I'd offer."

She thought quickly, sensing he wanted an answer now and not later. Was this something he had done with Kerry in the past, asking her for her *womanly* opinion on certain things?

Or could this be something he was doing just with her?

It could be his way of trying to make up to her after their misunderstanding over the journals, although she had thought they left off on good terms. If that was the case, she couldn't very well turn him down.

"Very well," Josie said. "I'll go with you. I'll go talk with Kerry about it so she knows in advance. I will feel bad about leaving her with Ella, but Ella won't mind."

"Not necessary. We can bring Ella. It's about time she saw a little more of the ranch than just the house, the garden, and the chickens, don't you think?" He turned away without waiting for an answer. "We'll take horses. She won't get too tired. Meet you at the stable around dinnertime."

Josie watched him go, still with unanswered questions. She shook her head and went to get Ella, lifting her up into her arms. "Let's get you inside and washed up."

Ella patted her face with dirty hands, smiling.

Kerry was in the kitchen. "Oh, dear," she said at the sight of them and dampened a cloth. "What were you doin' out there, Ella? Rollin' in the dirt?"

Ella held out her hands for Kerry to wipe them down. "I help," she announced.

"Yes, you were very helpful with the gardening," Josie said absently. "Kerry, has Hunter ever wanted you to go and do some work on the ranch with him?"

"Well, no, I can't say that he has." Kerry dabbed at Ella's dirt-streaked face. "Why would he? That's not my place. Why? Did he ask you?"

Josie took the cloth and kneeled to finish cleaning up her daughter while telling Kerry what Hunter had requested of her. "I said that I would go with him, and he wants to bring Ella. It's just strange, don't you think?"

"Might be he values your input, is all. You already agreed, so you might as well get to it." Kerry looked down at Ella and smiled, and Ella smiled back at her. "Ella will have fun, I'm sure. Won't you?"

"Yes!" Ella agreed, though she certainly had no idea to what it was she agreed.

Josie suddenly recalled the letter in her pocket. "Hunter brought me some mail from town. I'd best go see what it's about."

"I'll keep an eye on her for you." Kerry scooped Ella into her arms and tickled her.

Ella's bright laughter followed Josie as she went to the parlor and sat in a chair in front of the dead, silent fireplace. She pulled the envelope from her pocket and ripped the paper open. Inside was a small, folded scrap of paper, cheap, thin stuff the ink had bled through in multiple places.

Josie unfolded the scrap and held the near-transparent paper up to the light to read it better.

"Josie,

I hope you been well since you went back to the valley with that Hunter feller. I ain't like the looks of him. And word is he's a dangerous man. Why else does he keep to himself all the time like he does?

You should come stay with me, before it's too late. I don't want you to get it in the neck. I'll treat you right, make you happy like no one else has. Once you're finally here, you'll never want to leave.

Just think on it. I hope I ain't got to do anything drastic to make you see it's the right choice to come and be with me.

-Clive"

Josie shuddered as she finished reading. Clive had been giving her strange feelings all along with how he kept saying she needed to come and work for him. These words almost seemed like a threat.

She folded the scrap of paper to put it back in the envelope and stood to take it to her room. She placed it on top of the dresser and set the mirror partially on top to hold it there in case of a draft.

I shouldn't write back. That will only encourage him.

Her continued silence would get the message across, she hoped.

She returned to the kitchen and took Ella from Kerry's arms, holding her close to her chest.

"What was the mail?" Kerry asked. She arranged carrots and potatoes on the counter, to wash and then chop up for dinner.

"Nothin' important," Josie replied. She tried to convince herself it was true. "Just some correspondence with someone I know, but don't want to talk to. You know, I'm glad that I left the motel and came back home when I did."

"We're all glad." Kerry flashed her a broad smile and Josie found it in herself to smile back. "I couldn't bring up the flour from the cellar while holdin' on to Ella. You mind fetchin' it for me?"

"I'll get right to it." Josie hurried away.

She lifted her skirts to go down the cellar steps, into the dark and musty room. She pushed all thoughts of Clive and his antics from her mind. He didn't matter right then.

She couldn't wait to go out with Hunter later and figure out what exactly it was about the fence he wanted her opinion on. Could she actually be useful to him?

Chapter Eighteen

Hunter had two horses standing outside the stable and was tightening the straps on a saddle bag when Josie walked over with Ella trailing slightly behind her. He looked over at them and smiled. Josie smiled back, though she had that nervous look on her face.

"Howdy," he said.

"Howdy!" Ella echoed brightly, leaving Josie and going right up to him. Where had she gotten her boldness from? Not from her mother, who was still staring at him with her eyes wide. He could see her pulse ticking at her throat.

She might calm down if they got down to it instead of standing around.

Hunter finished saddling the horse and moved into the introductions. He rubbed its neck while speaking. "This here is Granite. My horse. You and Ella can-- Hey!"

He interrupted himself, noticing Ella going behind the other horse, reaching up for its tail. Her fingers were already twirled up in the wiry hairs. Josie flinched and Ella froze, her head whipping around.

Hunter silently admonished himself for raising his voice and made an effort to speak quieter.

"Hey," he repeated. He moved to Ella in a few steps and hooked his arm around her, shifting her away from the horse. "Don't go around behind any animal. You could get kicked."

Ella looked up at him with her head tilted. Did she understand the danger of a horse's kick? He had seen a horse kill a wolf in one quick, almost casual movement. He prayed Ella never experienced anything like that.

Josie reached and took Ella from him, pulling her back to her side. “Maybe I should leave her with Kerry after all.”

“No, no, she'll learn.” Hunter waved his hand. “I want her with us.”

“To go look at a fence?”

She still didn't understand. He thought she would have picked up on the situation by now.

Hunter leaned his head back and looked up at the sky, checking the sun's position. “We should really get goin'. Come on, mount up. Your horse is Maggie May here. Calmest, most polite horse you'll ever meet.”

The mare having a human-like name made Josie give a slight laugh. She stepped up to it and took hold of the saddle horn, pulling herself up. Hunter lifted Ella up to her and Josie placed her daughter between her legs.

Hunter gave Josie the reins and placed Ella's hands on the saddle horn. “You hold onto this the whole time.” A cowboy would be shamed if he held onto the horn, but it was alright for a little girl.

Ella immediately removed one hand and waved at Hunter. “Howdy!”

Hunter chuckled while Josie rubbed her face. Maybe Ella had the makings of a cowboy. She had the bravado, the confidence.

Hunter mounted Granite, who made the pale brown Maggie May look like a deer fawn in comparison. He squeezed Granite with his knees and set off at a trot. He looked around behind himself and saw Maggie May following of her own accord. Josie was stiff as a startled cat in the saddle. He hoped she would ease up or else she was going to be sore.

He turned back around and they were off, crossing the grass for a line of trees in a part of the valley Josie hadn't yet been to.

Maggie May picked up her pace on her own, coming almost fully up to Granite's side. The horses turned their heads together and briefly nuzzled.

A rabbit burst out of a patch of weeds almost directly underneath Maggie May's hooves. She didn't flinch. Her flanks didn't so much as twitch. She just walked on, calm as could be, head bobbing ever so slightly as she followed behind Granite.

After that, Josie settled a little into the saddle, her posture more natural. She now had proof that her horse was calm, reliable. Hunter couldn't have been gladder.

They steadily approached the line of trees, the cool, dark shadows gathered beneath the branches. Just before reaching them, Hunter made a turn to follow along their edge until they reached an indented spot where the trees edged back to form a semi-circle. The partially enclosed patch of grass and ferns grew thick and verdant. The air was hazy with pollen, and fat bees droned lazily from one wildflower to the next. Birds sang in the trees, and somewhere out of sight a squirrel noisily crashed through the undergrowth.

Hunter stopped them and got off his horse. "We're here," he announced.

Josie looked around, frowning. "We are? I don't even see a fence."

"Josie," Hunter sighed. He walked over to her side and held up his hands. Ella reached for him and he swung her gently to the grasses, then reached up again for Josie. She was still frowning as he helped her to dismount.

He put his hands on his hips and studied her. "You still don't get it?"

"I don't know what I'm supposed to get," she said.

Hunter went to his saddlebags and took out a cloth-wrapped bundle. He peeled the fabric back to show several biscuits, which only increased Josie's confusion further. Her brow furrowed so intensely that he worried she would get a facial cramp. He could almost hear the questions running through her mind. Shouldn't he have brought tools to fix the fence? What was she missing?

"Josie!" He started to laugh. "It's a picnic! Heck, I thought you would have figured it out ages ago."

"I don't..." She stopped. The wrinkles smoothed from her forehead. "You brought us out here for a picnic! Why, you could have just said that, Hunter Carson."

He laughed and handed the cloth filled with biscuits to her. They were still warm. Kerry had just finished making them before they set off. "I wanted it to be a surprise. I didn't know how stubborn you'd be. Guess I can show you a fence if you really want to see one, but let's eat first."

Ella walked up to Granite, sticking to his side, and reached up for the saddlebags. "More?"

"I brought more," Hunter told her, flashing a grin. "Josie, you go find us a good place to sit. We'll bring the food over."

"But I should help," she insisted.

"Nothin' for you to help with. We got this handled and the animals are fine."

The horses stood together, grazing contentedly on the juicy grass stems and sweet flowers. They would only be annoyed if Josie started to mess with them.

But she was still standing there and he figured he knew why. She didn't want to leave him alone with Ella just in case he yelled again. He had corrected himself earlier, though. She had to know that it was fine to leave them alone for just a minute.

She was going to stand there unless someone else acted first. So Hunter put his back to her and resumed digging through the saddlebags. Dismissing her. Though he was still very aware of her, hearing her take a step and pause, then finally move away for real.

Hunter took their picnic supplies and went to find Josie in the semi-enclosed clearing, Ella trailing along behind him like a duckling. The grasses were illuminated with shatters of evening sunlight coming through the trees. Ella waved her arms to push the fern fronds out of her way.

Josie was next to a fallen log when they reached her. "Find a good spot?" Hunter asked, coming around to her side.

"This log seems sturdy enough." Josie gave it a little kick. "It isn't caving in and there's no spiders. It's as good as any couch."

Hunter nodded and sat on one end. The other side of the log lifted up slightly beneath his weight. Josie was too small when compared with him to make a difference when she also sat.

They placed the food on the relatively flat, wide wood between them and started to eat, using cloth napkins as plates. There were slabs of butter to go on the fluffy biscuits, pieces of ham and cheese, boiled eggs, and crisp apples.

They ate mostly in silence. Hunter wasn't sure what Josie was thinking or feeling. She kept looking at him though, so he tried his best to seem relaxed to reassure her everything was fine. Ella sat on the grass facing them, her head on a swivel, turning as the birds chirped and the horses whickered. Crumbs rolled down the front of her dress and gathered in her lap, enough to feed a whole colony of ants.

Josie wiped butter from her fingers onto her napkin and tilted her head back. Hunter looked up, too. The broken-eggshell glimpses of blue sky seemed so very far away from them.

"This is nice." Josie spoke softly. "We should do this again."

Hunter popped the last bite of ham into his mouth. "Might be hard to find the time. I worked hard to make this happen."

Josie reached over and touched his arm. "Thank you."

Heat climbed up the back of his neck. "You're welcome."

She pulled her hand away and clutched it in her lap. "Maybe we could have some of our other meals outside on the porch."

"Chow does taste best when it's eaten outside. I agree." Hunter nodded. "When I was a boy, I used to eat most of my meals outside."

"Really?"

Ella yawned and leaned back against Josie's leg. Josie stroked her hair.

"Really, I did," Hunter said. "'Course, it was because I didn't want to let Pa down. I would eat while I was workin'. I didn't want to take the time to sit. Any chance I got, I worked so I'd get ahead on chores. That's the only time my father was ever proud of me."

"He must have been a hard man."

"He was." Hunter sighed heavily. Josie reached over and took his hand. He looked down at her fingers on his and smiled slightly. "He always blamed me for Ma leavin' us. I knew that even when I was too young to *know* that I knew it. I always wanted his approval. I'd guess the only reason he left me the ranch is so it wouldn't go to no stranger."

"You weren't to blame," Josie insisted with sudden ferocity. "Havin' a child is hard on a woman. It changes her. It changed me."

"Well, I guess you *would* know better than me on that." He looked at Ella. "Yes, ma'am, I think I will try to find time enough for another picnic sometime soon."

Hunter turned to Josie. He realized he was as close to her as he had ever been, except when he grabbed her after she snuck into the cellar.

Her eyelashes were so long and delicate.

To look at them any longer would mean staring into her eyes. Fearing she would feel intimidated, he dropped his gaze and found himself instead looking at the pale peach-pink of her smooth, pink lips.

An absurd thought skittered through his head like a spider out of the shadows.

What if he kissed her?

Ella was drowsing. No one would be the wiser. A secret between him and her.

If we did kiss, what would that mean for us?

Josie abruptly stiffened and leaned away, putting a stop to his crazy thoughts. She was working for him. It just wouldn't be right.

She averted her eyes and grabbed up their napkins and stood. "We should go back to the house."

"Yes, I suppose we should," Hunter said softly. His mouth was dry. Why hadn't he brought anything to drink? "But one thing before we do."

"Y-yes?" she stammered.

"I asked Kerry to pack us the food, but she doesn't know this was just a picnic. She still thinks you came out here to help me with a fence. It's your choice whether you tell her the truth or not when she asks. We both know she'll ask."

Josie studied the grass. "I think this will be our secret."

Hunter rubbed his hand over her shoulder, then walked off to the horses. His full stomach was twisting as he gathered the animals and prepared them for the ride back. Maybe they *shouldn't* share a secret. Maybe they should just forget all about that brief, yet lovely and freeing moment where it seemed like they would kiss.

But it was too late now. They were going to have to live with their decisions.

Chapter Nineteen

Josie walked with Kerry to the door, holding Ella against her shoulder. Ella's breathing was slow and even, her arms draped limply around Josie's neck.

Kerry stepped out onto the porch and turned back. "I won't be comin' in tomorrow," she said. "I meant to tell you earlier, but then you went off with Hunter on your picnic."

"Oh, why won't you be coming?" Josie shifted her grip on Ella. She was getting heavier every day, it seemed like.

"A friend will be arrivin' and spendin' the day in town before she continues on East. I already told Hunter. Tomorrow won't be too difficult for you, I believe. And if you do need help, you can always ask him." Kerry gave a sudden and meaningful look off in the direction of the stable, where Hunter would be still. Josie had offered to help him with the horses and he had turned her away, telling her to instead go help Kerry so she could leave and get back to town before dark.

Josie bit her lip and suddenly she couldn't keep quiet about what had happened earlier. She had too many feelings about all of it and she needed to talk, though only a little while ago she had wanted to keep it a secret. "We didn't go look at any fence," she blurted out.

Kerry smiled and shook her head, her hands on her wide hips. "Well, I know that. I called it a picnic just now. You didn't say anythin' about it, though."

She hadn't noticed. Kerry had just said it so naturally. She stammered, "Well, that was... I mean... We did eat while we were out there."

"I know. I helped Hunter pack up the food. And he told me the same whopper about the fence. But I know. And don't worry. I won't tell anyone." Kerry winked. "Who would I tell, anyway?"

Josie couldn't find anything to say. Kerry laughed and walked off, saving Josie from having to decide. She called out a quick farewell and then shut the door.

Josie let out a heavy sigh and wrapped both arms around Ella. "It's time for us to get to bed, my dear."

Ella stirred as she was spoken to and yawned. "Hunter?" She rubbed her eyes with a small fist and looked around.

Josie took her to their room and laid her down on the bed. She sat on the edge of the mattress and drew the blankets up to Ella's chin, smoothing them down. "There. Nice and warm."

She bent over and pressed a kiss to Ella's forehead.

Ella tipped her face up and kissed her chin. "Mama go to bed?"

"Very soon," Josie promised. Kerry had brought her a night dress that her daughter no longer used and she wanted to see if it would fit. If it did, it would certainly be more comfortable to wear than the too-large, very old dresses owned by Hunter's mother before she had left.

"Okay." Ella smiled and closed her eyes.

Josie went to the dresser to get the night dress and set it out. She started to remove her clothes.

She was careful not to stand in front of the mirror as she undressed, or to look at her unclothed reflection..

Her mind wandered as she folded her clothes and set them aside to wear again the next day. Her heart ached for Hunter and his abandonment. If his own father blamed him, then that was all he would have learned growing up. He would believe it was his fault, no matter what Josie said to him.

She knew what it was like to feel responsible for a wrong she hadn't committed.

Her own mother, Marie, had passed in childbirth. Josie blamed herself for that. But what could be done about it, except to try to be a woman her mother would have been proud of?

Josie was lifting the new nightdress when she heard Hunter's voice right outside the bedroom door. "Josie, can I come in?"

She spun around, her mouth opening to give him a resounding *no.*

Ella leaped out of the bed and ran to the door.

"Ella!" Her voice squeaked.

Ella grabbed the door and tossed it open.

Hunter stood in the doorway. His eyes roamed around the room.

Josie felt it quite clearly when they landed upon her. She could only stand there and look back at him, helpless in her nakedness. His brow furrowed and then he stumbled back as he registered the sight of her. Old wounds covered her body, raised welts and discolorations.

His nostrils flared, his face coloring in with a red so vivid it seemed there was a flame beneath his skin, shining outward. And for a moment she saw Owen's face upon his body. His snarl was Owen's snarl. His anger was Owen's anger.

"Don't hurt me," she whispered.

"Hurt you?" Hunter flinched as if he was afraid she might be the one to strike *him.* "I ain't going to hurt you! Who hurt you, Josie? What happened to you?"

"Mama?" Ella's small face was troubled.

Josie had dropped her dress in shock when Ella opened the door for Hunter. She had no way to cover herself and it was far, far too late anyway. Yet, the need to do so was undeniable.

"Step out of the room, Hunter. Please."

His eyes flashed. "I won't. You tell me what happened."

"Hunter!" She stared at him, then gestured with a quick tilt of her head in Ella's direction.

Finally, he understood. He spun away and slammed the door shut behind him, the thin wood slapping into the frame. Josie jumped, unable to help it. That sound, the abuse of any door that barred Owen's way to her. Sometimes she awoke with a start from her dreams with that sound echoing in her head, believing that he was coming from her.

But he was dead.

He couldn't hurt her any longer.

Ella walked over to her and hugged onto her leg tightly. "Mama?"

Josie bent and picked her up. "It's okay." Her voice shook. She clenched her jaw, forcing herself to be strong still. "Back into bed with you."

Ella didn't resist as Josie brought her back to the bed and tucked her in again. She focused on the simple task, one that always was so pleasurable and now which filled her with dread, for when she finished, she was going to need to go talk to Hunter and explain everything to him. He might not even be able to understand. She had to try regardless.

But first, she put her clothes back on. Not the night dress, though. She would appear before him as a woman, not like a child creeping out of bed in the middle of the night.

Chapter Twenty

Hunter paced in front of the fireplace, his shoulders tense, breath whooping in and out of his heaving lungs. He was a caged animal with nowhere to go, nothing to do to escape this prison of rage he had found himself in.

He kept seeing Josie in his mind's eye, the damage to her body. None of the wounds had been fresh, leaving only scars, but still. What had she endured in her life? Who had forced her to endure it?

He feared he knew the answer and that only added fuel to the fire of anger raging in him, as the perpetrator was likely dead. He wanted to hurt the one who had hurt Josie.

His senses were heightened. He easily heard it when Josie lcft thc bedroom, though the shutting of the door was only the slightest thump of contact. He moved to the hall to meet her as she walked down it.

Her eyes flew wide and she jumped back, clutching at her heart. Her body shrank in on itself, her head twisting away from him.

She thinks I'm going to hurt her.

And all at once, he understood everything. Every single incident flew through his head in a rush, like cattle in a stampede. All the times she flinched at a shout, or started at a loud noise. The way she stiffened when he touched her, when he even approached her too suddenly.

He suddenly saw himself as she must see him, a man much larger than her, who could do anything to her if he so desired. He had never done anything to harm her, but he *could.* He had the potential to do so. That was why she feared him, because another had instilled that fear so deeply into her.

Though his anger still burned, and burned even hotter still, he took several steps away from her. Then, he sat down. He willed his facial muscles to relax, forcing the snarl off his lips. He clutched at his knees to prevent his hands from forming into fists, all in the name of appearing less threatening.

She stared, her green eyes wild and animalistic with her fear. Her hand remained up by her heart as if protecting it. She licked her lips and dropped her eyes to the floor. "I'm sorry."

Hunter made himself breathe deeply in and forced a slow measure to his voice. "I'm the one who's sorry. I didn't mean to walk in on you. I thought, with the door opening, I was being invited."

"I understand. What did you... want?" She crept slightly into the room.

"I noticed you had put a handkerchief in one of the saddlebags. I didn't want you to forget about it." He took the scrap of cloth from his pocket and leaned forward to place it on the arm of the chair across from him, sitting back again to give her space if she wanted to get it. She didn't move.

"I really am sorry, Josie."

"It can't be undone." She abruptly heaved a sigh and moved to sit in the parlor, though not in a chair where he could reach her. "You want to know what happened. I'll tell you, but you have to promise we won't talk about this again. At least, not in front of Ella. She doesn't know that I'm..."

"But she must have seen them before?" He shifted in his seat, uncomfortable with the subject of her nakedness, the parts of her he had seen along with those old injuries. It wasn't couth.

"What I mean is that she doesn't know I'm not supposed to look like this." Her eyes begged him to understand. "Maybe one day, I'll explain so she can understand, but right now, she's too young. I don't want her to think that her mother is strange. Or broken."

"You are *not* broken." Hunter leaned forward, gripping his knees tighter.

"He certainly tried."

"Tell me who. I'll kill him." He didn't want to sound frightening, but he meant it. Someone who could do such awful things didn't deserve to be breathing.

"Someone already beat you to that," she said quietly.

"So it was Owen." He swore bitterly. "That man was crazy as a loon. Could have had a whole good life livin' on the ranch your father left him. Purty wife, purty daughter. And he done went and messed up every part of it."

Josie said nothing. She wiped at her eyes with one finger, which drew his attention to that little hook of a scar he had noticed before.

"You can tell me," Hunter said. "If you feel up to it. Then, I promise we won't speak of it no more. If we ever do, you'll be the one to bring it up, not me."

She shot him a look of gratitude. "It started not long after we were married. At first, it was just pushin' and shovin'. But it got worse very quickly. But he was careful. He never hurt me anywhere that anyone would notice."

Doubtful if anyone would have intervened even if they had noticed, Hunter thought, clenching his jaw so tightly that his ears popped.

"Your eye," he questioned, when he could unclench his jaw enough to speak.

She touched the little scar. "He did that on the day he was killed. At breakfast. He still had his fork in his hand. I'm lucky. If it was just a little higher, I'd have lost my eye."

Hunter swore again. "Don't talk like that. You were not lucky."

"I have to think about it like that," she whispered.

"Why?" He was on his feet without meaning to stand. "You didn't deserve none of that. If you were lucky, ain't none of it would have happened. If you were lucky, your father wouldn't have been such a fool to leave you and the ranch to that man."

Her eyes were so weary as they lifted to him. She held up her hands, weakly, and let them drop again. "If I think about it any other way, it hurts me too much. I'll... I'll break."

The crack in her voice was too much. His control snapped like a frayed rope. Though he would have done anything not to frighten her, he simply couldn't hold himself back any longer.

He moved toward her, and dropped onto the couch at her side. She flinched away and normally he would have backed off, but this was out of his control. He reached for her, folding his arms around her, pulling her in against his chest where she held still and trembled.

He closed his eyes and bent his head over hers. There was so much inside of him, under his skin. He didn't know what he would do, or say. The words just came out of him from somewhere deep inside, a part of him that was just as broken as she was.

"I will never raise a hand against you, Josie. Never. I won't let no one else hurt you, either. You're safe here."

She remained stiff and quivery in his arms, unmoving. He expected nothing else and did not blame her.

Then, she let out a shuddering breath and her cheek touched his chest. He could feel her heart pounding. He held her even closer, pressing her body to his.

"I swear to you," he said.

She lifted her head and met his eyes. "Thank you."

A single tear tracked slowly from the corner of her eye, trickling over the scar and along the line of her cheekbone. Hunter swiped it away with his thumb. Her skin was a little worn and rough, but firm and warm.

Josie tilted her head, leaning her face into the palm of his hand.

He held her in her vulnerable state, capable of doing anything, knowing he never would. That was what set him apart from Owen, from other terrible men. He would not do something just because he was capable of it.

I want to kiss her.

The realization came as an unpleasant jolt. But what man wouldn't want to kiss the pretty woman in his arms?

But, he wouldn't. He would not take advantage of her.

Josie's green gaze fumbled for his. Her eyebrows lifted and her lips parted, though no words emerged. Her chin tilted upward ever so slightly.

No.

Even if she also wanted to kiss him —even if he wasn't misunderstanding all these signals— he still could not allow it.

He forced himself to let go of her and shifted back until their bodies no longer touched, though she had left an imprint upon him that wouldn't soon fade. He could still feel her beating heart, the warmth of her form against his chest.

"I think you had best get back to your room." His voice was hoarse. "So Ella don't miss you."

"She's asleep." A pause. "But you're right. I should get back to her in case she wakes up."

"Tell me that I'm right again. Music to my ears."

Josie stared at him and he silently cussed at himself for his foolish attempt at levity. Then, she huffed a breath that was almost a laugh and stood. "I won't. You've got too much confidence already."

He laughed a little too hard at this response. Josie shook her head and moved away, to the hall. She put her hand on the wall and spoke without looking at him, her voice shaking, wet with tears. "Thank you."

Before he could respond, she walked away. The bedroom door shut a moment later.

Hunter slumped back on the couch and put his arm over his face, sighing heavily. All his energy had flowed out of him, leaving his limbs wooden. He was more tired than if he had just worked for a full day, and without the satisfaction. Yet, there was a different sort of satisfaction. He had learned more about Josie, finally putting together the missing pieces of her past.

He did wonder what he was supposed to do now. What *they* were supposed to do after having grown closer like they had.

And what of his sudden desire to kiss her? What sense was he supposed to make of that?

He heaved up to his feet and headed down the hall to his own room. The only thing he was certain of was that he needed some rest. He couldn't even begin to think of answers until after he had gotten some sleep.

Chapter Twenty-One

A hand in her hair, fingers wrapped in the strands, cruelly pulling her head back. Josie tried to speak and no words came out. She grabbed behind her for the assailant, clutching at clothing, nothing substantial.

A voice in her ear, indistinct and slurred. She tried to yell out her confusion and still couldn't make a sound. Her throat was tight, as if she was being choked.

Her assailant moved around in front of her and it was Owen, the hilt of a knife protruding from his chest. And then it was Hunter, but then he was a hulking wolf, lunging for her, fangs flashing.

She jolted upright in her bed, a scream locked in her throat. Cold sweat covered her face, running like tears down her cheeks. The back of her head ached from having her hair pulled. But it had only been a dream, hadn't it?

Josie rolled out of bed, the sheets sticking to her sweating body. She saw her true assailant at last: Ella, sleeping, strands of red hair captured in her fist. Rubbing her sore scalp, Josie managed to unlock her voice enough to laugh slightly. It had only been a dream after all, spurred on by her daughter grabbing her, likely during a dream of her own.

Josie sat down on the edge of the mattress and smoothed her hair back. Her heart still galloped in her chest, reluctant to slow, her body hesitant to believe what she had gone through wasn't reality. Of course, she knew Owen was dead. She knew Hunter was not a wolf, nor any type of monster at all.

He was a good man. Their conversation last night was proof enough of that. Her heart just wasn't quite as willing to believe that yet, and for good reason.

Josie listened and she heard Hunter as he spoke with Kerry, the sounds coming from the direction of the kitchen. His deep rumble made her smile. He had been so kind to her the night before. She hadn't even known he was capable of such kindness. She was glad to have been wrong on that account.

But they did need to talk about what had passed between them, something that was more than simple understanding.

She knew he had wanted to kiss her. And she had wanted to kiss him, too. Such an absurd time for it, not at all appropriate, but his kindness and his embrace had inspired feelings in her that she could hardly make sense of. When last had she felt tingles like that, the tickliness of a caterpillar walking on her skin? Surely not since she was just a girl and the attention from boys was new and exciting and desirable.

Unfortunately, it couldn't really mean anything. She had been vulnerable, in an odd, open state of mind. Perhaps she had misread the cues. Maybe there had been no cues at all, just her own desires reflecting back at her.

She wasn't certain. A talk with Hunter would sort it out. She'd have to catch him later and speak with him on this.

There was the rest of the day to get through, first. She needed to go and help Kerry with breakfast.

Wait.

Kerry?

Now with something else to puzzle over, she knew she couldn't wait any longer. She leaned over the bed and kissed Ella's face all over, cheeks and nose and forehead, until she awoken with giggles. "Mama tickle me!"

Josie drew her warm, sleeping daughter off the bed and into her arms. "It's time for breakfast, my little one."

"Okay." Ella yawned and leaned her head on Josie's shoulder. "Pancake?"

"Oh, I'm sure we can get you a pancake." Josie stroked her hair and headed out of the room, to the kitchen.

Kerry and Hunter stood at the counter, each holding a steaming mug of coffee. They glanced over as Josie entered. Hunter looked concerned about something. Her?

"Did we wake you up?" That was Kerry. "We was going to let you two sleep a little longer."

"No, I just happened to wake up." Josie frowned at the older maid. Her friend, if she was honest. The only friend she'd had in years. "I thought you said that you weren't going to be here."

Kerry's cheeks turned pink. "Yes, well, it seems that I got my dates mixed up. My friend is comin' into town tomorrow."

Josie laughed a little. "Oh, alright."

"You'll make the same kinds of mistakes when you're my age." Kerry held out her hands for Ella. Josie passed her daughter over and Kerry bounced Ella in her arms. Ella giggled, her flaming red hair bobbing. "Good morning, little one. What would you like for breakfast?"

"She wants pancakes," Josie said, at the same time as Ella chirped, "Pancakes!"

Kerry looked at them both and smiled. "Yes, we can do that. We'll have pancakes. Do you want some bacon, too? And how about some fried apples to go on top of the pancakes?"

"Yes!" Ella clapped her hands together. "Fry apples."

"Come with me into the cellar and help me, won't you?" Kerry bent and Ella hopped out of her arms. "You're so big and strong. You can carry the apples."

"I help Kerry," Ella agreed, and set off for the cellar steps. Laughing, Kerry rushed after her.

Josie watched them, smiling. Hunter cleared his throat and she swung back around to him. "W-what?"

"You want some coffee?" Hunter moved away from the counter and got another mug out of the cupboard.

"That would be nice. Thank you."

He brought her a mug of the stuff, black, though she personally preferred some sugar. But she wasn't about to complain. She took the cup from him with a murmur of thanks and sipped the hot, strong brew. To her surprise, the bitter edge wasn't all that unpleasant, and she took a longer drink than before.

Hunter leaned on the counter, his eyelids lowered, his long lashes stark against his suntanned cheeks. "I can't say that I slept too good. Can't imagine you did, either."

"I didn't," she admitted, and drank more of the coffee he had given her. "I had a bad dream before I woke up."

"What kind of a bad dream?"

She looked into the darkness of the coffee in her mug and supposed it would be a bad idea to mention Owen. "I dreamed you were a wolf."

"A wolf, huh? Maybe you heard one in your sleep an' put it into your dream." Hunter shrugged. "We get them around sometimes. Not so many as we did in the past. People hunt 'em, sell their pelts."

He clearly didn't understand the significance. Or perhaps he did and was ignoring it for the sake of levity.

For the sake of normalcy.

Josie listened to Kerry and Ella coming back from the cellar with what they needed to make breakfast. She needed to remember that. They would be having breakfast, and then there would be dishes to wash, other chores to do, other meals to plan for. Life had to go on. That was what Hunter was telling her, that in spite of everything, the day would go on.

Ella rushed into the kitchen with an apple in each hand. She went straight to Hunter and showed him. "I help," she announced.

"And a very good helper you are," Kerry replied, coming in with everything else they had gone down to get. "Josie, I just realized we're gonna need a few more eggs. Do you mind going to the coop to get some? We can worry about cleaning it later, but will you check the feed too, while you're there?"

"Of course," Josie replied. "Stay here with Kerry, Ella."

Ella sat down in the middle of the floor and started to eat one of the apples she held. Kerry chuckled. "I knew I had a good reason to bring extra."

Josie headed out of the house. The day was already very warm, working its way to being fully hot. The chicken coop was stuffy, smelling of soiled straw and musty feathers. Chickens clucked around her feet, forcing her to navigate carefully around them as she checked their feed and then took the freshly-laid eggs from their nests. With the eggs gathered in the front of her dress, she went back to the house.

Hunter's voice carried from the dining room. "Nice job. Let me see if I can do better."

Ella suddenly squealed with laughter. "Me, me! Me turn!"

Hunter laughed, too. "Okay, fine, here. Your turn again."

Curiosity sparking inside her, Josie crept to the doorway to see what they were doing.

They sat at the table together, a giant next to a fairy, with a collection of small brown things between them. Ella grabbed one of the brown things and flicked at it, missed, and flicked again. The hard little object skittered part of the way across the table, where others like it were scattered.

Hunter took one of the objects and flicked it, sending his all the way across the table and off the edge, onto the floor. Whatever it was struck the wooden floorboard with a minute *tink* and bounced off into a corner, rebounding again to come to a stop by Josie's feet. Taking care not to crush the eggs, she crouched and picked up the flicked object. It was an apple seed.

Hunter sent another of the seeds sailing across the table and Ella laughed again, rocking back and forth in her chair.

Josie palmed the seed and stepped away before she was noticed watching them as they played their game. She didn't mind that she was going to have to do some extra sweeping, not at all. The only important thing was that they continued to bond. Now that Hunter understood the life she had lived, and therefore also the life Ella had lived, he would be gentler, less likely to yell. That was her hope, at least. It was a tentative hope and she wasn't ready to fully commit to it, but it was good to have that hope regardless.

"Josie, are you back inside?" Kerry called out from the kitchen. "I swore I heard you come in."

"I'm here." She went into the kitchen and removed the eggs, placing them on the counter next to the other ingredients for the batter. Kerry was peeling and chopping apples, obviously where the "game pieces" for Hunter and Ella had come from.

"I was startin' to think you'd gotten plumb lost." Kerry chuckled. "You don't mind fixin' up the pancake batter yourself, do you? Then we'll let it rest while I fry up these apples."

"Of course." Josie settled into the work next to her friend.

The periodic bursts of laughter from the dining room kept her smiling. She found herself looking forward to spending breakfast with everyone, and to the rest of the day, as well. She couldn't imagine much that could ruin this.

Chapter Twenty-Two

A handful of days blurred by, life resettling into normalcy. Hunter took his chance at breakfast, over a spread of eggs and bacon and good, strong coffee.

"I was thinkin' on somethin' recently," he began.

Josie flicked her eyes over to him. When their gazes met, he felt a spark, a strike of iron against flint. "I knew you were actin' strange," she said.

"I ain't," he protested.

"You've been actin' *too* normal, is the thing." Her smile made his heart skip a beat, his traitor heart with no right to be feeling such things for her. He just couldn't deny how pretty she was when she smiled. A light came into her eye, a glow of new spring life.

"What is it that you were thinkin' of?" Kerry jumped in, curious as always. If Hunter died, she'd probably get in the grave with him to see what it was all about.

"Well, my thought was that I could take Ella off your hands for the day, *Josie.*" He made sure Kerry knew who he was actually talking with. "You're always workin' so hard, I thought you could use a break."

Josie's brows drew together, her smile fizzling out in but a moment, like a bucket of water tossed into a fireplace. "Thank you. I appreciate it. But I don't know that she's old enough."

"Sure, she is. Old enough to follow me around a few hours." He looked at Ella, sitting in her chair next to Josie. She used a scrap of bacon to eat her eggs instead of a fork, something a cowboy would have done; it made him smile, since she had probably copied that from one of the ranch hands.

"She wants to follow me around anyway. You've said so yourself," Hunter reminded Josie. "It'd give you some time to focus. When she gets tuckered out, I'll bring her home for a nap."

Josie chewed on her lower lip while looking at her daughter. She was clearly torn. He didn't want to push her, but she needed to learn to trust him. He was nothing like her dead husband.

"She'll be safe with me. You know that." He looked at her as if Kerry wasn't in the room with them, watching, observing, figuring out that something had changed between them.

Josie looked back at him and then gave a slight, single nod. "If she wants to. I'll ask her." She turned to Ella. "Dear..."

"Want Hunter," Ella informed her, without looking up from her eggs.

Hunter laughed. "That's that, then." He could see Josie was still worried. He would save his breath on trying to convince her with words. He would show her when everything turned out fine.

After breakfast, he took Ella by the hand and led her away. She trotted along at his side to keep up with his longer steps. He slowed down so she wouldn't get tired out, and to give himself some time to think as he realized there was an important aspect of all this that he had missed.

What were they actually supposed to do?

He wouldn't take her anywhere near the cattle. Too dangerous. Perhaps it would be best if they went to the stables and he could introduce her to all the horses, let her pet them and give them treats. She could assist him with cleaning, and perhaps they could play a game of hide-and-go-find.

Ella stopped walking and pointed up at the top of the stable. "Bird!"

Hunter peered up. A small, round bird perched at the very apex of the roof. He recognized quite easily the buff underside, the distinctive black cap and white eye markings. "That's a chickadee."

"Chicky-dee," Ella echoed.

He bent and picked her up, letting her sit in the crook of his arm. She nestled in, her head on his chest. "That's right. Let's go see all the horses. They need food and water and clean straw. You goin' to help me?"

"Yes! Let's go!"

He brought her into the stable and introduced her to all the horses one at a time. Remembering her brief earlier interactions with the animals, he kept a close eye on her, ensuring she didn't stand too close to a hoof that could kick and didn't wander into their blind spots.

When Granite bowed his huge head to sniff at Ella, Hunter stared, awed. His horse's head was bigger than Ella's entire body, once again putting it into perspective for him just how small and fragile she was.

Had he really expected Josie to be fine with him watching over her?

But she *had* agreed, astonishing him further. She truly did trust him.

His resolve hardened. He would be deserving of that trust.

They spent the next while in the stable with the horses. Hunter showed Ella where all the different feed bags were, and she even fetched water with him to fill their troughs. She was too small to actually lift a full wooden bucket, so he gave her one with just a little bit in it. The pride on her face when she dumped her tiny contribution into the indicated trough made his heart glad. She thought she was helping, doing a great job, and he thought she was doing great, too.

He moved on to cleaning the stalls, using a pitchfork to stab up clumps of the soiled straw and placing them in a wheelbarrow. Ella scrunched up her nose and wanted nothing to do with that particular task, though she enjoyed the part that came after. Spreading out the clean straw on the stall floors was great fun for her. She gathered up an armful of the dried, golden grass, and tossed it out as far as she could from where she stood. The lighter pieces fluttered in the air after the main clumps had already hit the floor.

Somewhere around the last stall, she stopped throwing the straw with such vigor. Hunter kept an eye on her. She was lagging, her energy waning fast. He might not have had much experience with children, but he did know about young animals. He had seen this behavior often with calves and even chicks. They could fall asleep at a moment's notice, even while standing.

Hunter went to her and put his hands on her shoulders. He leaned over her so that he was looking at her sweet, round face upside down. She peered up at him from underneath heavy eyelids, her smile lazy. A big yawn nearly split her head in half.

"About time for a nap, huh?"

"No," she protested, and swiped at her eyes with her fists. "No nap. Stay with Hunter."

Hunter scratched the back of his head, thinking on it. Were she a boy, he'd let her lay on the bales of clean straw.

Well, heck, what did it matter if she wasn't a boy?

Hunter crouched and pointed at the bales. "You can lay down over there, chickadee." The nickname escaped without him thinking about it. It just felt right.

"No," she said.

"Yes," he insisted. "Just a little nap. When you wake up, we can keep having fun."

The look she gave him was skeptical, surprisingly shrewd. No cow calf had ever fixed such a perceptive stare upon him.

"Okay," she said, after a long while of staring at him. "You stay here?"

"I'll be right here," he promised. The stalls were done, but there were other things to clean and he liked to check over the horse tack on a regular, frequent basis to catch any fraying or weakened parts.

Ella gave him a hug and scampered off. Hunter turned away, smiling. He didn't know much about Owen's interactions with Ella, but he supposed they couldn't have been good ones. Maybe he could be the father figure that she needed.

The father figure he wished he'd had.

I'll have to watch myself. Make sure I'm celebrating her accomplishments instead of correcting her all the time. Josie would like that, I'm sure.

Hunter grabbed the wheelbarrow full of soiled straw and, after reassuring Ella he would be coming back, he took it outside to dump it. As he was on his way back, he heard something, a strangeness from within the stable. The soft keening caused all the hair on his body to stand on end. No horse had ever made a sound like that before.

"Ella!" he gasped. He rushed in.

She sat on the floor, clutching at her knee.

He saw blood, a bright line of it marring her perfect skin.

There was no time to think. He snatched her up off the floor and ran out of the stable, sprinting across to the house. He slammed the door open with his shoulder. Josie's voice rose up in fear and he headed for her, finding her in the parlor with Kerry. His heart pounding, he took in the scene in a single moment. Between the two women was a tray with a teapot and cups and cookies. They had been taking this rare moment to relax.

Josie leaped to her feet and ran to him, reaching for Ella. "My baby! What happened to her?"

Ella wailed as soon as she was in Josie's arms, burying her face in her mother's neck. Kerry grabbed up a napkin and pressed it to the cut on her leg, stopping it from dripping on the floor.

"I-I don't know," Hunter stammered. "I came back from the stable and found her like this."

Josie stopped and stared. "What? You left my daughter alone? You were supposed to be watching her!"

“I only left for a minute! Less than a minute!”

A sharp sound cut through their tension. Kerry clapped her hands together twice. “You two can have your argument some other time. This little girl needs help.”

“Right. I’ll go fetch a doctor from town!” Hunter turned.

“She don’t need a pill.” Kerry glared at him. “Take too long, anyway. What she needs is her mama.”

Josie put her back to Hunter and got into the chair next to Ella, stroking and kissing her as she whimpered.

Kerry kept her unhappy stare fixed on Hunter. “Put yourself to use, now. Bandages. Hot water.”

He rushed off to do as he was told, his throat tight. Maybe his father was right and he couldn’t do anything properly. He should have known better than to leave Ella for any length of time, even seconds. She never stayed in one place. Her fall, her injury, it was all his fault.

What if she had a permanent disfigurement from this? He’d never be able to forgive himself.

He came back to the parlor as Kerry was cleaning up the cut using one of the napkins from the tea tray. It was deep and nasty, with bits of wood stuck in it. No doubt she had fallen right onto the hard wooden floor of the stable, probably while running.

Kerry took what he had brought and dipped the napkin in the bowl of hot water. She slowly and carefully cleaned up the cut, picking out all the wood slivers, then wrapped a bandage around it. Ella whined and kicked her other leg. “Hurts!”

“I know it does. But look, it’s all done.” Kerry tucked in the edges of the bandage to secure them and sat back. “You should be feelin’ better already.”

Ella grumbled and tucked deeper into her mother's arms.

Kerry picked up the bowl and the soiled napkins and carried them away. Her receding footsteps went into the kitchen.

"You let her get hurt."

Josie's voice was a mere sigh of wind.

Hunter stared at the floor. "I got nothin' to say to defend myself. I messed up. I thought she'd be fine." He couldn't stop talking, even though he'd just said he couldn't defend himself. He ached for something to take this blame off his shoulders. "I keep thinkin' of her almost like a doll. I forget she's got a mind of her own. I *know* she's stubborn and don't listen half the time, but it's so easy to overlook that. But it ain't an excuse. I'm sorry."

Josie closed her eyes. "I know. I'm not mad, because I understand."

"Not mad?" He couldn't let himself believe that. He put a hand on top of his head. "You should be crazy mad. Angry as all get out."

"But you didn't hurt her. She just fell." Josie stroked Ella's hair. "And she don't blame you, either. I bet you that if I let go of her right now, she'd go right over to you."

"Probably shouldn't try to find out. She shouldn't be walkin' on that leg until it starts to heal up."

"Then, why don't you come over and sit next to her so she won't feel like she has to get up?" Her stare was pointed, direct.

Hunter stared back at her. He couldn't figure her out. Women were such mysterious creatures. He never had all these questions about himself when he was taking care of horses.

He looked at Ella, and he had never seen her look less interested in spending time with him. She didn't really need him, anyway.

"I'm thinkin' I'll just leave it to you." He twisted around and hurried away, brushing past Kerry. His chores called to him, not because they needed to be done, but because they were his escape. They always had been. He was only good for ranching, nothing else.

All of this could be a sign he needed to spend less time with Josie and Ella, and more time on his job. His father would have approved of that.

Chapter Twenty-Three

"Hunter?"

Lingering outside his office door, Josie clasped her hands together and awaited a reply. The faint glow sneaking out from below the door told her he was in there.

What she wanted from him seemed absurd given what had occurred earlier, but there really wasn't any other option.

After a bit with no response, she gathered her courage, lifted her fist, and rapped her knuckles on the wood.

"Come in."

Swallowing hard, she pushed the door open and crept in. Hunter sat behind his big, old desk, a coffee mug at his elbow. There were papers spread out before him, loose, yellowed. He picked up his mug and sipped whatever liquid was inside. Setting the cup aside, he said, "I thought I heard someone out there. Wasn't too sure of it, though. You doin' okay?"

"I am." Josie nodded. She crossed the threshold and walked in, the big shelves and their many books a soothing presence. She didn't feel penned in. Instead, there was a sense of expansion. Perhaps not every one of those books held a story, but there was the potential there, and that was especially what mattered right then.

She walked up to his desk and peeked down at the papers. Lists and numbers. "What are you working on?" Her own brashness made her blush and she quickly amended her question. "If you don't mind my asking you."

Hunter gave a slight smile. "It's just records," he said.

"Records of what?" Again, she was too bold, asking about these things that were no concern of hers. He hadn't seemed to mind the last time, though.

Hunter took one of the papers and turned it around. It still made little sense to her. The words were abbreviations, the numbers without any correlation that she could see.

"We got to keep track each year of what we buy, sell, use, and get rid of," Hunter said. "Every year, things get more expensive than the last. You know what I mean? It takes a lot of tin to stay alive. So we track it all to make sure we use everythin' we have and don't keep around what doesn't work anymore. Might cost a bit now to replace a worn saddle, but the cost of doctors and medicine for a man who breaks his leg when that saddle fails would be far worse."

Hunter took back the paper he had used as an example and tapped them all into a neat stack.

"Is the ranch running well so far?" She hadn't considered what might happen if Hunter lost his farm.

Hunter nodded. "We're stayin' about even with last year so far. Don't got as many calves in the herd, but the ones we do are quality. We'll make plenty when we sell them."

She let out a relieved sigh. "I'm glad."

"I'm sure of that." He tipped his head back to drain the last drops from his mug. "You come to learn about bookkeepin' or is there somethin' else?"

Josie lowered her head and fiddled with her own fingers. "You might have noticed that the sun's gone down. I've been trying to put Ella to bed, but she won't settle in. She misses you. I think if you went and saw her, maybe brought one of your books to read her a story..."

Hunter rubbed his forehead and massaged the bridge of his nose. "I don't know about all that. She maybe don't need to spend more time with me today."

Josie tapped the top of his desk hard and stared at him. "If you feel so bad about what happened, you should work to make it right. Ella doesn't blame you and neither do I. These things happen, so there's no use in hidin' in here and pretendin' otherwise."

His dark eyes flashed and he half-rose from his chair. "I'm not hidin'."

"Well, now you're standing. So why don't you just come back to the records in a bit? Ella is important. Do this for her."

She didn't like challenging him and would have preferred not to. He was just being silly, that was all. She knew she was right and so did he. All that remained to be seen was how stubborn he would be.

Hunter walked over to his shelves and Josie moved to stand at his side. He ran his thick fingers over the spines of the books, then crouched down and resumed his search. She found herself staring at the top of his head, his thick, dark hair. She had a great urge to touch it and see if it was soft, and she gripped the sides of her dress instead.

He rose with a slim volume in hand. "Look at this."

Josie held out her hands and he placed the book in them. Their fingers touched, and warmth traveled through her veins. She could feel another blush coming —she had never blushed so much around any man before— and sought to distract herself with the book.

It was a plain thing, drab blue in color, without any words on the front, back, or sides. She flicked through pages packed densely with printed words. Drawings interrupted every few pages or so.

"I'm not an artist," Josie said slowly. "But are these... bad?"

Hunter laughed. "Yes, ma'am, they are. Now, the story behind this, Pa had a friend with this idea that he would get some stories published. He went off to New York City and got his books printed. It was a farce, though. The printer took his money and left with the job half-done. So he came back here to Deadwood and gave them away. I'm pretty sure he would have tried it again and lost more of his money before Pa talked him out of it. That's what you got there."

"What is the story about? It won't be too much for a little girl, will it?"

"It's a series of short stories, actually. And he wrote them for children. The stories aren't good, but Ella can't tell the difference, can she?"

"Even if she can, I'm not sure she would say it. She'd be afraid you would stop reading if she complained. And what are the stories about?"

"Deadwood," Hunter said, surprising her. "Actually, it's about a rabbit, a walkin' and talkin' one that goes around tryin' to dig up gold. And he goes into town, meets people and gets into trouble. I ain't read it in a long time. I don't remember too much."

"Well, we'll find out together, I suppose." Josie moved to leave the office.

Hunter's bulk was at her back, keeping pace with her. If she reached back, she'd have touched him.

She walked with him into the bedroom. Ella lay under the blankets, her face scrunched. She looked over and as soon as she saw Hunter, her entire expression lightened. She pulled her arms out from underneath the blankets and reached for him. "Hi! Hi, you."

"Hi, yourself." Hunter brushed past Josie. His side touched hers and the graze of contact was like getting much too close to a fire. And yet she was drawn to him, like a woman lost in a blizzard. She was between two extremes, isolation and intimacy. There was only one correct option and she was afraid of it, because it hurt as much as it felt good.

Hunter sat down on the edge of the bed and Ella hugged him. He touched her hair, the book balanced on his muscular thigh. "How's your knee?"

Ella reached for the book, ignoring his question. "Story?"

"That's right. You want to hear a story?"

"Yes!" She scooted in closer, laying her head on his arm. "Story! Mama come listen, too."

Josie walked over and sat at the foot of the bed, giving the two their own space. If she went and sat at Ella's other side, it would feel too much like they were her parents, and Hunter was not. There was no sense in pretending he could ever be anything like that. She still expected that they would leave one day when the time was right.

Hunter opened the book and started to read, his low voice a rumble that reverberated through the bed. Listening to him was like listening to a refreshing rainstorm, one that held no danger for her as she lingered in her house, safe and warm and dry. She felt like she could fall asleep if she tried.

Her thoughts wandered away from her as she listened to the story, not really hearing the words he said. Hardly aware that she was doing so, she asked herself why she still wanted to leave, and where she would go when she did? She never thought about the future in concrete terms, but she needed to.

Did she want to buy her father's ranch back from the bank? Why would she want to go there, to a place filled with such terrible memories of the pain Owen had brought upon her?

And if she wanted to go somewhere else, then where? And what would she do? She didn't want to be a rancher or a farmer. She had many other skills, but she had already gone though most of her possibilities in the area when she was working to keep the bank from taking the ranch away. Was she meant to leave in search of other opportunities? But Deadwood was all she knew.

What if I do stay with Hunter forever?

Her eyes strayed to him as he read to Ella. They had already come close to kissing. She was beginning to trust him in ways she hadn't thought she'd be able to trust again. If her feelings toward him continued to grow...

Hunter suddenly met her eyes and she flinched in surprise. The corner of his mouth turned up in a grin and he nodded down at Ella. Her daughter was asleep, slumped limp into his side.

That was what he had wanted, to show her Ella was asleep, not to catch her looking at him.

She tried to look calm as she moved around the bed to settle Ella down on the pillow and tuck the covers in securely around her. Hunter shut the book and slipped out of the room.

After a moment, Josie followed. She pushed the door shut and turned to him. The air between them had a static pre-lightning charge to it, raising the hairs on the back of her neck. "Thank you."

"'Course. These stories is only a few pages long. I figure we can do one each night that she wants a story." Hunter smiled again.

"I agree. It's a good idea. I can read to her some nights that you're too busy."

"I'll make the time," he said gruffly. "Say, I saw that letter on top of your dresser. The one I brought you from town. I kept meanin' to ask what it was and never got around to it."

Josie reached behind herself and felt the cool, dimpled wall. "Clive. Owen's cousin."

"The one you said is better than me at communication." His heavy brows cast darkness over his black eyes. "What'd he want with you? Did he ever bother you like Owen did?"

"No. Well, to tell the truth, I hardly ever saw him after I married Owen." Josie chewed on the inside of her cheek, thinking. "He just was trying to get me to go stay with him. He said that people... think you're dangerous."

The angry-bear look was back, the one that frightened her. Hunter's shoulders rose and even his mane-like shag of hair appeared to bristle, like the fur of an agitated mountain lion. "People always think what they don't understand is dangerous. It don't mean nothin'. Unless you believe him?"

She said nothing, looking away. If she lied, he'd know it. If she told the truth, he'd be hurt. And the truth was she thought he did have the capacity to be dangerous... just like everyone else. He wouldn't settle for that reasoning, though. He would take it too personally.

Snorting, he pushed the book at her. "You can keep this in there. I trust you with it."

"Thank you," she murmured, unsure if he heard, as he was already moving away.

Was he angry with her? She hadn't felt threatened, exactly. But there had been a bitterness in his words.

It couldn't be that he was... jealous?

Josie looked down at the drab book in her hands and shook her head. No, there wasn't any reason for him to be jealous. She didn't belong to him.

She didn't belong to Clive either, even though he seemed to believe that.

Suddenly exhausted, she retired to her room for the night, wrapping herself around Ella.

Chapter Twenty-Four

Josie's scream split the calm valley air in twain, sending startled flocks of birds bursting up, briefly darkening the sky as their wings blotted out the sun. Hunter was already running before her scream faded out, still holding the hammer he had been using to make repairs on the side of the stable. He spat nails from his mouth and shouted for her.

"Hunter!" she cried.

Terror chased at his heels as he rushed in the direction of her voice. Kerry burst from the house, also running, her eyes wide. Butch was leaving the tool shed, squinting in the sun. He yelled out a question to Hunter, who ignored him, saving his breath for running. After a moment, he heard footsteps and the jangling of a laden belt as Butch joined in the run behind him.

"Hunter, get over here!"

She stood in front of the chicken coop, both hands plastered to her face. Hunter reached her side, grabbing her around the shoulders and pulling her back, away from whatever danger had her so fearful.

She turned her face up to him and he saw she was dragging her skin down with her hands, stretching her pretty features into a grotesque mask. He grabbed her wrists, forcing her to stop. "What is it? Tell me!"

She wouldn't answer him, shaking her head from side to side.

"Boss..." Butch's voice.

Hunter turned and saw his ranch hand standing at the entrance to the chicken coop, just as Josie had been. Kerry was walking over, too.

Butch held out his arm, stopping her. “No. You ain’t need to see this, Miss Kerry. You should talk Josie back to the house.”

Kerry shouldn’t see it? She was no delicate flower.

Kerry walked over and hooked her arm through Josie’s. “Come on, then,” she said, voice low and gentle. “Let’s go. You need some tea, dear.”

Hunter left the women to sort themselves out and joined Butch at the coop. Butch stepped aside, but Hunter had already seen enough.

Every single one of the chickens was dead, and their deaths had not been pleasant. The evidence was everywhere.

Hunter put a hand to his stomach as his middle swirled with nausea. He had put sick animals down before. He hunted. He had assisted in messy births, and slaughtered cattle for their meat.

And still nothing compared to this... massacre.

“Do you think an animal did it?” Butch walked into the coop, stepping around what he could.

Everyone knew that if a fox or wolf broke into a pen with animals, the bloodlust overcame them and they would kill everything. But even such incidents showed signs of eating. And these wounds were too cleanly made.

“A man did this.” Hunter removed his hat and held it by his side. “I don’t know why. I ain’t wronged anyone.”

"Look there." Butch left the coop and pointed at the ground. Red smudged led away from the coop, in the direction of the river. The dust had been kicked around, the assailant's attempt to cover their tracks.

"I'll follow it. You go back to the house, just in case."

If the person responsible is still in the area, the women could be in danger.

Butch nodded, his jaw clenching. He didn't need to have the reasoning explained to him. "Be careful."

Hunter grunted in response and set off. The red smears went on for some way before fading, though there were still footprints and crushed patches of grass to follow. His pulse throbbed in his ears. He felt like he could see everything, every individual blade of grass, every leaf, every smeared pebble. He took all of it in, missing nothing.

As the river came into sight, he finally lost the trail. They were always going this way to fetch water, crushing the grass themselves, leaving their own footprints. He couldn't differentiate.

But like a hound dog determined to see the hunt through to its end, he pressed on to the river and stood on its muddy bank with his hands on his hips. He looked up and downstream and growled swears under his breath.

Whoever had done this had gone to the river to wash the blood from their body to keep from drawing unwanted attention to themselves. They had then likely walked inside the river for some distance before exiting. Hunter could go looking for that exit point, but there was no telling what way the person had gone. He'd just be wasting time if he did that.

He couldn't ask any neighbors if they had noticed anything suspicious in the night, as he had none. He was alone, out of the way. Which meant whoever had done this had sought him out to do it.

This was a targeted attack.

“Hunter!” Harry’s voice broke into his thoughts. He ran over, huffing, his hair wild. Skidding to a halt at Hunter’s side, he bent over and clutched his knees while getting his breath back.

“Harry? What are you doin’ here?” Hunter asked.

“Butch caught me as I was ridin’ up and he told me all about it,” Harry gasped. “I followed the blood until I saw you. What in the blazes is goin’ on around here? First, that bull in the hollow and now this.”

“I don’t know,” Hunter growled. He paced the riverbank, mud sucking at his boots. He tore his hat from his head and raked his fingers through his hair. “I ain’t done nothin’ to anyone.”

Harry stood back, watching him. “Could it be someone from the past? Someone still mad about a bad business deal?”

“It don’t make any sense!” Hunter threw his hands into the air. “When you’re mad with someone, you go up and fight them. You don’t creep in like a fox and kill their animals.”

“Unless they got drunk and weren’t in control of themselves.” Harry’s proposal was weak. He didn’t even believe in it himself, adding, “But I never saw a drunk that did anything like this."

“What I don’t get is why I didn’t hear anythin’,” Hunter said. “If he was killin’ them, the chickens should have been makin’ a fuss.”

"Chickens ain't too bright," Harry countered. "They would've been asleep. If he did it fast..."

"Which means it *really* wasn't a drunk," Hunter said, and Harry nodded. No drunkard moved so fast and decisively as that

"We'll have to get the sheriff out here." Hunter sighed heavily. "Maybe someone in town knows somethin'."

"I'll go get him," Harry offered. "I'll be back fast as I can."

Hunter nodded and clapped him on the shoulder. "Thank you."

Harry's normal cheer was nowhere to be found, his lips twisted with a dark, wry amusement. "You keep losin' animals and the ranch goes under, I'm out of a job."

Hunter snarled. "This ain't getting' to that point. Long before then, I'll be waitin' out here in the dark. And if I catch the criminal, I'll wring his ugly neck."

Harry headed back to the ranch. Hunter stared into the water of the river as if its shallow depths might hold some answers for him, though of course, he only found more questions.

And worries.

Nothing like this had ever happened until Josie came into his life. This couldn't possibly be related to her. Could it?

Chapter Twenty-Five

Josie stood at the window, watching the men ride in. She recognized the sheriff at the front, a huge man, though not so large as Hunter. The sheriff rode astride an enormous dark brown stallion. The bare patch on the stallion's shoulder was an unpleasant paleness, a disruption.

"They say that that horse fought off a mountain lion one night," Josie murmured to Kerry at her side. "The sheriff was ridin' alone and got ambushed. His horse saved him and got that scar."

"You don't really think of horses as bein' able to fight off predators, but they can be dangerous," Kerry replied. "That scar's almost in the shape of a sheriff's badge. Isn't that funny?"

Josie couldn't even pretend to smile. She braced her hands on the windowsill, leaning closer to the glass until her breath misted on the crystalline surface. Ahead of the sheriff was Harry, and behind him came one of the sheriff's men.

Josie turned and looked at where Hunter stood waiting for them, sweat from the hot sun beaded on his arms. She wondered what he was thinking, if he was afraid or just angry.

Kerry took her arm and pulled at her, guiding her away from the window. "It won't do you any good to stand there and fret, now."

"Kerry..." Josie blinked back sudden tears. "What if we're all in danger?"

Kerry clicked her tongue. "Are you a chicken, Josie?"

"Whoever could do something like that to poor, defenseless animals might not care about stopping at animals!" Her voice rose, unbidden. She turned away from Kerry and wiped hurriedly at her eyes to get rid of the tears that slipped out.

She didn't know how to explain what she was feeling.

She knew chickens were killed for their meat. She had killed them herself, though she had hated the task. The sounds, the smell of blood, the bits of feather she kept finding everywhere...

But there was a difference between a purposeful death and this needless slaughter. When a chicken was killed for food, it was eaten. The insane person who got into their coop had not wanted the chickens for food. All he had wanted was to kill them.

How terribly dark did a person have to be to do such a thing? And, presumably, he had done it out of anger at Hunter. To use innocent creatures for one's own terrible purpose was...

Kerry moved in front of her, putting her hand on her cheek and patting briskly. "I know that you're havin' a hard time,' she said, gentle, yet firm. "But the men will get it sorted. In the meantime, you got to think about something else."

"What?" Josie murmured.

Kerry tilted her head to the side, indicating something. Josie turned. Ella stood in the doorway, her eyes large and watchful. Tucked under her arm was her stuffed bird.

"Mama?" Ella ventured.

Josie realized that she had been forgetting to consider how her reactions would look to Ella. Her daughter had already been through so much. She didn't need to endure anything more.

Josie rushed over to her and dropped to her knees in front of Ella. "Well, now, look who it is," she exclaimed, forcing cheer into her voice. She tickled Ella under the chin and kissed both her cheeks. "It's the most beautiful little girl in the whole world!"

Ella stared, her brow furrowed. "Mama?" she asked again. She knew something was amiss.

Josie tickled her again and stroked her hair, smoothing the unruly flaming locks. "*My* beautiful little girl," she said. "Do you want something, Ella?"

Ella's scrunched expression relaxed, which Josie noted with relief. She had decided to be convinced that everything was okay. "Mama, play with me."

"Play? Okay, what game?"

"Chase me!" Ella exclaimed, and dashed off before Josie had the chance to suggest a different game.

Kerry started laughing. "You'd best catch her, I think."

"How is this a game? It's what I spend all day doing!" Josie dashed out into the hall, just catching a glimpse of Ella ducking into Hunter's office. She chased after her.

Ella was attempting to crawl underneath Hunter's big desk. Josie leaped over and grabbed her by the ankle.

"No, no!" Ella shrieked. She gripped the underside of the desk with all her strength.

"I've got you now!" Josie panted. She took hold of both Ella's ankles and pulled her over, with Ella squealing all the while. She pounced on her daughter, tickling her all over while Ella writhed and wiggled in a not-quite genuine attempt to free herself.

Technically, the game of chase had ended with Ella being caught, But Josie knew it wasn't enough to satisfy her daughter.

"I'm losing my grip on you!" Josie exclaimed. She allowed Ella to pull away from her. Ella crawled away fast on her hands and knees, jumping up again when she reached the door.

This time, Josie was right behind her, following her back in the other direction, toward the kitchen. Then Ella was at the door to the cellar, opening it.

"Careful!" Josie cried, her heart lurching up into her throat.

Ella squealed at the sight of her and scurried down the cellar steps. Josie threw herself through the doorway, watching as Ella navigated the steps with ease. She went down much slower herself, into the dank stillness.

The shadows swathing the barrels and baskets was thick, impenetrable. She lingered in the faint pool of light before the stairs, squinting into the dark for a sign of Ella. Her straining ears searched desperately for a laugh, at the same time as she was hoping she wouldn't hear the squeaking and scrabbling of a rat.

Nothing, no sound. She wouldn't be able to end this so quickly. Holding her breath, she edged out of the light, the dark enfolding her in its thick grasp. Her heart skipped beats. "Ella?" she whispered.

Still nothing. How could it be that her usually giggly daughter was being so quiet? She would just have to accept it and find her the proper way.

She moved around the barrel of apples, and her foot thumped on something both firm and yielding, a sack of flour. She fumbled ahead of her with her arms, her grasping fingers encountering dangling dried meats and cheeses.

There!

A paleness in the dark. Ella's leg was sticking out from behind a crate.

"I've got you!" Josie leaped for her and grabbed her leg. As soon as her fingers fell upon the object, she knew she had been mistaken. The wrinkled, leathery thing in her hands was an old carrot.

From her side came a flash of movement, and then a small, warm body was tackling her, knocking her over. Josie screamed, and then she realized what had accosted her, partly because it was laughing and kissing her cheek.

"Ella!" Josie wrapped her arms around her and buried her face in her hair. Ella smelled of dust and old vegetables. "You got me!"

Ella lifted her face and grinned; Josie's eyes had adjusted just enough to see it. "Now me chase you?" she suggested.

Josie shifted off her back and onto her knees. Ella crouched beside her, dirty, still smiling. Josie brushed some of the dust and cobwebs from her hair. "Oh, I don't think so. Are you hungry, maybe? Do you want a snack?"

"Yes," Ella agreed happily. She stood and held out her hand.

Josie took the tiny hand in hers and they moved around the obstacles together. Then, Ella paused. She stood in front of the blocked-off tunnel system, her lips pursed.

Maybe she's remembering Hunter carrying her through there after the storm. After he rescued her when I couldn't.

"Ella," she said. "Come on."

Ella obediently turned away and they headed to the light. There really wasn't enough room on the narrow steps to go up together so she sent Ella ahead of her. She moved to follow, and a sudden thought struck her, pinning her immobile to the hard packed-earth floor.

The tunnel!

Josie broke free of the paralysis that had gripped her and rushed up the few steps until she reached Ella. She picked up her daughter, slinging her over her shoulder. Ella yelled out and kicked her legs. "Mama!" she laughed.

Josie held tight to her and hurried up the rest of the steps and back past the kitchen. Kerry was just emerging from Hunter's room with a basket full of laundry when Josie saw her and rushed up to her.

Kerry took one look at her and set the laundry down. "What is it? What's happened?"

"I need you to watch Ella for a bit," Josie said quickly, and handed her over. "I have to go tell Hunter something. I had an idea."

"An idea about... what?"

Josie wasted no time in talking about it. She needed to get to Hunter.

She rushed outside and there he was, waving a farewell to the already-distant riders. She called out his name and hurried over to him. "The sheriff left already?"

"He said there was nothin' he could do here." Hunter's eyes were dark and dull, devoid of any shine at all. "The criminal isn't in the area anymore. No one for him to arrest. You know, I used to like him, but that's a real lack of gumption right there."

"I have to tell you something, Hunter." She touched his muscular arm, trying to bring his attention back to her.

He was lost in his complaints about the sheriff, unable to pay attention to her. "There's plenty he could be doin'. I'd do it all myself if I had the authority. But all he said was to summon him if I found out who did it, and he'd make the arrest. Well, that's the point of a lawman who only does his work after the fact? Ain't he supposed to work to make Deadwood a safer place?"

She did agree with everything he had said, but she needed him to listen. She grabbed his hand and squeezed hard. "Hunter, I was down in the cellar with Ella, and I thought… What if this person came through the tunnels?"

He finally looked at her, though he didn't seem to really be seeing her. "What?"

"The tunnels!" she insisted, pulling on his hand. "The person killing the animals could have come through the tunnels."

Hunter frowned. "No one knows about the tunnels outside of my family."

"I found them on my own. Someone else could have."

His frown deepened and he rubbed the back of his neck. "Well, I suppose that is possible. It don't make sense, though. After killin' the chickens, why not go back through the tunnel? The trail led away."

Josie winced at memories of what she had seen, which she wouldn't soon forget. "I don't know. But it's a possibility. Don't you think so?" She suddenly realized the true significance of this event. "What the intruder did to the chickens, that could have been us!"

Hunter slowly pulled his arm away from her. He had been a bit cold ever since that night when she made the mistake of telling him what Clive's letter was about. She wished that he would put that aside for right now and comfort her.

Hunter said, "I guess this means it's time to finally do what I've thought about doin'. I'll have to go off into the mountains and bring back dirt. A lot of it. It's not goin' to be easy. Or fast." He sighed. "Easier than ranch work, though. Some of the hands might be talked into doing it."

"I would feel safer with the tunnel sealed," Josie told him. "At least where it meets the cellar."

"I'll see what I can do. Is that it? Or did you need something else? Because I have a lot of work to do now. There's... cleaning to be done." He pressed his lips together.

She didn't even want to think about it. She backed away with a shake of her head. "I'm sorry."

"Sorry for what?" He turned away. "You didn't do this."

She watched him go, her chest tight. What if all of this was her fault, though?

What if the person who did this was someone she knew? Like...

Clive?

But he wasn't that type of person. Was he?

Josie groaned and rubbed her face. She didn't like mysteries. All she wanted was for the culprit to be caught and for this to end.

Chapter Twenty-Six

The town unfolded before him, bustling mostly with women eager to catch up on their work after yesterday's day of rest and worship. As he approached on Granite, they stared and ushered their children to get out of his path. Still, safely navigating with all the people and the other horse riders and the carriages was an impossibility.

Hunter dismounted and took hold of Granite's reins to lead him through the throng. The enormous gelding moved with surprising delicacy for a creature his size, stepping around a dog that ran out in front of him and stopping for a child that Hunter somehow hadn't seen. The boy was utterly unaware of having nearly been crushed under enormous hooves.

"Excuse me, sir." A polite voice from his left made him turn. A woman stood out in front of what everyone thought was the town's best bakery, though he considered their goods to be overpriced and of subpar quality. "Sample of our new bread, sir? Studded with blueberries and nuts."

Hunter started to wave her off, then reconsidered. Bakers were always awake very early to start their work. "You didn't happen to see anythin' suspicious about a week ago, would you? It would have been very late at night, or just before dawn."

She frowned and shook her head, then turned to the woman standing next to him. "Sample of our new bread, ma'am?"

He growled and walked away to the general goods store. He tied his horse out front next to the mare that was already there, and they sniffed each other in a curious, friendly manner. Hunter made sure he had his money on him and headed inside.

The store was stuffy, but cooler than being outside. A boy, nearly a man, was stacking up apples in a precarious triangle. Hunter could smell them, fresh and sweet. His stomach growled and he regretted not grabbing some of that free bread from the bakery woman.

"Hey, boy." Hunter raised a hand to get his attention.

The boy turned around, gradually looking all the way up Hunter's body to his face. He took a small step back and bumped against his apple tower. Several pieces of fruit cascaded off the top of the stack, slapping hard on the floor.

"Aw, heck," the boy grumbled. He bent and picked up the apples.

Hunter grabbed one that had rolled against his boot. "Sorry for startlin' you."

"That's alright." The boy shrugged. "These'll be bruised-up now, though. Jacob don't like it when I drop things, but I got clumsy hands."

"I'll buy them," Hunter said. "My fault anyway. I'll feed 'em to my horses. They won't mind the bruises."

The boy shrugged again. "If you want them. Can I help you with somethin'?"

"You mentioned Jacob Aberdeen. The owner. Where's he at?" Hunter walked over and placed his apple on the counter. He added some candy next to it; Josie would enjoy a treat after the recent disturbing events.

"He's been ill this past week," the boy said. "I'm watchin' the store for him. Me and a couple others."

Hunter searched his memory, now knowing he recognized this boy. "You his nephew?"

"Sure am. George's the name." George walked over and set the other bruised apples next to Hunter's. "This it for you? Did you want to talk to Jacob?"

"I got to grab a couple more things. You wouldn't happen to know anyone sellin' chickens, would you?" Hunter paused. He considered not mentioning what he wanted to talk to Jacob about. They had made plenty of deals and were friendly with each other. He'd rather talk to the man himself than this inexperienced relative.

But what was the point in holding his tongue? The sheriff had probably already told other people the reason he had gone out to Hunter's ranch, and if not the sheriff, then his man certainly had. And if people were talking, perhaps information had surfaced. The sheriff might not act on such information. Hunter would.

Hunter motioned for George to keep him company as he moved around the store, grabbing a few other things that he didn't really need. It was only polite to pay him back for the time spent talking. "Someone killed my chickens last week. I need to replace 'em. Can't be comin' out to town to get eggs every couple days."

"Well, I think that old couple living out on Harmony Road was lookin' to downsize," George said. "You could see what they got. I'm sorry to hear it, about your birds. I don't know anythin' about it, unfortunately. You think my uncle would?"

"Not really, no." Hunter worked his way back to the counter and George began to calculate what he owed. "Just thought he might have heard something. Ah, well. That's a good idea about visiting the Hammonds, though. Might head by there before I go home."

The Hammond homestead was in the opposite direction of his ranch. Mr. and Mrs. Hammond were certainly getting on in age, and they were all alone, their grown children having gone further West. They might well be eager to get rid of some of their animals to lessen their workload.

Hunter paid and accepted the change George counted out for him. He thanked him and made to leave.

“Hey, uh, I don’t know if you already was goin’ there, but you might check at the saloon. Them fellers there are the sort to know about that kind of thing, ain’t they?”

Hunter turned back as George ventured the idea. “I wasn’t fixin’ on it, but it’s a good idea. Thank you.”

George smiled. “Sure. Hope you find out what you want to know.”

“So do I.” Hunter thanked him again and left. He brought his purchases to Granite and put everything in the saddlebag.

The saloon wasn’t too far distant. Hunter left Granite where he was, seeing no need to untie and retie him.

As he approached the saloon, he heard music, the clattering of dishes. Someone yelled out in a slurred voice, and a sharp response flew back.

Hunter lifted his head. That was Clive shouting at someone. He was unsure why he hadn’t thought of Clive until right then, though of course he would be running into him seein’ as he owned the saloon.

Hunter paused outside, took in a deep breath, and stepped into a cloud of alcohol fumes. Several people sat at the bar, with others scattered intermittently at the tables. All were drinking, and some had plates of fatty meat and roasted corn before them.

It was more people than he would have assumed would be present so early in the day, and right on Monday, too. He tried not to let his disgust for these people show on his face as he walked among them, heading for the bar. There was a reason he didn't often go to church. People went to worship to absolve themselves of their guilt just so they could go right back to sinning.

Hunter pulled out a stool at the bar and sat.

Clive walked up in front of him, already setting a glass down. "What'll it be..." He choked on the final syllable as he saw who was in front of him. "What do you want?"

"Your tone changed quick. There a reason for that?"

Hunter watched, mildly fascinated, as Clive forced his features into an arrangement befitting that of the amiable bartender. His lips went up. The corners of his eyes crinkled. Yet it was all a farce, a dead mask.

"I just don't see you here much. Caught me off-guard, is all." Clive shrugged woodenly, his shoulder rising and falling. "What'll it be?"

"Coffee, if you've got any hot."

"Alright." Clive shrugged again with that dead smile still hanging on his lips. He left and returned again with a steaming mug, sliding it across to Hunter. Some of the hot liquid slopped up over the rim and trickled down the side.

Hunter took a careful sip. The taste was awful, not at all worth the burn to his tongue and lips. "It's good," he lied. "Thanks."

"Sure." Clive leaned forward on the counter. "How's Josie?"

Hunter looked at the drab, ordinary man peering at him with so much excitement and hunger in his gaze and his stomach was sick from more than the awful bitter coffee. Clive was like a too-eager hunting dog, almost quivering. It just wasn't right.

"She's fine," Hunter said. He tried to remain civil sounding, like he didn't know that Clive had been telling Josie bad things about him. "There's been a skeersome situation out on the ranch that's got her all upset, though. The rest of us aren't none too happy, either."

"What sort of a situation?"

One of the other patrons at the bar lifted a hand to flag Clive over. He ignored them entirely, and they got up and walked out, seemingly without paying. That also didn't sit right with Hunter. How was a man meant to run a business like that? Were Clive's feelings so powerful he would overlook all else just to hear about Josie's life?

Hunter made himself focus and informed Clive of the slaughter of all his chickens. "You wouldn't know anythin' about it, would you?"

Clive drew himself up, squaring his narrow shoulders. "What are you implying? That I had somethin' to do with it?"

Hunter stared for a few long moments, watching the other man's mask, searching for a crack, a sign of what was truly underneath. Clive stared back at him, his face slowly turning red. Hunter couldn't tell if it was anger or a flush of embarrassment.

"No," he said at last. "I'm not implyin' that at all. But you get all sorts in here. Thought maybe you'd have heard someone plannin' it, or braggin' about it after. Or maybe someone who's talked unkindly about me in the past."

Clive pursed his lips and rolled his eyes up to the ceiling, where cobwebs draped in lacy strips from the rafters. Hunter had the impression he was only pretending to think.

"No, I don't recall anything that might help you." Clive gestured around at his establishment. "Like you said yourself, I get all sorts here. There's always some fuss happenin'. People are always fuddled. They say and do things that don't make no sense. I don't try to make sense out of any of it anymore. I'd go crazy, myself. So, sorry, but even if someone stood right there in the middle of the room and said they'd gone and killed your chickens, I wouldn't have been listenin' anyway."

"Fine." Hunter dropped some money on the counter, more than enough to cover the bad coffee. "You do hear anythin' I hope you'd let me know. If you care about Josie as much as you seem to, you'd want this matter put to rest, same as me."

"I'm sure that I care for her more than you."

Hunter lifted his eyebrows. "That right?"

"It is." Clive slapped his palm down on the bar counter. "I've known her longer than you have. I don't know why she's livin' with you. Bein' off all isolated in that valley can't be no good for her. Or her daughter."

"Well, it's what she chose." Hunter rose from his stool. "And you can't choose for someone else."

He turned to leave. Clive muttered under his breath, "I'll do what I want."

Hunter turned back, his irritation growing. "What was that?"

"Nothin'. I think you'd best leave my establishment. And maybe you'd best never come back."

The others in the bar turned to look their way. Clive's voice was rising, attracting attention. He didn't seem to notice. He sure had a way of blocking out things that he didn't want to notice.

"I didn't plan on it," Hunter said.

"Good. 'Cause I don't take kindly to being accused."

"Don't think I accused you."

Guilty conscience?

Clive picked up the money Hunter had left and tossed it on the floor. Coins scattered. One drunkard, Buck, crouched down to pick them up. The sight of a grown man groveling on the floor for a handful of coins was pitiful, and Hunter decided he'd had enough for sure.

If anything else was said to him, he didn't hear it. It was his turn to block everything else out and focus on only one thing, and that was getting back to his horse so he could go back to the ranch.

But first, a trip to the Hammonds to ask about chickens.

Chapter Twenty-Seven

Three young hens huddled in their nests as Josie filled their feed container. One clucked anxiously, and another ruffled up her white-speckled feathers. As Josie scattered more feed on the ground to encourage them to scratch and forage, she wished there was something she could do to reassure the uncomfortable birds that they were safe in their new home. Hunter had brought them home a full two weeks ago and they had yet to settle in. They seemed not to recognize the routine of feeding and egg-collecting; they were every bit as startled as the first time whenever anyone entered the coop.

As for laying eggs, they weren't doing much of that, either. They were young, and should have been laying regularly, but were not. Kerry had suggested they would lay better when they had settled in, though no one knew when that would be. And Butch had said adding more hens to the flock would be beneficial, which had yet to happen.

Josie finished with the feeding and exited the coop. She stood outside looking in at the birds, the poor things. She, and she alone, had a different theory as to their discomfort.

She had witnessed it a few times before, enough to believe in it. Animals were aware of things that people weren't. She had never mentioned it aloud to anyone else for fear of being labeled as a crazy woman with fanciful ideas, but she felt that anyone else who had been around animals for a time knew it to be true as well.

Maybe the chickens were disturbed by the sense of death still lingering over the coop, a black cloud of destruction. Everything had been cleaned up, the blood washed away with many buckets of water, yet the space would never be the same. If she closed her eyes, she could still see it so clearly.

Maybe moving the coop entirely would have been best.

Josie went to find Kerry in the kitchen. Ella stood on a chair by her side, helping to crumble butter into a flour mixture for a pie crust.

"No eggs?" Kerry asked, without looking up. She vigorously rubbed her hands together until the butter-flour mixture resembled a coarse cornmeal.

Josie held up the single egg she had found, a diminutive thing less than half the size of a normal egg.

Kerry smiled slightly and took the egg with her dusty hand. "Well, it should be enough for the pie. We just need it for a wash on the top crust."

Josie nodded. She put her hands on Ella's shoulders. "You're doing so well."

Ella looked up at her with a smile, a smudge of butter on her lower lip. Josie used her dress to dab it away.

"You didn't happen to see Hunter out there, did you?" Kerry asked, to which Josie shook her head. Kerry sighed. "Well, alright. I guess I'll just talk with him when I see him next. Probably at dinner."

Kerry started to add the rest of the ingredients to the bowl of pie dough. Josie lifted Ella and took her to the sink to wash her hands.

"What did you want him for?" Josie asked, while scrubbing Ella's hands with soap.

"I know someone sellin' some ducks," Kerry replied, mixing the dough. The muscles in her wrinkly, deeply tanned arm flexed rhythmically. "We never had ducks before, but I know they get along well with chickens. And I do love a nice duck egg. Have you ever had a duck egg?"

"No. I had duck once for a holiday dinner though, and didn't like it much."

"The eggs are much different. So lovely and rich."

"Well, if you think it would be a good idea..." Josie dried hers and Ella's hands. "He's been cold to me lately. To you, too. Do you think he'll even care?"

Kerry touched her arm. "He's been havin' a rough time of things, that's all. Lots on his mind. He does get like this and he doesn't mean anythin' by it. Just have to wait for him to work his way out of it in time."

"Talkin' about me, huh?" Hunter stepped into the kitchen. The heat of outside poured off his big body. He smelled of sweat, his hair plastered to his head with it. Josie did appreciate the sight of him like that, the proof of how hard he worked. Owen had never looked like that.

Ella scurried over to Hunter and hugged him. He ruffled her hair and bent to speak to her. "They been talkin' about me?"

"A little," Kerry said, with a small smile. "What's that you got there?"

Josie noticed the papers stuffed into Hunter's pocket for the first time, several of them.

Hunter straightened and turned, blocking his pocket from view. "Asked Harry to pick up mail for me. That's all."

Hearing Hunter's clipped tone, Josie frowned. Was he hiding something from her?

Or was she being suspicious for no reason? Because she was worried and upset?

Hunter walked away, his footsteps fading as he went deeper into the house.

Josie bit her lip, hesitating, then quickly make up her mind. "I'll be back in a moment, Kerry," she said, and ducked out of the kitchen.

She checked the office. Hunter wasn't there. She moved to his bedroom door next, which was shut. She listened closely and heard him moving around, a door sliding open and shut again. Lifting her hand, she prepared to knock.

The door swung open before she had a chance and Hunter stepped out, knocking into her. It felt like colliding with a wall. Josie stumbled, but his arms were already around her, firm, strong, holding her upright. She managed to get her feet underneath her and straightened. "I'm sorry..."

"Sorry," he said at the same time. He huffed a slight laugh and let go of her. His hand slid down her arm, fingers lingering briefly on hers before dropping away entirely. "You wanted to talk to me?"

Now that she was standing before him, she struggled to recall what she had wanted. Mostly what was in her head was the feel of his body against hers, the strength in his muscles.

"Josie?" he prompted.

She forced herself to focus. "Have I got any mail? Did you ask Harry to check?"

"I did. Nothin'. Sorry." Hunter stared down at her. "Were you expecting any?"

She shook her head. She had just been wondering if Clive had written to her again, as it was strange that he would give up after the contents of that last letter. Saying so didn't seem very wise, however. She didn't feel like upsetting Hunter.

He continued to stare at her. "I feel like you're not tellin' me the truth here, Josie."

"It doesn't matter," she whispered.

"Of course, it matters. So that means you were lyin' to me?" He leaned down, putting his face close to hers. His breath was sweet from Kerry's special water mixture. "You want more letters from Clive? So he can tell you all the ways I'm dangerous?"

Josie flinched back. "Hunter, no. I just meant..." She gave up. The day was too hot for this and she was too unsettled. They wouldn't be able to have a normal conversation. "Never mind."

"Josie..." He leaned away and sighed heavily. "I suppose you can want his letters. That's your choice. You ain't my wife and I can't stop you."

"You wouldn't be able to stop me even if I was your wife!" She curled her hands into fists. "I'm tired of men tellin' me what to do. Why can't a woman make her own choices?"

Hunter laughed. "They can, when they're outlaws with persuaders."

"Persuaders?"

"Equalizers. Six-shooters. Guns, Josie."

"Oh." She looked down at the floor, freshly-swept earlier that day.

"I'm only teasing you. Though, I might feel better if you did have a gun on you."

"What?" All of this was too confusing. She shouldn't even have tried to talk to him until later, if at all.

"I don't like Clive," Hunter said, as if she hadn't figured that out for herself. "And I don't like what's been happenin' on my land. It feels like there's snakes in the grass. How about it? Would you want a pistol to keep around when you're on your own, just in case?"

How has this become a talk about pistols?

"No, I don't want a gun," she replied, frustrated now. "The way Ella is, she'd get ahold of it."

"It don't have to be loaded. Just somethin' to show off if you need to."

"I don't want a gun!" she repeated. "This is ridiculous. I just came to ask about mail. Actually, what I really wanted to suggest was movin' the chicken coop to a different spot. So the chickens will feel better."

Hunter put his hand on his hip. "You mean so you'll feel better."

"What if they can smell the blood?"

"Birds can't smell. Anyway, we took care of all that. But if *you* want the coop to be moved..."

She waved her hand and turned away. "Forget all of this. Just go back to work."

She walked away, confused as to what exactly had just happened. They hadn't been talking to each other, not really. Everything they said had a slithery quality to it, sliding around some bigger subject they hadn't acknowledged. She was too tired to figure it all out.

And why had he suggested a gun? To taunt her, knowing she would never accept his offer?

Maybe he really thinks there's danger around and I should be prepared.

As she came back to the kitchen, Kerry was waiting for her. "I heard shouting. Are you alright?"

"I am," she lied. But Kerry, unlike Hunter, didn't challenge her. She just shrugged and turned away.

Josie stood there with her shoulders slumped and wished that she *had* been challenged and could get back into arguing. Even that was better than silence.

Chapter Twenty-Eight

Only a circlet of black amidst the stars showed where the new moon was hiding. Crickets droned wearily in the tall grass, even the insects suffering in the heat of deep summer. An owl hooted, a sad and lonely sound.

Clive related very much to that owl, wherever it was. He too was sad. And lonely. In dire need of companionship to give his life some form of meaning.

He dismounted from his horse, a small black mare he had favored for many years. She was old now and not much good for riding long distances. But she was perfect for this dark and moonless night, able to move unseen in the shadows.

Clive guided his mare by the reins to a small, withered tree. He looped her reins securely around a branch and patted her neck. She turned her head and nudged into his shoulder, whickering.

“Quiet, girl,” Clive whispered to her. Her ears swiveled and she swished her tail. “That’s it. You stay here. I’ll try not to be too long.”

She whickered again and he winced. He hadn’t wanted to do this, but it seemed she was giving him little choice. He couldn’t take the risk of other animals hearing her and answering her, alerting people to his presence.

Clive removed a bag he had tied to his saddle, a pouch filled with oats. He held the pouch in front of his mare. Her delicate nose twitched, nostrils flaring. She allowed the feedbag to be placed over her mouth. He secured the straps of the pouch at the back of her head, making sure she couldn’t shake it off.

The treats would keep her busy, and the pouch might muffle any further sounds she made.

Clive looked off at the horizon. He judged dawn to still be a good amount of time away and moved off, following the gradual downward slope of the land. Black mountains rose ahead of him, but he was going down, into the valley. While he was nervous, his mind was clear, his senses open. He supposed some people would be feeling guilty if they were about to do what he was. Guilt wasn't part of it, though. In fact, he was rather excited.

And determined. His resolve had hardened over the weeks and days.

He would accomplish his goals. And it started with sneaking onto Hunter Carson's land for a final time.

The buildings were before him, still a good distance away. A single light burned in the house's window, a gauzy yellow pool of glow splashed upon the siding and the grass. By now, Clive knew that light meant nothing. More than likely, everyone was asleep.

Still, he took his time. He stuck to the valley wall, lingered in the shadows of trees, tucked himself behind bushes, waiting and watching and listening. Hunter was on edge at this point. He might be sitting somewhere in the dark to spot intruders, or have the ranch hands doing guard duty themselves.

No matter how hard Clive looked, he saw nothing. He listened and heard only the exhausted crickets, the discontent murmurs of the horses sweating in the stable.

He forced himself to be unaware of the minutes flashing by, the inevitable approach toward dawn. He couldn't mess this up by rushing.

He had stumbled upon the tunnels by accident while hunting in the mountains. There had always been faint rumors of such tunnels, though no one knew where they were, what they were for, or even if they were real. So many stories passed through his saloon that he had thought nothing of them until he came across them himself.

How astonishing it had been to discover one of those tunnels went straight to Hunter's cellar. He remembered exploring it, emerging amidst the flour and vegetables, hearing voices overhead.

It must have been God who made those tunnels just for Clive, because one of those voices he heard up above was Josie. The coincidence was too perfect not to be a miracle.

He had used the tunnel to return many times in the night, exploring the land, even going into the guest house. What a shock it had been to find an old woman sleeping there! And he was sure she had seen him, though he had never gotten a visit from the sheriff about it.

He had killed one of Hunter's cattle, and killed all the chickens. And he had written Josie many letters about Hunter, making up stories of dangerous things he had done, implying he was the one hurting his own animals.

Still, she continued to live on the ranch. She hadn't run into Clive's arms like he so desperately needed her to.

Why couldn't she understand that he loved her?

He could no longer wait for her to reach that conclusion on her own.

It was time to stop acting like a boy and enact a true plan like a man, time to treat this like it was a war and he was the general who would win it. He would end what he had started all that time ago when he stabbed Owen.

Moving silently, breathing slow and even in spite of his racing heart, he worked his way over to the stable. Some of the horses were aware of him, shifting around, nickering quietly, but too hot and tired to cause a fuss.

From the stable, he moved to the garden, lush even in the dark. The tomato plants sagged under the weight of their fruit, while the corn stalks stood proud and tall. Cucumbers and squash covered the loamy soil with their thick vines. There were beans pods hanging in clumps, and onions and potatoes, too.

Clive removed his knife from his belt, freshly sharpened just that morning for this purpose.

He stepped into the garden, leaves swishing, vines tangling at his boots. The smell of green growing things was so thick as to be sickening.

He crouched and started cutting. Indiscriminately. Whatever stalk or stem he touched, he sliced and sawed. He pulled up the onions and potatoes and cut them into pieces. The reek of onions stung his nose, made his eyes water. He blinked hard and continued, slashing the cucumbers, felling the corn stalks.

He stepped on the fallen tomato plants, crushing the fruit to a pulp, their seeds squirting in satisfying gushes on the thirsty earth.

It took a long time. By the end of it he was sweating, covered in dirt and vegetable juices. His fingers stung from multiple small nicks with his knife. But it was done. The garden was gone.

When Josie saw that, she would wonder how they would feed her precious little daughter, Emily, or whatever her name was. They would eat the food in the cellar and then buy more from town, which would be a financial burden. Her eyes would be opened to more flaws here.

Clive stepped out of the dead garden plot and moved toward the chicken coop. An assortment of odd objects by the front porch of the main house caught his eye, glittering and shiny even in the absence of moonlight. He turned and stepped closer.

Wheelbarrows of dirt and muddy shovels.

Hunter was having his tunnel filled in.

Clive turned away and resumed going for the chickens. He hadn't felt like using the tunnels on this night and he was right not to have done so. Another blessing from God, surely.

Too little, too late, Hunter. You haven't stopped me.

Clive came to the coop. The new chickens were asleep, unsuspecting. He moved in and did what had to be done.

Now Josie would see the problems here couldn't be fixed. They couldn't buy more chickens. They couldn't pretend nothing was happening. There was danger and it would return time and time again.

A door creaked open.

Clive froze with his dripping knife by his side. He knew that door sound by now. Someone had just stepped out of the main house.

He dropped to his hands and knees and rolled into the shadow of the chicken coop. Hardly a breath later, Hunter's massive shape moved through the dark, in the direction of the outhouse in the back.

Clive clutched the dirt, digging his fingers in. He pressed his face down to the ground and squeezed his eyes shut.

After a short time, Hunter returned, grumbling something under his breath. He went around the front of the house and the door creaked again.

Clive remained where he was. His heart wouldn't stop hammering in his chest, thudding the ground. An hour passed. The very edge of the sky began to turn from black to coal. He could wait no longer.

Rising to his feet, he crept back the way he had come. Leaving was faster than entering and before long, he knew he had put a safe distance between himself and the ranch. He started to run, and he didn't stop running until he reached his horse. She shied away from him, but he grabbed hold of her bridle and tore the feed pouch from her face. Her ears flicked back and she lifted her lips to show her huge flat teeth.

"Don't you bite me," Clive whispered, and swung up onto her back. "I'll kill you if you bite me. You're almost too old as it is."

She half-reared, lifting her front hooves. He dug his heels into her and spun her around, and he pushed her at a full gallop back to town. She was straining and blowing, covered in a froth of sweat by the time he got back. He allowed her to slow and took her to his house, putting her in the stable. There wasn't time to remove her tack or wipe her down. He would do that later. Right now, there was more work to be done before the people of Deadwood woke up.

Clive went inside his house. He spent most of his nights sleeping in the back of the saloon, to the point where some didn't even realize he had a house relatively nearby. He would use that to his advantage.

He went around lighting lanterns, enough to work by. Then, he grabbed a hammer, nails, and every bit of spare fabric he had. Old clothes, rags, spare bedsheets. He brought them all into his spare room to make a pile.

He intended to cover as much of the walls as he could with what he had, and buy more to finish it off. The fabric would dampen any sound.

He'd have a gag in Josie's mouth until she learned better than to scream. Still, he wasn't going to take the chance of anyone hearing her.

And when he was done, he would close the curtains on that window and hammer boards over the inside.

He would need rope. Maybe even a chain.

And sewing supplies. Books. Dresses.

He would fill this room with things a woman liked, and he would keep Josie in here until she learned that she belonged to him. It would take time. He knew that. He was prepared to wait, as he was a patient man. He'd already waited for so long even though she was meant to be his.

One day, she would agree to marry him. And he would invite Hunter to the ceremony.

Chapter Twenty-Nine

"We're lucky."

Josie pushed the heel of her hand down hard into the bread she was kneading, stretching it out on the counter. "It doesn't feel like we're lucky, unless you mean bad luck, Kerry."

Kerry dipped a finger into the pot of water she was heating up to add to the laundry basin, testing the temperature. "No, I mean good luck, Josie."

Josie flipped the bread dough over and slapped the lump down again. "It's terrible luck! I'm starting to think the law in Deadwood is downright useless. They never, ever catch the criminals!"

"I can't comment on that." Kerry shook her head. She added another piece of wood to the stove and stirred the burning embers, encouraging them to consume the new fuel. "But most folks would be *starvin'* at this point. No chickens, no garden, no leavin' their property. But we got us everything in the cellar. We're not wanting for anything right now and I would call that good luck."

Josie kneaded the bread dough hard enough to rip holes in the elastic mixture. She sighed and lowered her head. She wanted to trust in what Kerry said, she really did. But she couldn't let her guard down enough to allow that sort of positivity.

Two weeks since a shadow in the night came and murdered their new hens, tore up the garden. Hunter was tense, a pacing mountain lion. He refused to let anyone come or go except for Henry, Kerry, Ezra, and Butch. All other ranch hands had been sent away to find different work. There could be no visitors, not even the sheriff or his men; if they wanted to meet with Hunter to discuss the crime, he was the one who went to them.

The only *good* thing was that there had been no further incidents. But who knew how long the momentary peace would last?

"Josie, would you quit beatin' on that dough and let it rest?" Kerry lifted the pot of simmering water from the stovetop. "I forgot to get Hunter's laundry from his room. Would you mind bringin' his things outside so they can be washed?"

"Okay," Josie muttered. She formed the squashed dough into a round shape and plopped it into a greased bowl to rise. Dusting flour from her hands onto her dress, she left the kitchen and peeked into the parlor to check on Ella. Her daughter drowsed on a chair, enjoying a midmorning nap.

Josie put her fingers to her mouth and nipped at one of her nails, tasting flour and salt. Ella had been picking up on the turmoil in the air even though they were all careful never to speak of the bad events in front of her. She had also seen the destroyed garden patch for herself, and had been asking where the chickens were, why they no longer had scrambled eggs with their bacon in the morning. She knew, though she was too little to understand. The weight of it all had her tired and she was napping more frequently.

At least I know where she is when she's asleep.

Josie left the parlor and continued on to Hunter's bedroom. She pushed the door open and stepped through. The air was thick and hot in there, every breath laced with a mixed musk of man and animal. She tried not to look at anything too closely as she went to the corner of the room where she knew his laundry basket to be. The basket was full of sweaty, mud-stained clothes, a sign of just how hard he had been working recently.

She hefted the basket on her hip and turned. A small article of clothing fell off the top of the pile and she bent to pick it up.

What she had thought to be a sock, or perhaps a handkerchief, wasn't clothing at all. It was an envelope, creased down the middle, slowly unfurling like a flower hesitant to bloom in early spring. He must have forgotten it in one of his pockets.

Josie shot a look at the bedroom doorway. She simply couldn't be caught picking up and looking at something else that didn't belong to her.

It's sealed. He can look at it and see that I didn't read the letter inside, even if I move it.

She took the envelope by the very tip of the corner and lifted it, standing. She shuffled over to his oak dresser and set it down on top of the old, scarred surface where he would easily find it.

But it wasn't his name written on the front.

It was *hers.*

She swallowed and licked her dry lips. A letter from Clive? Why hadn't Hunter given her her own mail? Had he just forgotten about it when there was so much else going on around the ranch?

Josie took the letter and put it in her pocket, since it belonged to her. She adjusted the laundry basket on her hip and went to find Kerry out on the porch, adding articles of clothing to the basin of hot water.

"Whew." Kerry wrinkled her nose. "That stuff smells. Go on and add the worst into the water while it's at its hottest."

Josie sorted through the basket, selecting the worst of the stained shirts and pants to add into the steaming water. The smell coming out of the basin was reminiscent of soup left out on the counter for a few days.

"Thank you," Kerry said. "I'll just handle this. Why don't you go on back inside and make sure his room is tidy? Goodness knows he probably isn't taking care of his things."

"Are you sure I should do that?" Josie touched her pocket, feeling the paper envelope crinkling. "He might get upset."

"No, he'll feel better having a nice, tidy room to sleep in. I'm sure of it." Kerry used a stick to swirl the clothes around in the water. A scum of oil and dirt formed on the rippling surface. "He was so happy when he was spending that time with you at the picnic. He'll be pleased that it was you who made his room nice."

Josie held up her hands. "Sometimes, I feel like he likes me, and other times it feels like he doesn't want me around at all."

"Well, you know what you got to do when he acts like that, don't you?"

Josie shook her head.

Kerry lifted the stick out of the water and gestured with the dripping end. "You tell him to shut up unless he can be kind."

"I could never do that!"

"Why not? You remind Ella when she's forgettin' her manners, don't you?" Kerry waved her away with the stick. "Go on, now. Before I make you do the laundry instead."

Josie managed a small smile and left Kerry to her unpleasant task of cleaning Hunter's filthy clothes. She checked in on the still sleeping Ella and then went to Hunter's room. She stood in the doorway with her arms crossed over her chest. It *did* need cleaning, she admitted to herself. The floors had boot prints marked in mud and there was a plate on the nightstand with the remnants of a past meal.

She grabbed a broom and started to sweep the floors. The muddy boot prints wouldn't be cleared away so easily. She crouched and chipped at the flaking ridges with the edge of the dustpan. When she had removed the worst of it, she went and brought back a damp cloth to wipe away the remnants.

She took the cloth to the kitchen to wring it out in the sink. Hunter was there, leaning one hip on the counter. He held a biscuit leftover from breakfast, plucking off fluffy morsels and popping them into his mouth. He glanced up as she approached. A smile slowly formed on his lips. "Hey."

"Hello." She pulled in a deep breath, very, very aware of the shape of the letter in her pocket. "How, um, how are you?"

"Better. I was hungry." Hunter dropped the last piece of biscuit into his mouth and chewed. "I looked in on Ella. She's still asleep."

"Thank you." Josie dropped the rag in the sink. She gripped the edge of it, looking at her smeared reflection in the metal.

Hunter moved to her side. Her body warmed where he pressed against her. "Somethin' interesting down there?"

She glanced up. "No. Not really."

He shrugged and shifted away. Shadows marred the skin underneath his eyes, the whites of which were stained with red.

“Are you okay?” She reached for him, placed her hand on his shoulder. His muscles were very tense. “Maybe you should be taking a nap like Ella.”

He chuckled and placed his hand over hers, holding it to his shoulder. “Maybe. I don’t want to set a bad example for her, though. Shouldn’t show her that I’m tired. I got to be strong. Though,” and he turned his head away, “I s’pose it isn’t my place to try and influence her. I’m not her father.”

“But she does look up to you.” Her heart ached. He looked so sad and worn. She stepped closer to him, resting her cheek on his shoulder. “You were good with her during the picnic.”

“Thank you for saying so.” He heaved a great sigh, the swelling of his chest pushing her. “It’s strange that I got so much to worry about and what I’m focusing on is Ella. It’s not that I don’t want her to see me resting. Everyone should rest when they need it. I just worry she’ll be upset if she thinks I’m not strong enough. She needs me to protect the ranch. I *need* to protect the ranch and I can’t.”

“Oh, Hunter.” Josie put her arms around him. His heartbeat was an unsteady thumping, at odds with her own. “She wouldn’t think that. No one would think that. What’s going on is out of your control. We just have to get through it.”

Hunter leaned back, squinting down at her. “When did you become so positive?”

She blushed and looked away. “I just don’t like it when you don’t feel well.”

"Well, it did make me feel better. It's good to know that you have faith in me." He straightened and set his jaw. "We *will* get through this. No matter what. And I'll figure out how to be a better figure in yours and Ella's lives."

"You could ask for advice," she told him. "You don't have to figure it all out on your own when there's people around who know what to do. If everyone tried to figure things out on their own, we'd never make any progress."

"True." Hunter took her hand. She slid her fingers between his and squeezed. "Do you think we could go for a walk together tonight?" he asked.

"A walk? Of course. Should I bring Ella?"

"No, just the two of us." He rubbed his thumb over the back of her hand. She caught her breath at the sudden rush of tingles in her blood. "I'll ask you some questions about Ella and what I can do to be better for you two."

Josie smiled and she squeezed his hand again. "I'd be happy to tell you anything you want to know. And maybe I'll ask you some questions of my own."

"Is that right? What sort of questions you got for me?"

Why didn't you give me my letter?

"I'll think of something," she said.

"That's somethin' I know about you for sure. You're always thinkin'." Hunter released her hand, their palms and fingers slipping apart with a cascade of sparks. "I should get back to my work."

"Me, too. So there won't be anything to distract us from our walk later."

Hunter tipped his hat to her. "See you then."

He strode away, standing taller than when she had first walked in and seen him. The proud, powerful figure he cut gave her a little confidence in regards to their situation. He was so stubborn that there was no way they wouldn't get through this. He wouldn't allow for anything else.

She would do her best to support him. She had to believe in him, because doubting wouldn't help anything or anyone.

Maybe he really had just forgotten the letter in his pants pocket because he was too busy thinking of so many other things. She would just ask him about it instead of worrying over it.

She resumed cleaning his room, humming softly as she finished cleaning the floors and tidying up all the little things out of place. By the time she left it spotless, Ella was up from her nap and the bread dough needed to be shaped for its final rise before baking. Always, there were things to do, and the time passed quickly from lunch to dinner. She tidied up and then left Ella with Kerry to work on a dessert for later.

Hunter caught her as she was heading down the hall, holding his arm out to stop her. "I got to check on the horses. Why don't you go on and get a head start? I'll meet up with you by that old stump near the pine trees."

Josie agreed and he headed off, banging the front door open and crossing to the stable at a near-run. She caught the door before it could slam shut and stepped out herself. With dusk on its way, the air had cooled and dampened, a welcome reprieve from the heat of the day. Fireflies drifted lazily on faint drafts of wind, blinking their tiny lights.

Crickets leaped out of her way as she walked through the dark grass to the stand of pines, the old, blackened stump right nearby them. She pulled in great lungfuls of the fresh air and trailed her fingers over bumpy seedheads. She so rarely had time alone to herself. How refreshing it was not to be thinking of the next chore and watching over Ella.

That had to be why Hunter told her to go on her own. He was so kind to think that she might enjoy herself. She wondered how to thank him for that kindness. Could she sew him a new handkerchief?

Maybe a kiss on his cheek.

She reached the old stump. Dewy cobwebs stretched between shards of gray, broken wood. She leaned against it and looked up at the purpling sky.

Something moved behind her, crushing the grass. She started to turn, expecting to see a raccoon or a fox, some nocturnal critter emerging from a den.

A shadowed figure loomed over her. In the next instant there was pain exploding through her head, down into her neck. The dusk sky seemed to collapse around her, falling, draping over her and ensnaring her in darkness.

Chapter Thirty

Hunter looked all around for Josie as he neared the stump where he told her they should meet up for their walk. He couldn't see her, though there was something white on the ground at the base of the black stump.

"Josie?" he called out. His yell echoed off the high walls of the valley, fading out without so much as a hint of a reply. He kneeled down next to the white thing and picked it up. His groping fingers encountered paper, and he suddenly knew what it was. He even recognized the exact crease on its surface, one he had made when he folded it up and stuck it in his pocket.

This was Josie's letter. He had picked it up from the post office a few days ago, to add to the growing pile. She must have found it.

All at once, his skin prickled with heat. He held the folded envelope and scanned the area for some sign of Josie, straining his hearing. There was nothing at all, no one nearby to keep him company. It was only him and the fireflies twinkling in and out of the growing shadows.

"Josie? Josie, you out here?"

Still nothing, just the crickets.

Muttering a swear, Hunter turned on his heel and went to the house. He went into the kitchen to find Kerry. "Where's Josie?" he demanded. "You seen her?"

Kerry looked up from where she stood at the counter. Ella sat on the countertop with her legs folded, plucking the seeds from halved cherries; smudges of red on her lips showed she had been sampling the little red fruits as she worked, rather than waiting for them to be baked into a pie.

"Josie?" Kerry repeated, and his heart dropped clear out of his chest, into his stomach. "I thought she was going to take a walk with you. That's what she said to me earlier. She ain't out there?"

"I didn't see her at our meetin' spot." Hunter held up the letter. "I found this on the ground near it, though. She was out there for sure. I thought maybe she came back in for somethin'."

"What is that?"

Hunter gave her the letter. Sweat beaded on his forehead and he swept it away with the back of his hand. "A letter she got, that I forgot to give her."

Kerry looked up sharply. A strand of blonde hair fell from her bun. "Don't you think you can lie to me, Hunter. You didn't forget to give this to her, did you?"

"That Clive was sendin' her tons of letters. This is the fourth or fifth one." His throat and eyes burned. "I didn't like it. I don't like him."

"You kept her letters from her." Kerry put her back to him. She took Ella by the hand and swung her down from the counter. "Dear, you go off and play. The adults have to talk."

Ella looked back and forth from her to Hunter. "Where's Mama?"

That's what I'm trying to find out.

"Go on, chickadee," Hunter told her.

She looked at him, giggled, and scurried off. As soon as she had gone into another room, Kerry rounded on him. She shook the letter in the air between them. "It don't matter how much you don't like Clive. This is her mail. You had no right to keep it from her."

Hunter pushed her hand down so she would stop waving the letter in his face. “I was protectin’ her. That man is trouble, a snake.”

“Protectin’ her,” Kerry repeated. She slapped the letter down on the counter. “Lyin’ to her, actin’ like a snake yourself. If you got feelings for someone, you don’t hide things from them. You give them the whole truth and let them decide for themselves.”

Hunter took off his hat and raked his fingers through his hair. Josie really had come to mean a lot to him, in ways that he didn’t fully understand. If he had given her the letters, Clive might have gotten into her head and scared her away.

“You should have trusted her to do the best thing.” Kerry swept cherry stems and pits off the counter, into her palm. “She’s come to know you. She’s got doubts, but she’s smart. She would have been able to see for herself that a man who writes five letters is desperate and untrustworthy. If what you’ve got to say is worth listening to, it only takes one.”

Hunter paced to the opposite end of the kitchen and back again, needing to move, to release some of the tension building up inside him. “She didn’t open that envelope. It’s still sealed. What’s that mean? Where is she?”

“What about the other letters?” Kerry tossed the fruit scraps into the trash. The red stains on her hand resembled blood. “Are they still in your room or did she find those? She was cleaning there today.”

He turned and left to go check his room. Ella sat on the floor in the hallway. She gave him a cheerful wave. He stepped around her and ducked into his room. He went straight to his dresser, where he had the letters hidden away beneath his shirts. As he dug for them, he thought he caught a faint scent in the air, a sweet, floral remnant of Jose's presence.

The letters were still there.

Hunter grabbed up the stack and brought them back to Kerry. "Not a one is opened," he said.

Kerry chewed on the inside of her cheek. "That is odd. But she doesn't need to have opened them to know you were hidin' them from her."

"But where is she?" he demanded. The longer they went without knowing where she was, the harder it was for him to breathe. "Are you sure she didn't come back here?"

"She didn't. Check her room if you want, but she isn't around." Kerry stared at him, her eyes clear and truthful.

He couldn't just stand there, though. He went and checked her room, and of course she wasn't there. Kerry was waiting for him when he rushed back to her. He grabbed her by the arm, his eyes wide. "Where could she be?"

"Well, she wouldn't just absquatulate without her daughter," Kerry said. She moved his hand off her arm, clucking her tongue. "Could be she decided to do some more walkin' on her own rather than wait for you. Might be she needed to think about those letters and all."

"I'm going to go find her. You holler for me if she does come back here."

Hunter turned and started to leave. Kerry was the one to grab him that time, her broad hand swiping his wrist. "You might be the last person she wants to see right about now, if she's upset with you."

He pulled away from the older woman. "I don't care. She can be angry with me all she likes, as long as I know she's safe."

She sighed and held up her hands. "Go on, then. If that's what you think is right."

"It is."

He went straight to the stable and saddled Granite as quickly as he could. The gelding shifted uneasily on his hooves, whickering, picking up on what Hunter was feeling. Hunter gave the horse a calming pat on the neck that his heart wasn't into and mounted. He snatched a lantern as he rode out onto the ranch. The moon was up and bright, slanting frosted rays across the valley.

Urging Granite up to a canter, they reached the meeting stump in no time at all. Hunter called out for Josie, pausing each time and straining to hear any response at all before yelling out again. Granite moved shyly, jerkily underneath him, sidestepping and huffing whenever he was halted.

Hunter rode into the pines, brandishing his lantern. The pale warm light stretched the shadows of the trees out into long black piano keys.

An owl shrieked out overhead. Hunter flinched, lifting the lantern high. A glimpse of feathers and the owl was gone, flying silently.

And there was only the sound of Granite's anxious breathing and the chirping of crickets after that.

Hunter rode from the stand of pines, across the grass to the opposite side of the valley, looping back around to the river and following its course to the waterfall at its source. He came back to the house and dismounted, leaving his horse outside. He rushed in, calling Kerry's name.

Kerry burst from the parlor, her eyes so wide they were rimmed with white. "Did you find her?"

"No!" Hunter took his hat off and tossed it on the ground. He grabbed the nearest thing, a coat on a hook, and dashed that onto the floor as well. Panting, he rounded on his maid. "She wouldn't go off without Ella!"

"I know that, Hunter!" Kerry stood up to him, raising her face. Her nostrils flared. "But now it's late. Wherever she's gone, she won't be found in the dark."

"Then you want to wait until morning to search more?" He reeled back, incredulous.

"Look. Calm down." Kerry reached up and cupped his cheek in her palm. "I'm sure she's gone off to think and will come back when she's done."

Hunter gestured to the inhospitable outside. "Need I remind you she nearly died on the mountain before we met her? That's not even considering the wild animals and the strange happenings."

"She'll find herself a place to rest. She might even be waiting to come back when we're all asleep. Or..." She didn't finish. "At first light, if she isn't back, you can take your horse and search for her again."

Or she might not come back at all. Hunter silently finished her sentence. He put his hand to his aching stomach. "What about Ella? She already knows that something's wrong."

"Which means that she will look to us to reassure her. We must act as if everything is normal, for her sake." Kerry lowered her voice. "We have to act as if the rest of this night is ordinary. We'll finish making the pie and have dessert. I'll take her to the guest house with me and we'll spend the night there. If she's entertained and kept busy, she won't be afraid."

"Fine." He didn't like it. This whole situation was too odd. He knew Kerry was just as afraid as she was and doing a better job of hiding it. Did that mean he really did have feelings for Josie?

The answer frightened him.

"If she's not here in the morning, where do you think I should look?" As he spoke, he heard Ella approaching, singing a little song to herself.

"The saloon," Kerry whispered. "Maybe she's gone to get Clive's side of the story once and for all."

Ella walked up to them and held up her arms. "More cherry?" she asked hopefully.

Kerry forced a chuckle and lifted the little girl into her arms. "Yes, we need more cherries pitted for the pie. Hunter, if you want coffee with your pie, you'll either have to wait or make it yourself."

"I'll make it. Soon as I go put Granite in the stable." He ruffled Ella's fiery curls, making her laugh. Even that precious sound barely soothed his nerves.

The worst thing would be for Josie to have gone to town. Thieves and other, worse criminals prowled night roads to take advantage of the unwary and vulnerable.

He made up his mind. She wasn't foolish enough to have gone off for no reason. She knew all the risks. Something must have happened that he was missing.

At first light, he would get on the road and pick up Harry at his place. They could cover more ground that way and they would find Josie somewhere.

They *would* find her. He would not stop at Clive's saloon. He would find her no matter where she had gone, because this just wasn't right.

Chapter Thirty-One

Josie sat on the thin mattress, her head leaning back on the wall behind her. Her arms, secured behind her at the wrist by thick ropes, had long since gone numb. Her ankles were similarly bound and devoid of feeling. She wished her head was in the same state. Her skull felt like it had been smashed like an egg, throbbing with every heartbeat. Focusing was not so easy. Her eyes kept closing. Every time she opened them, it seemed the amount of light creeping into the room past the boards nailed to the window had changed. The hours were passing. Dawn was approaching.

And she had no idea where she was.

Through the dark and her hazy vision, she took a long time to make out her surroundings. She was in someone's house, someone's bedroom. A woman's room, she guessed, from the vases on top of the dresser and the sewing box tucked away beneath the desk across from her mattress. Fresh flowers filled the vases. She identified them by their shape, the dark robbing them of color: sprigs of lavender, daisies, and puffy marigolds.

Part of her wanted to get up and explore her new environment, although she wasn't sure what she was expecting to find... or even how she thought she would move around with her legs and arms bound. Snaking from one ankle was a chain, bolted to a section of the wall. It didn't look as if it would let her get very far and she didn't feel like trying, wasting her energy lugging it around with her.

The door was probably locked, or at least secured from the other side.

There was little she could do to pass the time, wavering in and out of half-dreams. Hazy thoughts slid through her mind. Hunter. Ella. Was anyone looking for her?

They won't just think I abandoned my daughter, will they? They can't. I'd never. They have to be looking for me.

As the light outside brightened, voices rose as men exited their homes to go to their jobs. Horses neighed and roosters crowed. Someone shouted at the roosters, drunkenly slurring their words. And now she heard a woman singing, the sweet babble of a happy infant. Life went on without her. No one knew she was right there inside this house, held captive. She couldn't even scream for help. A gag jammed in her mouth and tied at the back of her head prevented her from making a sound any louder than a gargle.

The rag gagging her tasted faintly of soap. She wanted to vomit.

Footsteps suddenly echoed through the house, approaching the door. Josie sat upright, ignoring the bolt of pain in her head. She wriggled around on the mattress, the chain rattling with the uncoordinated movements from her stiff body.

A series of sounds came from the other side of the door, as if things were being moved out of the way. Finally, there was the click of a lock being undone. The doorknob twisted with a soft thump.

Josie braced herself to see her captor. Her sluggish, painful mind struggled to come up with a plan for what she could possibly do if this monster tried to hurt her.

The door opened. Light spilled into the room and she twisted her head away, wincing.

The footsteps approached, soft and careful. Whoever it was, they crouched in front of her, smelling powerfully of alcohol.

A hand cupped the side of her face, twisting her head to the front.

Clive's smile was a twisted vine. She couldn't look away from his face as he grinned down at her. His eyes held a hard shine.

No. No, it can't be Clive. He's too…

Too normal?

She had been wrong. All the warning signs were so clear to her now.

Clive hooked his finger into the gag, his nail scraping her lips. "I'm going to take this out so we can have us a talk. If you scream, you'll be sorry for it, Josie."

She made a muffled sound through the fabric.

"I mean it." His teeth clenched. "You don't want to know what will happen if you upset me."

Making noise only angered him. She stayed quiet that time, hearing her own heart pounding.

Clive pulled the gag down, leaving it to dangle around her neck like a necklace. "There, how's that? Better, I would think, huh?"

Josie pressed her lips together to muffle any noise she might accidentally make and nodded slowly.

Clive smiled, pleased with himself. He sat on the mattress in front of her with his legs folded and rested his hands on his knees. "You're probably real balled up, don't know what's goin' on. I'll tell you and you just listen like a good little woman. You'll see sense when I'm done talkin'. I know it."

I don't need you to explain to me. I already know what's going on. She bit her tongue and only nodded again. She couldn't see a weapon on him, but that didn't mean he couldn't hurt her. She knew exactly all the many ways a man could hurt a woman if he wanted.

"You're going to be my wife."

Josie closed her eyes. Cold crawled over her skin from head to toe. The urge to vomit was back again, stronger than before. She willed herself not to, frigid sweat prickling on her brow as she fought the bitter nausea.

He had her captive, tied up, and still somehow thought she was going to be his wife. This man was crazy, worse than Owen had ever been. Owen had acted on impulse when he hurt her. He never thought about what he would do, he simply acted when the urge struck.

Clive had planned this. He had been sitting on this desire like a hen on an egg, and now his plan was hatching and she couldn't stop it any more than she could halt the course of nature.

"I love you." Clive was shaking and sweating too, his face red as with a sunburn. "I've, I've always loved you since I first saw you, Josie. You're the most beautiful woman I've ever laid my eyes on. You make me... feel things. It ain't proper to talk about all these *manly feelings* you give me, but you got to know that's what you do to me. Do you understand? Say you understand."

A helpless little groan escaped her even though she was doing her best to make no noise.

Clive slammed his hand on the wall next to her head. His eyes were rolling like an enraged stallion's. "Say you understand! Say it!"

Josie struggled for her voice. "I... I..."

Clive swore and wrenched away from her. He paced the room, ripping at his hir with both hands. "No one understands me. Never have. Doesn't matter. You'll learn." He swung around and dropped to his knees on the mattress, so close she smelled his rank, hot breath. "You made a mistake in marryin' Owen. I saw how unhappy you were with him. And he told me all about the things he would do to hurt you. I don't care if that's a matter between a husband and wife, it was wrong. One night, he was jawing on and on to me and I couldn't take it any longer. I stabbed him."

It was you? You *did it?*

Josie stared at Clive, the man she had taken to be so normal and inoffensive. She would never have imagined he was the culprit. How could he kill his own cousin like that? And to talk of it so plainly to her. He clearly saw nothing wrong with his actions.

"I thought that you would see reason and come be with me, then. But no matter how long I waited, you didn't come. You didn't reply to my letters. You didn't even come to see me. Well, I got tired of waiting and I brought you here myself." He smiled and placed his hand on her leg. "Once you adjust, we're going to be so happy together."

His touch made her feel a squirming inside her, earthworms writhing in salted soil. She tried to pull away and couldn't move properly enough.

Clive gripped her leg hard, digging his fingers in. Her numb flesh stung. "I'm going to keep you in this room until you adjust to bein' with me."

"Will you take the ropes off?" Her voice quivered. "My arms are numb. My legs, too. I'm not very comfortable."

He sighed and sat back. He slapped his own leg and stood. "I'm sorry, I just can't do that yet. I know you can't be feelin' too good right about now and that does hurt my heart. You're just flighty, Josie. I can't be sure you won't do something we both regret. You know? No, for now, you'll have to stay with your gag on and the ropes tied. In a few days, we can try givin' you some freedom. Until then, you're just going to have to make do."

"I swear I won't do anything!" She kept her voice low, but urgent. "I won't yell. I won't bang on the walls. You can trust me."

If he lets his guard down because he thinks I'm cooperating, he might give me an opening to escape.

Clive sighed. "But I don't trust you. Not yet."

He looked at the boarded-up window. Josie followed his eye and really saw the walls for the first time. Curtains and bedsheets had been nailed to the walls, the gaps between filled in with newspapers. The room was a patchwork quilt of insanity.

How long had he been working on this? Creating this room to keep her in? She was sick to think of how much she had been on his mind, ensnared in his terrible thoughts. He had even thought to cover the walls to dampen any noise she might make. What else had he taken into consideration? What else did he have in store for her? Because he wouldn't be happy just keeping her in this room forever.

Clive looked back at her and smiled in that sickly-sweet, twisted way. "It's goin' to be hard to wait, but I'll manage. One day, you'll see how happy we can be. You'll be happy to be my wife."

Think, think. Josie, think.

“What about my daughter?”

“What about her?” The line of his smile pressed thin and he waved his hand, swatting away her question like it was just a fly. “I couldn’t bring both of you at once. She’s still at the ranch.”

“I want to see my daughter.”

“I’ll get her.” His eyes drifted away as he spoke. “But don’t you worry about it too much. Once we’re married, we can have our own children. You can have another daughter.”

Josie shuddered all over. She stared down at her lap and prayed silently to God, begging him to be watching over her, to help her get through this. When she looked up, Clive was moving, reaching for the gag dangling around her neck. She recoiled, twisting her head away.

“No, don’t! Please, Clive, don’t put that back in my mouth.”

“I’m sorry, Josie.” He sighed and touched her hair. Then, he slowly tightened his fingers around the strands, until she felt the tugging at her scalp. Her sore head throbbed horribly and she couldn’t keep a whimper from escaping. The pressure continued for several long, terrible moments until it abruptly eased.

Clive jammed the gag back into her mouth and stood. Straw from inside the mattress stuck to his knees and he dusted the golden fragments away. “I wish that I could stay and spend more time with you. But I have to go to the saloon and get to work. I’ll try to bring you some food in a few hours. You should just rest. Your head must hurt.”

It does. And that’s your fault. You’re no better than Owen. No, you’re worse.

Owen was a terrible man who had hurt her. Clive was *depraved.*

Josie squirmed on the mattress, making sounds through the gag. Clive stared down at her, then sighed again. He hooked his finger into the gag and pulled it from her mouth. "What is it? I have to leave now."

"Remove the chain?" She forced herself to look into his mad eyes. "So I can stand and move around a little? You know I won't be able to go far or do anything."

Clive nodded curtly and pulled a key from his pocket. He bent and undid the lock securing the chain to her ankle, the links falling aside with a heavy clatter. As soon as he was done, he put the key back into his pocket and stuck the gag into her mouth again. "I really do have to go now. I'll see you in a few hours, Josie, my love."

His cheeks suddenly flamed bright red. He turned on his heel and left the room in a hurry. Josie listened to him locking the door. She hoped he might not set up the barricade again. Those hopes were dashed at the sound of him working, the thumps and thuds of heavy objects hitting the door. Minutes later, when he had finished blockading her inside, his footsteps receded.

"Good morning, Nancy!" His voice came from outside. He was by the window, speaking with someone, showing her that he could be out there and no one was the wiser as to what he had done. The woman speaking to him, Nancy, was not suspicious of him at all as she asked him if he was headed in to work. She even gave him an apple from her basket before they bid each other a farewell and moved off.

She was well and truly alone at that point.

Josie sat back against the wall again, staying still to keep her head from hurting even worse. She actually felt sorry for

Clive. He had hurt her and he was crazy, but he was pathetic and blind. He'd just had such a nice, normal interaction with that woman. His whole life was probably filled with such nice interactions and yet he couldn't appreciate any of it. He was too focused on what he didn't have —Josie— to notice everything that he did have. A good job, a home of his own, financial stability.

All at once, she was angry. Where it came from, she wasn't sure. It flared up brightly inside of her, filling the whole of her, chasing away the shadows.

She couldn't just sit there and feel sorry for herself! That wouldn't accomplish anything. If she wanted to see her daughter again, she needed to take action.

If she wanted to see Hunter again...

She did. It didn't matter that he was misguided and gruff and sometimes acted in ways she didn't understand. He had been kind to her and was making efforts to change. He had shown her respect like no man ever had.

She wanted to see him again. She couldn't let her life be like this.

She forced her numb arms to move, wrenching them up and down behind her back. The rough rope was surely abrading her wrists, but she couldn't feel that yet. Everything from the elbow down was like wood. She kept working her arms anyway, waiting for the moment when her arms would awaken to pain.

She would be able to feel, then. She could maybe find some weakness in the rope and work at untying herself. When she had her arms and legs freed, she could try to escape. Even barricaded in, there had to be some way to break out and she would not stop until she had her freedom once more.

Chapter Thirty-Two

Harry drew his horse to a skidding halt next to Hunter and Granite. “Didn’t see her out that way. No footprints or anythin’.”

Hunter clenched his jaw and nodded. He had expected as much. They had been combing the area for a sign of Josie since just after dawn without finding a single thing. Their yells had only been answered by the barking of a stray dog.

“It’s time to go into town,” Hunter said. He applied pressure to Granite’s side with one knee and flicked the reins, pushing the steady gelding on to Deadwood. They had made their way closer and closer as they searched and were only a few minutes out from the first building. Already he could hear the shouts and laughs of children playing, see the people moving around on the streets, busy as ants.

Harry urged his own horse to move faster, keeping pace at Hunter’s side. His face was drawn and tense under the shadow of his hat. “Straight to the saloon?”

“Straight there,” Hunter growled. “To speak with that yellow-belly Clive. I would bet the whole ranch that he knows something, or had something to do with those. All those letters, his manner, his relation to Owen… I don’t like it.”

Harry had his eyes fixed forward on the town. “You get bad feelings about a lot of people.”

“This is different. There’s malice in him.”

“And if you’re wrong? He won’t take kindly to being accused.”

“I don’t care what he feels. I need Josie back. Ella needs her mother.”

"Well, I'm with you, boss. I got your back." Harry patted the pistol holster at his hip. Hunter was glad to see the gun. He had his own, but it never hurt to have another as backup.

They rode into town, stirring up plumes of dust. The horses' hooves thundered on the hard, dry earth. A group of children standing on the side of the main street turned and gaped as they rode by. The youngest one was hardly older than Ella, just an innocent little girl in a pale yellow dress, dark brown hair pulled back from her face.

Ella needs her mother. And I need Josie. I will not stop until she's home.

She was so special, that woman. She had gone through so much and some of her spirit had been broken, yet she was still strong. She was a good mother. She had stood up to Hunter and shown him changes he needed to make, something no one else had done. He needed to see her again and hold her and tell her all of those things.

They came to the saloon and dismounted. Hunter told Harry to tie the horses up and headed into the building without waiting for a response.

At least ten men occupied the saloon, sitting at the tables farthest to the back. They filled the building with their unwashed stench. Their clothes were ripped and stained, the hands on their mugs almost black with dirt. The wind and sun had darkened their skin, scarred their faces with deep, ugly wrinkles.

Bandits, Hunter thought, his mouth filling with bitterness. Were this his saloon, he wouldn't have served such men. Their belts bristled with weapons, knife and gun holsters on obvious display.

Several of the men spotted Hunter looking their way. One of them, a scrawny fellow with hair so blond it neared silver, lifted his finger to his throat and made a cutting motion.

Disgusted, Hunter turned away from them and went up to the bar. The barmaid behind the counter smiled sweetly at his approach, but the gun on *her* hip was obvious, too. This wasn't the type of woman who would tolerate much nonsense.

"Howdy," she said. Her voice was silky and deep, that of a singer. "What can I get for you, sir? Some whiskey to start your day off right?"

Harry entered, walking up to join Hunter. The barmaid favored him with a smile, her eyes shifting uneasily back and forth between them. They weren't sitting. She knew they didn't want a drink. She might have recognized Harry, but Hunter spent so little time in town she might not know who he was and would assume he was another bandit.

Hunter braced both hands flat on the counter. "Where's Clive?"

"Clive isn't in yet today," the barmaid replied. "He'll be along shortly. What do you want with him?"

"I want to talk to him, see if he knows something."

Harry jabbed his thumb in the direction of a door against the far wall. "We know there's room up there and he sometimes spends nights here. Is he up there now? If he is, we'd like you to go fetch him so we can talk with him."

Her smile dropped away and she shook her head. The line of her jaw hardened. "He ain't here. Anyways, he doesn't like to talk personal business at the saloon. He won't like that you're here, whatever you're wanting. It'd be best for you to leave and talk with him some other time."

Hunter grabbed one of the stools and swung his leg over it. "You don't mind if I stay here and wait for him to come in. He can decide whether or not he wants to talk."

"Now, I'm sure you two don't mean to cause trouble..."

Harry also grabbed a stool and sat.

The blond bandit abandoned his table and strode over, spurs jangling with every step. He had his hands on his hips, resting right above his pistols. "You botherin' this lady?" His voice rasped unusually. A thick burn scar encircling his neck gave the reason why. Someone, at some point, had tried to hang him.

I bet they had good reason for that.

"We aren't botherin' anyone," Harry said. "Just waitin' here."

The bandit gave a humorless little laugh. "You come to a saloon, you don't just sit around. You drink. You want a drink? I'll buy you one. Whiskey." He spoke to the barmaid without looking at her and snapped his fingers.

A glass of whiskey slid his way. He grabbed it and held it out to Harry.

"I don't...." Harry began, and the amber liquid struck his face.

The bandit started to laugh. Harry lunged up off his chair, knocking the empty glass from his hand to shatter on the floor. The bandit latched onto his arms and they grappled, knocking over stools.

The other bandits rose from their seats, hands dropping to their guns as they moved in.

Hunter lunged forward and yanked Harry free from the blonde bandit's grasp, shoving him back. "Enough!" he shouted. "This ain't solving anything. It's makin' things worse. We just want to talk to the owner. We don't want to fight."

"Looking for me?" Someone spoke behind Hunter.

He turned and Clive stood there, holding the saloon door open. Hunter recoiled at the sight of him. There was something not right about the man, a touch of unease that stuck out as even more obvious than his disheveled clothes and reddened eyes. He almost seemed to vibrate, as if glimpsed through flames. A muscle in his cheek ticked a regular rhythm.

Hunter pushed his sudden misgivings aside. Unhinged or not, this was the person most likely to know about Josie's current whereabouts. "I'm lookin' for Josie. You wouldn't happen to know where she is, would you?"

Clive's eyes were veiled as he gave a thin laugh. "Why would I know where she is? Isn't she supposed to be on your ranch? Or did she leave because she finally realized you weren't any good for her?"

Harry and the blond bandit were eyeing each other up, fists clenched. Hunter held his arm out in front of Harry. He prayed that he could get through this talk before the tension snapped like a thin branch and people started fighting again.

"Josie left her daughter in the middle of the night. I was supposed to meet her and I couldn't find her." Hunter leaned in closer. The smell coming off Clive was downright offensive. He hoped his disgust wasn't showing on his face as much as he feared it was. "I figured if anyone had seen her, you'd know about it."

"I haven't heard anyone say anythin'."

"Have you seen her?" Hunter pressed. Clive was squirmy and evasive. Hunter needed to make sure they were speaking the same language. "We both know she wouldn't just leave her daughter. Unless maybe somethin' happened to her. You can see why I'm concerned, can't you?"

For just a moment, Clive hesitated. A flash of doubt made Hunter hesitate, too. If Josie really had gone to see Clive, wouldn't he be boasting about it instead of pretending he didn't know anything?

Then, Clive's shoulders tensed. He lifted his head and drew himself up. "No, I don't see why you're concerned. It's got nothin' to do with you. Josie doesn't belong to you anymore. She never did."

"You're lying." All doubt was gone. He knew it now. The satisfaction in those last words, the smile creeping in. "You know where she is. Tell me!"

Hunter grabbed Clive's arm.

Clive yelled out and swung at him, striking him across the side of his face and sending his hat flying off. Then Harry was grappling with the blond bandit once more, their arms interlocked in a shoving match.

"Stop! Stop this now!" The barmaid screamed.

Hunter backed away, fumbling behind himself for the door. He saw the other bandits rising from their tables. Two of them knocked into each other and a brawl broke out between them, with half the bandits trying to break them apart and the rest approaching Hunter.

Clive launched at Hunter, his fingers clawing for his face. Hunter swung his arm, knocking Clive back. Then there was a bandit coming at him from the side, knife out for a strike.

"This ain't your fight!" Hunter shouted.

The bandit licked his yellow teeth and swung the blade, a silver needlepoint striking for the fabric of Hunter's flesh. He arched his back and the knife nicked harmlessly into his shirt. He kicked out as hard as he could and struck the bandit's knee. There was a crunch of impact and the man reeled back, howling, the cords in his neck standing out. He struck a table and toppled backwards with it.

The barmaid continued screaming. Someone else had come into the saloon from another door. Buck, a known drunk, staggered in, yelling unintelligibly. Outside, horses squealed and confused voices approached as townsfolk drew near to see what was happening.

Hunter grunted as Clive launched at him again, hitting him right in the stomach. And then Clive was a wild animal, a diseased raccoon, clawing and biting. Hunter stepped back and struck the door. He tripped and they went sprawling out onto the porch. The gathered crowd gasped and someone screamed. Hunter hadn't the breath to call out for help as he tried to get Clive off of him.

What am I doing? I have an advantage here!

Hunter wrenched around, straining his muscles. He rolled them over, his weight pressing down on the smaller man. Clive gasped and arched underneath him, biting off the sort of swears that would make a miner cringe. Hunter grabbed one of his hands and pushed it onto the wooden porch and grabbed for the other. Clive bit at him and Hunter yanked back.

Clive grabbed down by his hip, hand flapping like a fish. Hunter had no idea what he was trying to do —attempting to fight dirty?— and tried to get his hand.

Clive pulled his arm up. He had a pistol, finger trembling on the trigger. The safety was off.

Hunter threw himself backward.

At the same time, he heard the gun go off.

Chapter Thirty-Three

Gritting her teeth, with tears blurring her vision, Josie worked at the ropes around her wrists. Her arms were able to feel once more and they ached horribly from being pulled so harshly behind her. Her blood tingled. Her hands felt like they were being stung over and over by hundreds of bees.

But, she was making progress. The ropes had loosened ever so slightly and she could twist her hands to get her fingers on them. She pinched and plucked at the rigid strands. Ever so slowly, the knots were loosening.

Come on, come on, she thought. Throwing a glance at the door, she stopped her struggles and held her breath. Through the pounding of her pulse echoing in her aching head, she strained to hear if Clive was coming back. She feared this was a trick. He might not be working at the saloon after all. If he came back and found that she was trying to escape, there was no telling what measures he might take to keep her trapped.

She had heard of workers who stole from the mines and tried to run off with their ill-gotten gains. If they were caught, their bosses punished them. They didn't kill the thieves and therefore lose manpower. No, instead, the thieves were *hobbled* and sent back to work. When that was done, the thieves were unable to make another run for it.

When horses were hobbled, their legs were tied together to keep them from wandering far. Josie didn't need anyone to explain to her that the thieves received a much worse punishment.

She wasn't really sure if those stories she'd heard were real, or gossip. Maybe such tales were passed around just to keep workers incentivized not to steal. She didn't know. But

Clive must have heard similar stories, or worse. She didn't want him to get the idea that he had to hobble her to prevent her escape.

All she could do was trust that he wasn't going to come back soon. She had to work hard and make her way out of here before he did come back.

She commenced fumbling at the knots and found she could shove her finger between two strands. She reached in and yanked, and suddenly something came loose. Pulling as hard as she could, her arms finally came out from behind her. The pain was so fierce that she sobbed as she ripped the gag from her mouth, but she was free.

Swallowing back her cries of pain, she drew her legs up and tore at the ropes on her ankles. Her hands were an awful sight, abraded and gray from restricted blood flow. Her wrists were red, ropeburned.

Josie kicked the ropes off her ankles and clambered to her feet. Her legs were weak and she almost collapsed. Grabbing onto the wall, she managed to stay upright.

She shoved away from the wall, doing everything she could to stay on her feet. She staggered over to the door and grabbed the handle, twisting it. It rattled and wouldn't even turn. She pounded one of her sore hands against it and heard something fall on the other side. Her hopes lifted and she stepped back and threw her shoulder into the wood. The door bounced slightly in its hinge. Nothing moved on the other side that time.

Rubbing her aching shoulder, she turned back and rushed over to the window. Someone outside let out a high-pitched scream. Josie pushed her ear to the curtain covering the wooden boards over the window and heard shouting.

"Please don't let it be because of Clive." Her mouth was so dry from having the gag in it that she could barely whisper the words.

If he was out there and hurting people because of her, she wouldn't be able to forgive herself.

Josie tore at the window covering. The fabric ripped in several places where it had been nailed to the wall. She threw it aside and attacked the boards. The first layer had been put neatly into place, but the second layer, the one she was facing, was a chaotic piece of workmanship. The boards angled over each other at odd angles and the nails were all over, some bent over on themselves and embedded sideways into the wood.

Running her hands over the wood, she searched for a loose spot. She was able to get her fingers underneath one board and she pulled with everything she had. The board groaned, some of the nails squeaking as they were tugged loose.

Another scream from outside. A horse squealed. People were shouting. It sounded like a whole crowd of them.

Desperate, Josie spun around and rushed around the room, yanking the sheets off the bed, throwing the sewing box onto the floor. She ripped open the dresser drawers, peering into each one. Women's dresses and undergarments. Tiny outfits meant for a little girl.

She pulled the last drawer fully out of the dresser and smashed it onto the floor. Panting, she walked back to the door, ready to tackle it again.

And then she saw it.

There was a hammer in the corner of the room, leaning on the wall.

Josie grabbed the hammer and rushed back to the window. She used the back of it, slotting it behind the board, and pulled. The board popped off, falling onto the floor.

She winced at the loud noise. There was no stopping now. She kept going, pulling off another board.

From outside, there was the high, swift sound of a gun firing.

Josie jumped and almost dropped the hammer. What was going on out there?

She pulled off several more boards and finally a section of the window was freed. She crouched and stared through.

Clive!

He was running down the street, pistol in hand. There was blood on his face and clothes.

Josie tore off another board. Her breath came so fast she was getting no air at all. She could feel no part of her body except for her aching head.

"Clive!" A deep voice snarled out. Another man ran from the direction of the saloon, chasing Clive. He was a lumbering wildman, his hair in a mane around his face.

Hunter!

There was something wrong with him. As he ran, he kept his arm close to his chest. There was blood on the ground, trailing behind him.

In a moment, she understood. When Clive knocked her out and took her away, Hunter must have started looking for her. He would have known she wouldn't leave her daughter.

And now he was hurt because of her.

Josie lifted the hammer and swung it with all her strength, slamming it into the window. The glass shattered in an almost musical manner and flew out onto the street. She swept the remnants away with the side of the tool and stuck her head through the gap.

"Hunter!" she screamed. "Hunter, I'm in here!"

Hunter swiveled to a halt and spun in her direction. He slipped in the dust and his own blood, almost falling. Then, Clive was turning back, throwing himself onto Hunter. They collapsed onto the ground, exchanging blows. Hunter was trying to get the gun from Clive's hand and Clive was trying to point it at him.

"Careful, Hunter!" Josie tried to push herself through the window. The gap was still too small. She jammed the back of the hammer behind another board and started to pull it off.

Outside, the gun fired again. She heard it strike the side of the house, saw the thin circle of light where it had passed right through.

She looked out again, crying Hunter's name. The men were in such a brawl she couldn't tell what was happening, dust pluming up around them. The crowd she had heard was running over, the sheriff at their head.

Suddenly, Hunter went sprawling away from Clive. He rolled over, something silver in his hand. He'd grabbed the gun.

Clive scrambled at him on his hands and knees, his eyes wild and white in his dirt-smeared face.

Shoot him, Hunter!

She opened her mouth and then, as she was yelling, the words that came out were different. "Don't shoot him! Don't shoot, Hunter!"

Hunter brought his arm around and slammed the side of the pistol into Clive's face. The crack of metal against bone shot into the air. Clive stopped in his mad scrabbling and touched the side of his face. Then, he collapsed onto his side.

Hunter rose to his feet and shoved the gun into the sheriff's hands. He said something to the other men. Turning on his heel, he rushed to the window. "Josie! Is this Clive's house? Are you alright?"

"I'm fine. Get me out of here!" Tears sprang into her eyes. "I want to go home."

"You done real good so far." His dark eyes found hers and held them. "Need you to hold on a little longer, Josie. You got a hammer?"

"Yes." She raised it. "I'll remove the rest of the boards." Her arms were shaking. She didn't know how much more she could do.

"No." Hunter shook his head. He still had his arm clamped to his side. The blood on his skin was vivid cherry-red. "Stand to the side a good distance."

She obeyed, moving back and away from the window. Wood and glass burst into the room as Hunter gave the remnants of the window a mighty blow with a piece of firewood from outside. Josie lifted her arm to her face, protecting her eyes from the flying splinters.

"Come on, now." Hunter leaned in through the broken window with his arms outstretched. "Come to me, Josie."

She went to him and he swept his arms around her, lifting her off her feet and pulling her through the window. Her feet hit the dirt and she clutched at Hunter to keep herself from falling.

His arms enfolded her. She buried her face in his chest, finally able to catch her breath.

"Oh, Josie." His voice shook. "I was so afraid for you."

"But you found me." She ran her hands up his muscular back, into his tangled hair.

"I felt the saloon would be the best place to find you." He suddenly pulled back, holding her by her shoulders. "Are you okay? He didn't hurt you?"

She shook her head. She didn't want to divulge the details of what exactly she had gone through. His eyes softened and he pulled her in against his warm, solid body once more. That was when she felt wetness seeping into her clothes and remembered.

"Clive shot you!"

"He only got my arm," Hunter murmured. He stroked her hair. The pain was bad, but the feeling was too good to resist. She was cared for, gently comforted. "I'll be fine."

"We need to get you to see the doctor."

"In a moment. Josie..." His hand cradled the back of her head. "I realized that even though I still got lots to learn, there's one thing I know for sure. I... I love you."

She drew back a little in surprise, staring up into his dark eyes. They were gentle as a warm night and she could see her own reflection in them. She touched his cheek, felt the scruff of stubble. He leaned his face into her hand, his eyelids lowering.

There was so much she wanted to say to him in that moment, but the sheriff was coming toward them and their time together was running down to mere moments. She would only be able to say one final thing before they would be interrupted. They would have to explain the situation, maybe several times, maybe together and also separately, and after that they would have to make the journey home. It was going to be a long and difficult day to endure.

But after that?

That was what she had to think about, what came next.

Josie stroked Hunter's face and she whispered just for him, too quiet for the sheriff to hear even just a few steps away. "I love you, too."

Against all the odds, she did. She never would have imagined anything like this back when she was sneaking into his cellar to steal food from him, or when she was first working for him just so he wouldn't bring the law down upon her. Something, somewhere along the line, had changed. She saw past the gruff exterior to the softness within, saw him for who he was. Flawed, but hard working. A loner, but with love in his heart. Love for Ella, love for her.

Something inside of her had also changed through all of this. She had felt so tired, so downtrodden by everything. Now she knew that she still had so much strength left in her. She could get through anything, and she hoped he would be there with her while she did.

The sheriff walked up beside Hunter. He started to speak.

Hunter held up his hand. "Only a moment, Sheriff. I got to do somethin' first."

Josie frowned. She started to speak and ask him what he meant by that. Then, she realized his face was lowering toward hers and she understood. She tipped her face up to his, her eyes closing. His lips touched hers, firm and warm. A rush like a high wind swept through her body, taking away all her aches and pains. She felt like she was on the back of the fastest horse the world had ever known, just flying across the ground.

This is what it's supposed to feel like.

She clutched her arms around Hunter's neck and kissed him, ignoring the dirt and the blood getting on her clothes.

The only other man she had ever kissed was Owen and that was at their wedding ceremony. He had never kissed her again after that. She'd had no idea it could feel so good to be putting herself in this vulnerable position. And to know that Hunter would never hurt her like that? She never wanted it to end. If only this moment could be an eternity.

The sheriff coughed.

She was back to reality in a moment, realizing what it must look like, an unmarried man and woman embracing like this in front of everyone. There went her reputation. But she really didn't care as much as she should have. Let these people think whatever they wanted. She knew who she was.

The kiss lingered a fraction of a heartbeat longer before Hunter pulled away. He kept his arm around her as he turned to the sheriff. "I'd say I'm sorry, but I ain't," he said roughly.

The sheriff looked vaguely amused before becoming serious again. "Let's get the pair of you to the doctor. We can talk there."

Hunter looked down at Josie. "You can walk?"

"I can." As long as he was with her, she had the strength to go anywhere.

They set off, the three of them, the sheriff leading the way while they straggled behind. They passed the crowd surrounding Clive. Everyone was talking at once, their voices mingling. Beneath the other voices, Josie thought she heard one in particular.

"Josie..."

She ignored the faint plea. With her head high, she walked on, leaving Clive behind.

Chapter Thirty-Four

Hunter held open the door to the sheriff's office for Josie and stepped in after her. The building was dingy and dusty, with only a few pieces of hard furniture around. Sitting in one of those uncomfortable chairs was a familiar face.

Harry stood up and strode over to Hunter, clapping a hand on his arm. "You lived!" he crowed. "I wasn't so sure, seein' the way Clive was going at you. Didn't know the scrawny guy had it in him."

Hunter winced as Harry came very close to slapping his bullet wound. "I wasn't going to let him be the end of me. I had to make sure Josie was safe."

He turned to Josie and she gave him a tired smile. He pulled one of the chairs over and motioned for her to sit. She lowered into the seat and leaned her head back with her eyes shut. He rubbed her shoulder, his heart aching for her and what she had gone through during those hours alone in Clive's clutches. The doctor had wrapped her hands and wrists in bandages. Hunter hadn't taken notice of their condition before that. He had been too preoccupied. He had no idea what was beneath those bandages and his stomach twisted with his fears.

Harry moved to his side again. "I'm glad you made sure I was safe, too. You're a true friend for leavin' me with those bandits to fend for myself."

Hunter rubbed the back of his neck and shifted on his feet. "I'm sorry, Harry."

Harry shook his head. "I'm only jokin' around. It was fine, in the end. Once you really started having yourself a brush with Clive, everyone lost interest in me. The only thing that's hurt is my pride."

"That'll heal in no time." Hunter sat down in another chair next to Josie. "The sheriff send you over here?"

"One of his men did, once they figured out I wasn't injured at all. He on his way?"

"He left us at the doctor and said he'd meet us here." Hunter touched his wounded arm and grimaced.

Harry let out a whistle at the sight of the bloodstained bandage. "Doesn't look too purty."

"He was aiming for my chest," Hunter said. "I moved in time and he only grazed me. Sure is bleedin' a lot, but the doctor said it wasn't anything too serious."

Josie spoke softly with her head still leaned back. "You'll be doing work on the ranch tonight just like nothing ever happened."

"That's true." He smiled. "The work won't wait around for me to heal."

She lifted her head and fixed her tired, yet bright green eyes on him. "You won't be doing it alone. I'll help you out."

"I'll help, too," Harry said. His determination not to be left out was a little amusing and Hunter chuckled softly. "You could also let the other ranch hands back onto the property now, for some extra help. Get things back to normal."

Before Hunter could say anything, the door to the office thumped open and the sheriff walked in. He glanced at the three of them and gave a slow nod. "You're all here. Alright. I'll get your stories just to have on the record, but we won't be needing to talk as much as I thought. Clive already told us everything we need to know."

Hunter moved his chair closer to Josie's and put his arm around her shoulders. "Did he, now?"

"Sure did." The sheriff leaned his hip on his desk and crossed his arms over his chest. "One of my men trained under a doctor for a time, took care of him while you two were bein' patched up. Clive was jawing the entire time we were checking him for injuries. Josie?"

"Yes?" She looked at him, her lips pressed together. "He told you that he's the one who murdered my husband?"

"He did." The sheriff sighed. "Who knew that we had the murderer in town all along? Right under our noses. And Hunter, he told us how he was sneakin' onto your property, killin' your animals and causing damage."

Hunter shook his head slowly. He had suspected Clive played a part in all this, but the depths of this depravity were astonishing. He hoped he never had to experience anything like this ever again.

"With all of this coming right out of his mouth, we arrested him," the sheriff said. "And hosting those bandits in his saloon, and shooting you... There's no way he could possibly have walked free."

"Then, he's in jail now?" Josie leaned forward. The harsh line of her mouth quivered. "He's been arrested?"

"He's been arrested." The sheriff's voice softened as he looked at her. He seemed repentant, perhaps sorry he hadn't been able to find her husband's killer before now. "And I got no doubts the judge will make sure he stays there for a long, long time. A man like him shouldn't walk around with the rest of us."

"I agree with that," Hunter said. "So, what do you need from us now?"

"I'll just talk with you one at a time, make sure there's nothing Clive left out of his stories." The sheriff motioned to Josie. "You want to come join me in the back office there?"

Hunter touched her hand. "You want me to come with you?"

Josie held his hand but shook her head. "No. I'll be fine on my own." She rose to her feet and spoke to the sheriff. "Let's get this over with."

"Right this way." He motioned for her to follow him. They went off and the door closed behind them.

Hunter got up from his chair and walked the floor, suddenly restless with Josie out of his sight. Harry watched him. "How you feeling, boss?"

"Relieved," Hunter said. "Impatient, too. I just want to get on home and start livin' life like it's supposed to be lived."

"It'll be easy to get back into it," Harry said. "Now we know Clive was responsible for all of this, we can be sure that there's not going to be any more strangeness on the ranch."

"Yes. We can get chickens again. I've missed eggs." Hunter laughed at himself, but it was true. He just wanted to live a simple live with simple pleasures, with Josie by his side. "And we can replant the garden. Josie will love doing that. Ella will love 'helping.'"

"What are you going to do about the tunnels?" Harry asked. "You blocked off the entrance into your cellar. But those tunnels are still there. Someone else might stumble across them. They can dig through and break in if they really want to."

"I think it's time to put the tunnels to rest," Hunter said. "They've been a part of the ranch for as long as I've been alive, but they've got no purpose. I'll have to try to remember where all the entrances are and get those blocked up, too. Maybe I can get some of the foremen from the mines to collapse them with some dynamite. Let's see someone get through them when they don't exist anymore."

"Dynamite? You haven't had your fill of excitement so you want to blow some things up?" Harry was shaking his head.

"*Carefully* blow some things up," Hunter stressed.

Their talk was interrupted as the door opened and Josie stepped out. Hunter glanced past her at the sheriff, who gestured for him to come inside. Hunter stepped into the small, even dingier and dustier room.

"You can sit, if you like," the sheriff said. "But I don't think this will take us that long. I just need you to run through the trouble you've had on your ranch and give me the estimates of the tin you've lost because of Clive. I don't doubt the judge will be putting him to work so he can pay you back."

Hunter held up his hand. "You can tell the judge this when you see him. I don't want any money from that man. I don't want to see or hear of him ever again. So long as he's nowhere near me and my family, I will be happy."

The sheriff looked at him steadily. "Your family. You know that woman's a widow, homeless. She's come on hard times clearly through no fault of her own, but she's still got all that in her past."

"She's family," Hunter said firmly. "I know about her past and she knows about mine. That's about all anyone needs to know. If they got an issue with her reputation, or mine, they can come and say it to my face."

"Alright, alright." The sheriff held up his hands. "You don't got to be defensive with me. I'm only trying to get the important parts of the story. Do you mind telling me the estimates for the damages anyway? The judge will use the information when he gives Clive his sentencing."

"That's fine." Hunter ran through the list. He knew every plant in the garden that had been destroyed. The sheriff had to get out a piece of paper to write everything down.

When Hunter was finished, the sheriff folded up the paper and tucked it into his shirt pocket. "If there's anything else to tell me, you should say it now. The moment you set foot out of this building, I'll consider your involvement to be finished. Justice'll move fast. No time to wait."

No time to wait now that the mysteries have been solved for you.

"There's nothing else," Hunter said. His arm ached and he was tired. He just wanted to go home.

They stepped out of the office. Harry had taken a seat next to Josie. He was telling her about his pregnant wife and the preparations they were making for his child. Hunter caught his friend's eye as he walked over and gave him a nod of approval, silently thanking him for keeping Josie distracted.

Josie rose as she saw Hunter. His heart filled with the urge to have her near, he held out his hand. She took it without any hesitation and they stood close together as polite farewells were exchanged with the sheriff. The man walked them to the door and saw them out.

They stepped out onto the dusty street to a number of stragglers, mostly women. One of the young ladies, hardly more than a girl, stepped up to Josie. She pushed her sunhat back, peeking out from underneath the wide brim.

"Is it true?" she asked.

Hunter stepped between Josie and the woman. “Is what true?”

One of the few men standing there outside the sheriff's office spoke up. “That she was bein’ held captive in Clive's house.”

“That's the word going around town,” another man said. He adjusted the tortoiseshell spectacles resting on the bridge of his nose. “Might I speak with you about it, miss? For the newspaper?”

Hunter snapped his fingers. “None of you talk to her. This isn't any of your business. And you.” He pointed at the newspaper man. “I'll be readin’ the paper. I know I'll see an article on this. I can't stop that. But if what's written there is lies and speculations, the newspaper office is going to be getting a visit from me. Hope I'm understood. Now, clear out of our way. We're leaving.”

No one seemed inclined to move to let him through. He shrugged and, keeping ahold of Josie's hand, walked forward. They parted before his broad chest to avoid him running into them and he continued on with her and Henry bringing up the rear.

Their horses were still in front of the saloon, shifting anxiously and yanking their heads around. All the fighting and the guns going off had spooked them. They would have run off if they weren't tied.

“Poor things,” Josie murmured. She released Hunter's hand and walked up to Granite. She placed her bandaged hand on his neck and stroked his thick gray coat. “It's been a long day for all of us. We should get home and give them some extra apples when we're there.”

“That sounds like it would be a good idea to me.” Hunter walked up to her side. “He gave Granite a few pats on the flank. The horse turned his head and whickered, his ears twitching irritably. He stamped his back hoof and flicked his tail.

"Look at him," Harry said. "He's scolding you."

Hunter gave the horse another couple pats. "That's how I know he'll be fine." He stepped into the stirrups and swung his leg over the saddle. Reaching back down for Josie's hand, he said, "Come on up here."

Josie took his hand and he pulled her onto the saddle in front of him. He smelled her sweet, familiar scent and felt her body against his. An ease filled him. In his heart, they were already back on the ranch.

Hunter pressed the reins into her hands. "You know what to do."

She twisted around to smile at him, then faced forward again. As Harry got on his own horse, she flicked the reins. "Home, Granite," she said.

***

They rode up in front of the house around noon. The front door banged wide open and Ella rushed out. "Mama, Mama!" she cried.

"Ella!" Josie dismounted and dropped to her knees on the ground, sweeping Ella up into her arms. She was laughing and crying slightly as she hugged her daughter and pressed kisses all over her face. "My darling, my baby!"

"I miss you, Mama!" Ella leaned back and took Josie's face in her hands. "Where you go?"

Josie sniffed and shook her head. She put her hands over Ella's, gathering them up to give them yet more kisses. "I went to town. I missed you, too."

Hunter slid out of the saddle, grunting a little as his arm was jostled. He put his hand on Josie's shoulder. She looked up at him and sniffed again, then smiled. She lifted Ella into her arms and stood. "I won't be going to town for a while, I think. I'd rather stay here on the ranch and get back to normal."

"Back to nermehl," Ella echoed.

Hunter wrapped his arms around both of them. "Normal sounds great to me."

"You're back!"

They all looked around, including Harry, as Kerry rushed out of the house and trotted over to them. She swept her arms around all of them, squeezing tight. "I thought I heard horses! I was in the cellar. Ella was down with me and then I turned around and she was gone just like that. Oh, I am so happy that you're back."

"We're happy to be back," Hunter said.

Kerry suddenly looked them over with a harsh frown that hadn't been there before. "You're both hurt!" she exclaimed. She rounded on Harry. "Are you hurt, too?"

"No, ma'am."

"Well, at least one of you made it back safely. Hunter, Josie, you come right on inside. You both need something to eat and drink." Kerry spun around and marched back to the door.

Hunter looked at Josie and she looked back at him. "You go on in," he said. "Cuddle Ella and eat. I'll be right in when I've gotten Granite into the stable."

"Don't worry, boss." Harry took hold of Granite's reins. "I'll get them settled. You can both go in and get some food. I'll come after. Maybe Kerry will allow me to have some grub, too."

Hunter nodded his thanks. He put his hand on Josie's lower back and urged her to the house. They all went inside and Kerry busied herself at once with fixing them some coffee with whiskey stirred in to take the edge off their pains. Harry came in and she brought them all leftover biscuits and butter to hold them over while she took Ella into the kitchen to fix up lunch.

They sat in the parlor to eat and drink. Hunter and Josie shared the couch. He kept having to look over at her to reassure himself she was still there and safe.

This could all be a dream, he thought. He might wake up any second to find that it was dawn, that Josie was still missing and in peril.

She caught him looking at her and smiled. Her green eyes were soft as spring leaves just unfolding from their buds, full of newness and life.

This *was* a dream, he decided, but a good one.

Harry shoveled two biscuits into his mouth and stood. "Well, I could sit here and watch you two makin' eyes at each other. But I'd rather go make myself useful. I'll get some work done and come back for lunch."

Hunter tore his gaze away from Josie for just a moment to look at Harry. "That'd be much appreciated."

Harry left the house, the door banging shut behind him.

Hunter turned back to Josie. He could hear Kerry moving around in the kitchen while Ella asked a stream of questions. Knowing they would also be able to hear what was going on in the parlor, he leaned close to Josie and spoke low. "How are your hands?"

Josie dropped her eyes to the bandages. "They're not as bad as the doctor made them seem with all of this."

"Could I see?" He wanted to know exactly what she had gone through.

Josie hesitated. She frowned and her jaw moved as she bit the inside of her cheek.

"It's alright." He put his hands over her bandages. "You don't have to."

"No, I want to. I'll show you." She moved his hands aside. She plucked at the bandages until she found a loose end and unwound it, creating a pile on the arm of the couch. When one hand was bare, she uncovered the other.

Hunter slid his hands beneath hers and inspected them. "He had you tied up, I know. I saw the ropes. You freed yourself."

"It wasn't easy."

He had no doubt that every part of what she had gone through was the hardest thing she had ever done.

Her hands were covered in little cuts from the rope fibers, and rashlike abrasions from scrapes. Her wrists were encircled with similar abrasions, red and shiny.

"The doctor said there might be scarring. He said he couldn't be sure, that it depends on me." She sighed. "What's a few more scars?"

"Josie." He enfolded her hands gently in his and leaned to press his lips to hers, just for a moment. He drew back because he didn't want Kerry to catch them without an explanation, but he could have kissed her for much longer.

"I've seen your scars. And you know what I see? You, beautiful. And strong. You'd already saved yourself by the time that I got to you."

"You helped me the rest of the way. I couldn't have done it without you." Her cheeks were turning pink.

"Sure, you could have. But I am glad I was there to do what I could." He picked up the bandages to wrap her hands in them again. "I love you, Josie. I really meant that."

"I love you, too." She smiled the sweetest, prettiest smile. "Does this mean I don't have to work to pay you back anymore?"

"We both know you paid me back a long time ago." He finished wrapping her hands. "No, you're not my maid no more. Unless you want to be."

"I'd rather be something else to you. If you don't mind."

He chuckled and put his arm around her. "We can talk about that. Soon. Maybe tomorrow, after we've all had some rest. For now, why don't we go into the kitchen to see if Kerry could use some help with Ella?"

They walked into the kitchen. Kerry stood at the stove stirring a pot of beans. Ella sat on the counter nearby, eating a biscuit. She looked up with her face covered in crumbs and smiled. "I helping!" she announced.

Josie laughed and went to her, lifting her into her arms. She dabbed the crumbs from her daughter's face and kissed her cheek.

Hunter leaned his hip on the counter and looked around at all he had, smiling. Everything he could ever need was right here.

Epilogue

Deadwood, South Dakota

3 weeks later...

The first thing Josie noticed upon stepping out of the house that morning was the temperature of the air. Though the sun was well up in the sky, the winds sweeping down into the valley were cooling and moist. Summer was at last relinquishing its hold over the world.

The next thing she noticed was Hunter standing at the end of the porch, his suit struggling to encompass his muscular form. The seams and buttons were straining. He stood in an uncomfortable manner, the fine fabric at odds with his usual working attire of an old shirt and well-worn trousers. He had brushed his hair and looked wonderful with the shaggy mane slicked back from his face to show off his dark eyes. They shimmered with all the colors of fall in their depths as he turned to look at her.

He had his hands on Ella's shoulders. By some miracle, Ella's new dress was still perfect, bright yellow with white lace. The satin ribbon in her hair was also yellow, tied into a shape reminiscent of a flower.

Ella saw her and let out a happy chirp. She twisted out from Hunter's grasp and rushed over with her arms out. Laughing, Josie knelt and swept her up into a tight hug. As she stood, she at last allowed herself to look out past the porch boundary, to the people gathered there. Kerry was at the very front, in a yellow dress that matched Ella's, with her husband by her side, her children and grandchildren spread out around her. And standing with them were other townsfolk, Harry and his pregnant wife, the sheriff and his men, Arthur from the hotel, and many others. All of them wore their best dresses and suits, and their kindest smiles as they regarded her and Hunter.

Josie looked at the beautiful women in the crowd. They wore their hair in buns or pinned up in elaborate fashions. Necklaces encircled their necks and golden bracelets dangled from their wrists. They had wedding bands and lacy shawls on their shoulders.

And there she was before them all, in a dress she had sewn herself over the past weeks. Her hair was down and only brushed, and she hadn't a single bit of gold or even silver on her person. Did they think she was beautiful, too? Or did they hide their secret thoughts behind their smiles and kind eyes, pitying her for the simplicity of her appearance on her wedding day?

Hunter held out his hand to her. She went to him and he put his hand on her waist. She looked up at him, and she saw there that he thought she was beautiful.

And that was all that mattered.

Someone strode up from the crowd, the priest from the church. He held a small Bible in one hand as he mounted the porch steps. He was a dashing figure in his gray suit, his hair a silver-white shock. The slate eyes he fixed first upon Josie and then Hunter were keen and welcoming.

He held out his free hand and shook with Hunter, then faced the assembly of townsfolk. "What a beautiful day for a wedding," he said, his voice crisp and clear. "And what a fine gathering of folks who have come to help celebrate this wondrous occasion."

A small, appreciative murmur went through those who had gathered.

The priest adjusted his white collar and opened his Bible. He read out a passage. Everyone was silent as they listened. Josie tried to pay attention, but she was too nervous, her attention wandering. She instead heard the horses in the stable, the clucking of the new batch of chickens in their relocated coop.

The priest closed his Bible again. "It is always an honor to unite a man and woman in holy matrimony. I consider it to be one of my most important duties, and certainly my favorite. For the future of mankind is in the hands of the next generation, and only through the forging of strong bonds will our descendants have the greatest chance of success. So, a marriage is not only about the man and the woman seeking unity. It is about their children, and their children's children, and all the other lives they will touch in their time."

Josie snuck a look sideways at Hunter. She felt her heart thumping hard in her chest. She hadn't thought of anything like that until now. Would she carry his children one day?

I want to know what it's like to have a child with a man who loves me.

The priest was still speaking. "Hunter Carson and Josie Murphy have endured much in their lives. We all know that. We've seen and heard their hardships. But they are here together now and will make each other happy. That, I am sure of."

He turned to them and said, "Hunter, do you take Josie to be your lawfully wedded wife? To have and to hold her from this day forward, for richer or poorer, in sickness and in health?"

Hunter raised his chin. "I do."

The priest faced Josie. His eyes were serious, but kindly, and his voice softened as he spoke to her. "Josie, do you take

Hunter to be your lawfully wedded husband? To support him in his endeavors and enrich his life, for richer or poorer, in sickness and in health?"

She cleared her throat and found her voice. "I-I do."

"I now pronounce you man and wife," the priest declared, sealing their union.

"Man and wife," Ella repeated.

The priest smiled down at her and chucked her underneath the chin. Josie looked out at the crowd, hearing their cheers and whistles, seeing them clapping for her. She smiled.

Hunter spoke to the crowd. "Thank you all for coming out here to celebrate with us. If anyone wants to volunteer to help, there's food and drink to be brought outside and set up on those tables over there. I know some of you brought your instruments. We can have us some music and dancing. Later on, there will be a proper dinner feast. If anyone has brought us gifts," he chuckled, "that would be the time to bring them out. Unless you want to give it to one of us in private, of course. I can't wait to speak with all of you and have us some fun."

More cheering, and people were chanting their names, and Ella's name, too. Ella beamed as if this was her wedding, her day to be the center of attention. But, of course, that was every day.

Hunter lifted his hands up. "Before we disperse, there's one more thing I want to do."

Josie frowned. *We didn't plan anything else for the ceremony, did we?*

He turned to her and she froze, fearing that there was something she had forgotten. He reached into his pocket and pulled out a small cloth drawstring bag.

"Hunter?" she whispered.

He turned the bag over and shook something out into his hand, something small and shimmery. He held it up, a fine gold chain necklace decorated with the palest gray-white seed pearls.

Josie gasped and put her hand over her mouth. No one had bought her jewelry before. She couldn't imagine how much it must have cost him. He could have used the money for ranch repairs, saved it up for a time of need. Instead, he had bought her this.

Had she any lingering doubts that he loved her, they would have all been erased right then and there.

Hunter moved around behind her and draped the necklace around her neck. His large fingers did the delicate work of securing the clasp.

Kerry cheered out and strode up the porch steps to them. She embraced Josie tightly, kissing her cheeks. Tears shone in her eyes. "Beautiful ceremony!" she sniffed. "I just knew you two would wind up married. You make such a pretty little family together."

Josie hugged her back. "Thank you," she whispered into the older woman's ear. "For being there for us through all of this."

Kerry gave her another kiss on the cheek. "My pleasure," she whispered back. She drew away and dabbed her eyes with a handkerchief. "Well! Time for me to get to work bringing the food out."

“I’ll help,” Josie said.

“Not on your wedding day, you won’t!” Kerry held up her finger, tutting. She turned to the priest, who was still standing there and watching them. “Anyway, there’s still one more thing to be done, isn’t there, Father?”

“That’d be right,” the priest said. “There’s the marriage certificate to sign.”

“You all can go take care of that in the office. I can start rounding up volunteers to help with the food.” Kerry went back down to the crowd. Some had dispersed and were already mingling, while others were fetching their instruments.

“Shall we head inside?” the priest suggested.

“Let’s go,” Josie said.

Hunter chuckled and went to open the door for her.

They all headed into the house. Josie found herself at the front, leading the way as if this was her house to show off.

It struck her that this *was* her house. This had been her home out of necessity but now it was simply home. She swallowed hard around the lump in her throat and pushed into Hunter’s office.

The priest laid the marriage certificate out on Hunter’s desk and offered a pen. “It’s a simple matter. You each just need to sign your names there and that will be all.”

Hunter took the pen and wrote his name in the indicated space. His lettering was simple and bold. He passed the pen off to Josie and she wrote her name underneath his. And that was it. They were truly, officially married.

She looked at their names together on that paper and marveled at them.

The priest took the pen from her and put it in his pocket, and lifted the paper. "Thank you both. I'll take this for the records. You'll be sent a copy for your own records. Be sure to check your mail soon. The only thing left is to give you both a final congratulations from me."

"Thank you," Hunter said.

"Thank you so much," Josie said.

The priest looked at her down the proud slope of his nose and smiled. "I was there, you know. At your father's funeral."

"You were?" Josie tilted her head. Hunter faded slightly into the background, giving them space to talk. "But it was the judge who handled that. And my previous wedding."

"That's right. I was sick at the time. I hadn't the strength to handle the matters on my own and the judge took over some of them for me. But I was able to attend the funeral, though I left before I had a chance to speak with you." The priest held her by the shoulder. "I knew him. He was a good man. He took care of you as best as he could."

"I know he did," Josie whispered.

"He would be proud of you right now."

She blinked away the tears that rose into her eyes. "Thank you for saying so, Father. I hope he would be proud of me."

"He's looking down on you with a smile." The priest straightened and sighed. "I had best get going. I need to be back in town."

"You won't stay for the party?" Josie asked. "The dancing and such wouldn't interest you, I'm sure, but there will be dinner. You're more than welcome to stay and eat."

"Thank you, but I have an appointment I must keep." The priest shook his head.

"I'll see you out," Hunter offered.

Josie shook her head. "You really can't leave without partaking a little bit. I'll go into the kitchen and wrap up some food for you to take."

The priest smiled. "Very generous. I won't say no. I'll be outside saddling my horse, then."

"I'll be back in a minute." Josie left after making her promise and went into the kitchen. Kerry, her daughter, and several other women filled the space, preparing to take the many dishes outside to the tables set up for the party.

Almost everyone who showed up to the ceremony had brought food with them. The assortments of pots, bowls, platters, and jars covered all the counter space and overflowed onto the kitchen table. There was roasted corn, a pot of beans, sliced apples dusted with sugar and cinnamon, rolls and biscuits and sourdough loaves, and many cakes, cookies, and tartlets. The blend of scents was sweet and savory, vegetal and spiced, all of a meal's courses combining into one complex perfume.

Josie stood holding onto the doorframe, watching as the women opened jars of pickled vegetables and sliced late season watermelons into chunks. Where was all this generosity when she was on her own and struggling? Now that she was no longer in need, here came the assistance. They would be eating these leftovers for days, perhaps weeks. She wouldn't have had to steal scraps of food from Hunter's cellar if she had had access to all this.

One of the women noticed her standing there and turned with a puzzled smile. She held a jar of pickles, the tangy brine bringing water to Josie's mouth. She had hardly eaten anything for breakfast due to nerves.

"Need something, dear?" the woman asked.

Josie looked at her and wanted to hate her for all that she represented. She wanted to hate all of these prosperous women who had been so wrapped up in their own lives they had shunned her, outcast her when she came looking for help and work.

Then, Ella was walking to her, weaving between the adults' legs. She had a cookie in one hand, a cinnamoned apple slice in the other. Her smile was brighter than the sun.

Josie looked down at her daughter and all of the desire to hate went away in a flash.

No one could have known exactly what she was going through at that time. She had been secretive and wary, unwilling to tell anyone her full story for fear of being pitied. They couldn't have known how desperate she was, or how to help her.

And they had their own lives. Every person in this kitchen, every guest at the ceremony, every person who lived in Deadwood, they all had their own families and jobs, their own celebrations and hardships to endure. She had no idea how many of them had been mourning their own losses or were struggling to get by. Maybe some of them could have helped her, but maybe some of them had simply been unable to.

Perhaps every person she saw was just doing their best and she shouldn't begrudge them for that. She should forgive them.

Not forgive. There's nothing to forgive.

She *accepted* them.

No matter what they had and hadn't done in the past, what mattered was that they were here.

"Josie, honey?" The other woman patted her on the cheek, rather briskly. "Are you feeling faint? Do you need something to drink?"

Josie pulled herself out of her musings. "I'm fine. Just... overwhelmed."

"I understand." The other woman smiled. "But you aren't supposed to be in here. Kerry said so. You're not allowed to help us."

Kerry, hearing her name, glanced over with a chuckle.

Josie explained that she was there to grab a few things for the priest before he left.

"Well, in that case..." The woman looked around and grabbed one of the many cloth bags laying around. "You can put his food in here. But after that, you really must step out. Kerry seemed serious when she told us not to allow you in here. If she sees you helping out, or even just thinks that you're helping..."

"I don't want to be scolded at my own wedding," Josie agreed. "I'll be fast."

She stroked Ella's hair and moved past, working her way through the other women with more difficulty than her daughter had. She grabbed cloth napkins and wrapped up some cookies and biscuits and filled a bowl with some of the vegetables and pieces of cured meat and cheese. She placed everything securely in the bag and took it outside with her.

The musicians were tuning their instruments, plucking their guitar strings and teasing their violins with their bows.

Some folks were already getting started with the dancing, but most were still milling around and talking.

Josie saw the priest standing next to his tall black horse. Hunter was elsewhere, occupied in speaking with a man holding a baby.

"Here you are, Father." Josie walked over and held out the bag. "Hunter left you by yourself?"

"He was annexed by that other rancher there," the priest said, laughing. He took the bag of food and bowed his head. "Thank you. Very kind of you. Don't forget to check your mail for your copy of the marriage certificate."

He mounted his horse and gave her a little wave and rode off.

Josie waved him a farewell and turned back. The different foods were being set up on the tables by now, drawing a number of guests over. And at last, there was music, the violinist playing idly in front of a dancing couple.

Hunter finished with his talk and made his way back to her, holding her hand and pulling her close to his side. He bent his head and spoke in her ear, his breath hot. "My beautiful bride."

"Your beautiful wife," she corrected. Her cheeks grew warm. "And you're my handsome husband."

"I ain't goin' to get tired of hearing that." Hunter tugged on her hand. "Come on."

"Where are we going?"

"Everyone's distracted right now because the food's comin' out. In a short while, they'll turn their attention to us."

Josie remembered her previous, smaller marriage, how quickly she had grown tired of thanking everyone time and again.

"While we've got a moment, let's dance." Hunter drew to a halt next to the dancing couple and the violinist. "Our first dance as husband and wife."

The man with the guitar began to play, and he was joined by a boy with a trumpet. The music swelled, bright and lively, echoing across the valley, bouncing off the high walls. The dancers noticed Hunter and Josie standing there and moved aside. Other guests noticed them too and surrounded them in a loose ring.

"Dance!" someone called out and others took up the cry, making a haphazard chant.

Josie reached and took Hunter's big, strong hands. Hers were almost fully healed after her struggles at Clive's house. All that remained of her injuries were the marks on her wrists, the faint red circlets. Still, even knowing she was healed, Hunter held her hands so gently in his.

He looked her in the eyes and mouthed, 'I love you.'

She mouthed it back.

They started to sway together as the music wrapped around them. All that mattered right then was Hunter. She didn't see the guests or feel them watching her. She only knew her husband's hands, his loving eyes holding hers.

***

Everyone danced, ate, and drank for hours. As Hunter had predicted, and as Josie had expected, they were congratulated again and again by everyone they spoke to. Even more guests arrived, those who hadn't been able to make it to the main ceremony, and the process would start all over again. However, it was certainly easier to endure than it had been the last time she got married, because the man by her side was one she loved. She was able to join in on the conversations, to make jokes and to laugh.

It helped that the seasons were changing, giving them another conversation topic. Everyone wanted to talk about the fall vegetables they were growing in their gardens, their preparations for winter, which would be upon them before they knew it.

"Are you going to go to the festival next month?" Josie heard that question upwards of a dozen times. And each time, she said that she would. She hadn't gone to a festival since she was married to Owen, and Ella had never been to one at all. Now they could attend as a family, all three of them.

Dinnertime approached and Kerry and the other women disappeared into the kitchen to work on the feast, while some of the men rearranged the tables. They brought out chairs and haybales and stacked up wooden boards to ensure there would be enough seats for everyone. Josie kept trying to help, but no one would let her do anything. She could only watch and talk and let everyone else take care of it all.

"Dinner's coming out!" Kerry backed out of the house and turned, holding a huge platter with a roast chicken. A procession of volunteers came behind her, bringing potatoes and gravy, cornbread, and green salad. Everything was arranged on the tables and they all took their seats.

Josie sat at the head of the table with Hunter by her side. She looked down at the rows of people on either side of her and everything once again felt very unreal. She had never experienced anything like this before. She reached for Hunter underneath the table and he patted her arm.

When everyone had been seated, Hunter led them in a prayer. "Thank you God for this day," he said, his deep, solemn voice ringing out. "The best day of my entire life so far. Thank you for this feast, these friends, and family members."

When he had finished, he took hold of a knife and sliced off a slab of chicken for himself, Josie, and Ella. The meat was so tender and juicy it was almost falling apart as he maneuvered the pieces onto their plates. He passed the platter on and the feast began in true. The dishes went around and around in a circle, passed from hand to hand. Everyone made sure their neighbor had a bit of everything and was taken care of in kind.

Josie watched as more and more food was piled onto her plate by Kerry. The simple, absentminded kindness of everyone providing and cooperating made her want to weep with joy. She lifted her fork and started to eat, giving herself something else to focus on.

The first present came drifting down the table, a misshapen lump wrapped in butcher paper, secured with dyed red twine.

"From Arthur!" someone from the other end of the table yelled over. "For Josie!"

Josie placed her fork down and undid the twine. She unfolded the paper to reveal a beautiful, warm wool scarf made of blue and white yarn. She wrapped it around her neck right then and there, over her wedding dress. "It's beautiful!"

"Knitted it myself, I did!" Arthur announced proudly. "Keep you warm all winter!"

And with that, like a dam breaking, other gifts were delivered to them from down the length of the tables. Some were wrapped, others in boxes, most presented just on their own. Hunter and Ella also received scarves, and they were all given new mittens. They received candy and coffee, a woven basket, decorative napkin rings, and a full set of silverware.

As the presents formed a pile next to Josie's and Hunter's chairs, a representative from the newspaper recorded them to be reported in the article announcing their union.

"Do you hear that?" Hunter spoke suddenly, lifting his head.

Josie listened. "What is it?"

"Sounds like a wagon's coming."

"A very late guest?" someone nearby suggested. "Plenty of grub left if they're hungry."

Josie kept listening and she heard it too, the sliding of wheels over grass, and wood creaking. She twisted around in her chair and saw it coming, a small covered wagon pulled by two oxen, one brown and the other black. Sitting on the front bench was a man in traveling clothes, his face shaded by the brim of his hat.

The guests stirred in confusion. Josie had no idea who the new guest was, and it seemed no one else did, either.

The wagon drew to a halt close to the stable. The driver stepped down from the bench and approached the tables.

"Don't that look like Clive?" someone said.

Josie's stomach cramped. She started shaking all over as the figure approached. It *was* Clive, exactly him. She recognized his stature, his walk.

Hunter rose to his feet. He grabbed Ella from her seat and thrust her into Kerry's arms, striding a few paces forward. "Hey!" he shouted. "What are you doin' here?"

Other people were also standing. The sheriff had his hand on his holstered pistol. His mouth was open, his brows furrowed. He had no idea that Clive was out and walking around. Had he escaped jail? Where had he gotten the wagon and oxen?

"I know I look like him." The man reached up and removed his hat. His hair was not drab brown, instead sandy blonde.

And his face was different, Josie realized. The chin was narrower, the cheekbones higher. As much as he looked like Clive, *he was not.*

The man held up his hands. "Don't make any assumptions now, alright?"

Hunter narrowed his eyes. "Your accent. Where are you from?"

"New Jersey," the man said. "The name's Travis."

"What are you doin' here?" Hunter growled.

Travis pursed his full, almost womanly lips. "The short version of the story is that Clive has died."

Josie put her hand to her head, dizzied. "He's... dead? How did he die?"

Travis turned to her. "Are you Josie?"

"Y-yes." How did he know who she was? She had never seen him before.

Travis reached into his pocket and pulled out a folded piece of paper. "You might know Clive was sent off to serve his jailtime in another city. He was doing some labor, had an accident. Turns out that he named me in his will. I don't know why. We're cousins, but not from the same half of the family. I've only met him a few times before."

Josie went to stand beside Hunter. "Cousins. Do you know the story of what Clive has done here? To me? To my husband?"

Travis lowered his head. "The letter had come details, not all. I'd like to hear the whole story in time. Maybe next week at some point? I got some settling in to do."

"Settling in?" Hunter frowned.

Travis said, "In his will, Clive left me his house and the saloon. I've been wanting a reason to move out west and figured this is my chance to do it. I will be reopening his establishment."

Hunter crossed his arms. "Seems mighty coincidental that you'd show up here on our wedding day."

"I had no idea it was your wedding until I got to town earlier." Travis's blue eyes were wide, earnest. "I asked around because I wanted to come and speak with you right away, get you to know who I was and what I'm doing here. Make some reparations. No one was as surprised as me by the timing of this. I brought a gift. I know it isn't much, but I had only a little time to buy something."

Travis pulled out a pair of porcelain salt and pepper shakers from his pocket. He held out his gift. "I know you've had hardships caused by my family members. I know I'm likely not welcome here and I accept that. I only wanted to let you know that I'm here and I plan to stay. So, if you ever do want to meet up and talk, I'll make the time for it."

Hunter started to speak, then stopped and looked down at Josie. He made a motion with his hand, tipped his head slightly. She understood. He was putting the decision into her hands.

She looked up at Travis's serious expression and she knew she could not rightfully judge him by the actions of his relatives. He was not them. He had done no harm to her, and he was trying hard to be friendly.

Josie held out her hands. Travis placed the salt and pepper shakers in her hands and stepped back. "Wait," she said. "You've had a long journey from New Jersey to here. Stay a time. Have some dinner. Please."

A wide smile spread across Travis's face. "I would like that."

Hunter sighed and waved at the other guests. "Someone pull up a chair for this man and pass him some food."

"Thank you," Travis said. "Both of you."

The sheriff spoke. "There's a spot on this hay bale over next to me, sir. Come and sit. I want to ask you some questions, if you don't mind. I didn't even know Clive had died."

Travis nodded to Hunter and Josie, and waked over to the sheriff. "I'll tell you anything I know," he said. "Maybe your letter just got lost in the mail."

The sheriff sighed. "Could be. It's happened before. Sit on down, Travis. Help yourself to some of these hot rocks here. And I see the platter of chicken makin' its way to us. Should be enough left for you."

Josie looked up at Hunter and took his hand. "Let's sit back down," she suggested. "And finish eating. Okay?"

"Alright," he said. "You're my wife now, so I got to listen to you."

Josie laughed.

***

The house was in utter disarray. So many footprints covered the floorboards that it seemed there was no floor at all, only strips of dirt. The furniture in the foyer was all out of order and the kitchen was filled with dirty dishes, too many of them to fit in the sink.

Josie held her sleeping daughter to her chest. "This is what it's like to have a party, is it?" she murmured. "When it's over, to be left with the mess..."

Hunter put his arms around her from behind. "That's the price to pay, for sure. Imagine how bad it would be if Kerry and her daughter hadn't stayed for an extra hour."

"It's going to be a lot of work to get things back to normal around here."

"I think it will go faster than you expect." Hunter rubbed his cheek on hers. "We can worry about it tomorrow. Aren't you exhausted?"

"I am," she said. She ached from her hips all the way to her feet, the lower half of her body one single pain. "I think I'll be asleep before I even put my head on the pillow."

He chuckled. "I'm going to go change out of this suit. I'll help you tuck in Ella after. You'll call for me when you're ready?"

"I will," she promised. She gave him a kiss on the cheek and headed to her room. Ella stirred awake when she was placed on the bed.

Rubbing her eyes, the little girl murmured, "Where Hunter?"

"He'll be here in only a moment." Josie stroked her hair. "Let's get you out of your dress and ready for bed."

When they had both changed out of their dresses and into their night clothes, Josie called for Hunter. He walked in and sat with her on the edge of the bed. Ella smiled up at him and he stroked her cheek gently. "You've had a long day, chickadee. Time to rest."

"Night, Hunter." Ella closed her eyes. Her body relaxed and she was asleep in moments.

Hunter tucked the blankets in around her, working so gently. Josie leaned her head on his shoulder. "Now what?" she whispered.

"Come outside with me."

She nodded and they left the room, making their way outside. The sky had never been so full of stars as it was on that night, every dazzling pinprick like a sugar crystal. Josie burrowed into Hunter's arms for warmth, her eyes on the sky.

"Hunter?" she whispered.

"Hmm?" He held the back of her head, caressing her hair.

"Will you be Ella's father?"

His chest rumbled with his laugh. "And here I thought I was already in that position."

Josie blushed and she tucked her face against him. "I mean, will you let her call you her 'Pa'? If she wants to. Well, I know she would want to. You are already like a father to her.

But do you want that?" A tremor passed through her as she awaited his answer.

Hunter lifted her face to his. "Of course, I want that. I love that little girl. And I love you."

She kissed him to tell him that she loved him, too.

THE END

Also by Nora J. Callaway

Thank you for reading "**Sheltered by the Mountain Man's Love**"!

I hope you enjoyed it! If you did, here are some of my other books!

Also, if you liked this book, you can also check out **my full Amazon Book Catalogue at:**
https://go.norajcallaway.com/bc-authorpage

Thank you for allowing me to keep doing what I love! ❤

Made in United States
Orlando, FL
03 August 2024

49867845R00173